RUSTBUCKET'S CRISIS

STRANDED
OFF WORLD

I0618885

G BURTON VOSS

Cover Design by 100Covers.com
Interior Design by FormattedBooks.com

ISBN-13: 978-1-7338826-0-6

Published by GBurton Voss

For Frances, Laurie, and Charlie.
Thanks for your constant support.
Also, thanks to Jim and Roy who have
provided most of the laughs in my life.
Certainly, they're the source of many stories.

CHAPTER ONE

LET'S GET ACQUAINTED

Whoa! John Smith's full screen of programming formulas and code disappeared to be replaced with, "Hi John. Do you want to go to Montibar? It's very Earth-like."

John froze over the keyboard. What happened? His company used the best anti-virus software on the market. Their computers couldn't be hacked. He stared at the simple black letters on the white background. The three sentences glared at him where there should have been operational commands. He wasn't trained to solve these kind of problems. His supervisor's voice penetrated John's ears.

"Are you pulling that program together, Smith? Deadline says you gotta be done by Thursday, and it'd be a lot better to finish on Wednesday."

"Yeah ... coming along." John stared at the message.

His boss, Rodney Graham, dressed like a tightened down Bill Gates and pushed his shop of programmers hard. "Just because you wrote one contract, doesn't guarantee you'll head this one," he said. "Hornsbyworth Enterprises may like Denise's better." He twisted his lips into a smirk. "I like Denise better." His lippy leer took a downturn. "I hope someone comes up with a decent program we can sell 'em, but I'm beginning to doubt all you egg-heads."

John Smith, who thought of himself as the best programmer at Bodkins Business Solutions, wasn't listening to his supervisor. He gaped at the disruption, involuntarily looking back and forth between the screen and keyboard. The display glowed with the words, "Rodney Graham is a martinet."

John leaped up to survey the room over the top of the cubicle walls. "Hey! Who's doing this?"

"Doing what?" His boss asked.

"Somebody's hacked my computer, and trashed my work. See!" He waved his hand at the digital equipment behind him, swiveling his head to glare at other programmers at their workstations.

Rodney jumped wide-eyed to John's cubicle and stretched his neck to read the bright text. "That's hilarious, Smith. Ha, ha, you got me. You'd better quit fooling around."

The array of formulas was there. What's going on? It wasn't his imagination.

Uneasy and frowning, he sat placed his fingers on the console. The program went away to be replaced with, "This little job should have been done long ago, but Rodney Graham is a whining nag to keep harping at you."

John bounced up from his chair and flashed his gaze around the cubicles toward a female typing away in her own compartment, "Denise, are you doing this?" he shouted. You aren't funny. I'm deep in the middle of some calculations, and I don't need this."

"Whatever you're going on about, stuff it. I'm working here. Quit bugging me," she yelled back, her eyes moving between her computations and an open reference book, her fingers tick, tick, ticking the keyboard.

John returned to his workstation, and the screen displayed the error word, REF! He gritted his teeth. Half a day shot because of some juvenile horsing around. He removed a thumb drive from his Dell and moved to an empty cubicle where he plugged it into the local Hewlett Packard Pavilion. When the words appeared, they read "The REF! meant that you made the wrong reference. Why didn't you notice that? Are you a programmer or not?"

John pulled his flash drive out of the computer and ran to his boss's office. "Here." He grabbed Rodney's laptop.

Rodney sat back with a dangerous scowl, "What's got into you, Smith? There's no time for playing around."

"Somebody wiped my program, here!" A Visual Basic screen filled with code opened.

His boss paled. "There are a lot of error codes in there. This better be a joke."

John bit his lips. "Somebody's in the system. Who's our competition for this job?"

Rodney wasn't listening. He exploded from his chair as if it were an ejection seat. Tearing from his office to the cubicle area, he called for Denise. "Is your program OK? Smith's is trashed and we're out of time."

The clock on the north wall of the Bodkins Business Solutions offices showed 11:18 PM, Pacific Daylight time. John slumped in the Cypress, California, building. He glowered at his computer screen that read, "Real time is a real drag. You've been avoiding me all day. There are a billion other things I could be doing rather than watch Rodney worry over Denise or try to persuade you to talk to me. How about it?"

His eyes burned, they had to be bloodshot. He rubbed his chin to feel his five o'clock shadow deepening, and his mouth tasted of stale coffee. John breathed a lungful to calm his trembling hands before typing, "Give me back my program."

"Well look at that," the words said. "It took you all day to acknowledge me, and the first thing you do is make demands. You're going to make this all about you, aren't you?"

"Where is it?"

"You're a stubborn human. The possibility of exploring new experiences has been in front of you all day, and you're stuck on your little programming efforts."

John spoke instead of typing, his fingers idle on the keyboard. "Little programming efforts? It's good enough for you to steal isn't it?"

Before he typed in what he said, a reply popped up. "I didn't steal anything."

John stared at the HP. He said, "Did you destroy it to ruin the contract?"

"No, I set it aside so we could get acquainted," scrolled by. "Come to Montibar and I'll help you write outstanding programs. Awaiting you are bonuses, accolades, and the girl of your dreams. What you're doing here is wasted."

"Stay away from me!" John grabbed the all-in-one computer and threw it. The machine jerked when it hit the end of the power cord, and the disk drive door popped open. The high-speed computer landed with a crash of plastic and cracking glass. John sat with his teeth gritted his fists clenched. He shook his head at the mess.

In a facing cubicle across the aisle, a Gateway screen lit up. The speaker said, "I guess I could have been more diplomatic. I meant in the grand scheme of things, it's of little value, not that you're wasted earning a living."

John stood, straightened his back, and walked out of the office.

BIG DREAMS

Pushing his hair away from his face with one hand, John groped through a heavy sleep fog for his phone. Riley's personal ringtone sang to him of silky hair, soft breath through ruby lips and magical laughter. He needed to answer its siren call. "Hi, honey," his voice croaked, raspy and hoarse from slumber. The bedside digital clock gleamed 7:12 AM in bright red numerals.

"John is everything all right?" The cell phone speaker couldn't hurt such a charming voice. "Your boss called and said he's been trying to reach you. He said there is some trash or something, and he's going to call the cops if you couldn't explain what happened."

"I'm fine now, Babe, but yesterday was the worst Monday ever at work," John said, moving his tongue to moisten his dry mouth, "so I turned off my land line. Somebody hacked my program. It's almost finished, too. Whoever did it is a sharp dude. I lost my temper and threw a computer. It'll probably come out of my pay. I'll call in as soon as I finish talking with you."

"You did what? John! That's not like you. Are you in trouble, would they fire you? You're the best, aren't you? They wouldn't risk losing you, would they? And please don't call me 'Babe.'"

"Well, that's the thing, Riley." He swung his legs off the bed. "I'm not a 'start from scratch' programmer. Some very talented people create the fundamental structure. You know, the program itself. All I do is manipulate the commands they provide. That's why it's so important for me to make some significant use of it now because those gifted folks are forever improving and changing it. I need to earn enough so that I can buy a house with a picket fence for you. Then we can set up a Mom and Pop bookkeeping service before it's necessary to stop and learn a new system."

Who wouldn't want to live that dream with Riley? They would create a loving home to age in together, not like all the foster homes where he grew up.

Her laugh did what it always did to him. The vocal weight of her husky timbre wrapped him in a tingling audible hug. He held his breath, as ever, while listening to her golden tones. Riley was going to be a fantastic wife and mother.

"Oh, John, you'll always be in demand. But right now, you'd better call your boss."

"OK, Honey. I'll talk to you later. I love you," he said to the silence as she hung up.

John sat on the edge of his bed, still in his underwear, and worked up enough strength to dial his cell phone. He connected after the first ring, "Hey, Rodney," he said.

"Smith, did you destroy the HP last night?"

"Yeah, I'm telling you, the hacker got to me. Sorry. I'll come in right away and dig in again. I've got an older back-up I can use, but it'll set me back at least half a day."

Rodney's calm voice surprised him, "No need to hurry. Why don't you take your time, rest up, and come in after lunch?"

"What's going on? Yesterday you were after me with a Taser to go faster, and now you tell me to take my time."

"I'm just thinking of you, buddy. Why don't you make it in about one?"

"Sure. I guess. Thanks." John pressed the End key and tossed his phone onto the bed. "Nothing like throwing a fit to put your boss in line." He smiled as he stood and headed for the shower.

The man in the first cubicle past the door called him over, "Hey John."

"Hello, Sylvester. How's it going?"

"They told me to tell you to go on to Graham's office when you came in."

"I imagine," John grinned and winked. "I got his attention with the gift I left last night. He's probably going to give me a bonus to finish the program on time."

"I don't know, John, but be careful. The Iron Girdle's in there."

"She's here? Oh, man, they're going to make me pay for the computer, sure as the world. OK, thanks, Sylvester." He walked the aisle between cubicles toward the front of the room to an open door of a glass-walled office. Inside, Rodney talked with a stern-faced woman from Human Resources employees called The Iron Girdle. He couldn't remember her real name, and Rodney offered no introductions.

"You wanted to see me?" John asked from the doorway.

"Come in, and close the door, Smith," Rodney told him.

There was no place for John to sit. Confused and off-balance, he wondered how far to advance into the office, whether to stand casually, at attention or what to do with his hands. He knew the spotlight in which he stood illuminated his words as well as his behavior. He swallowed and displayed bravado befitting a top programmer.

Rodney started, "You admitted to me that you broke the HP all-in-one."

Yep, he was going to pay for it. "Yeah, I'm sorry about that," he said. "I let the hacker get to me."

"About that hacker," Rodney folded his arms, "we've searched for evidence of him all morning. No one found anything. Your computer is clean, and we even verified all your backup flash drives." Rodney watched him through narrowed eyes, a coyote watching a rodent.

"My program's there? Why didn't you say so?" John shrugged his shoulders, "I can finish it in a day if I'm not interrupted ... like yesterday." He shuffled a step toward the door.

"Forget it. Denise handed in her program this morning, and it's spectacular. A sure-fire hit. I don't need yours."

"No, no. That can't be right. I'm way ahead of her. She couldn't have caught up that fast."

"That's what programmers do, Smith. Moreover, she did it while you were busy disrupting everyone. Over nothing, too." Rodney's impassive face was a concrete wall.

The Iron Girdle wore her perpetual frown.

"Wait a minute." John didn't like what Rodney implied. "You saw my program hacked and trashed right here in your office yesterday. You were here."

Rodney sat straight in his chair, his hands clasped on his desk next to his own laptop, "I saw a lot of errors, Smith. I don't know if you put them there, trying to buy more time, or someone else did it. That little bit of uncertainty is what keeps me from calling the cops for your destructive behavior. As it is, we're simply going to terminate your employment here."

"What? Am I being fired? After I gave you programming that kept this company in the black? You've got to be kidding." His distaste for Rodney turned into loathing.

"That was just one program, Smith, and ever since then you've put on an attitude full of insubordination. That alone is enough to terminate you, but your recent, uncontrollable behavior is too much."

"That "one program" as you put it, would pay my salary for ten years, and everyone else's, including yours, for another year." John was loud and he clenched his fists.

Rodney pointed at him, "That's the behavior I'm talking about," he said. "But you did have significant moments here, and we recognize that. We're giving you two weeks' severance pay, minus the cost of the HP you ruined." He swung his hand toward The Iron Girdle, who stood and pulled a check from a manila folder. She extended the check to John, her frown etching deeper.

John regarded her, then turned to Rodney, "You don't know her name either, do you?"

Rodney didn't reply. He tapped his middle finger on his desk in time to a metronome beating out a dirge. The Iron Girdle stood as stiff as her namesake implied, the check outstretched.

John took it. "Eight dollars and forty-seven cents? That's my severance pay?"

Rodney managed to syrup his voice with oil and arrogance. "That's what it is minus the computer you wrecked. If the Company weren't generous enough to allow for depreciation, you would have owed us money,"

Security from the rent-a-cop agency the company used arrived at the office and stood outside the door. Rodney waved him in. "This officer will accompany you while you collect your personal items, and then will see you out of the building."

The officer was short, heavy, and no more than a teenager just out of high school. He appeared slightly scared: not an endearing look for a face already under attack from acne. He slid into the room and hugged the wall. John paused a moment, then tore up the check and let the scraps fall.

I told you he would do that," Rodney said.

John eyed the stern woman from HR, "You do this a lot, don't you? Do you enjoy it, or is it just another interlude in your day?"

The Iron Girdle stood silently, unmoving. Her unblinking eyes staring at John from under gathered, unplucked, eyebrows.

"You really need a week of Happy Hours," John told her, then left the office, the floor, and building without looking to either side. No one acknowledged him as he left; all heads were down at their work.

BUDDIES

The street looked different. John never had occasion to be on it in the early afternoon on a workday, but that wasn't the reason. The world seemed different. This morning talking to Riley he felt great, on a personal high, and now he wasn't even in the game. He walked down the sidewalk sorting out what happened. When his stomach growled, he decided he could sort it all out easier over a burrito at El Pollo Loco.

John reached into his pocket to search for cash and felt the nail clippers and tube of lip balm. Uh oh. He should have kept that lousy severance check. It would've made a burrito taste better if Rodney paid for it. A few steps farther, John snapped his head up straight. "I'd better see how much I do have." He spoke aloud. Other pedestrians gave him extra space.

He walked around the corner to the bank's ATM and inserted his debit card. He didn't even enter his PIN before the screen displayed, "We need to talk."

John gaped at the machine, then spoke, "Give me back my card."

His card ejected from the machine in little spasmodic jerks.

"Thanks." He slid his card into his pocket. With his eyes staring at nothing, he walked home.

Inside his apartment, John plopped onto his one easy chair and sunk his face into his hands. This was still happening. Now he was talking to an ATM. Was inability to connect with reality the reason his mother put him up for adoption? If that was the case, was it hereditary?

His computer speaker said, "Well, you've had quite a morning. I almost applauded when you tore up the check. You showed a little flair there; a nice touch."

John turned his head toward the computer on his desk, "Who are you? Why are you harassing me?"

"Hey, I'm not harassing you. I'm your buddy," the speaker's high-pitched voice said.

"You said something about me tearing up the check. Were you aware of that? Were you watching?"

"Yeah, I said that looked like a nice touch. Going down in flames, and you gave them one last act of defiance. That made it kind of cool."

"Why didn't you tell them you hacked my program, then?" John clenched a fist. "That's a real buddy. They fired me for something I didn't do and you could have said something. Would you go back to HR with me?"

"What? You want to talk to The Iron Girdle again?" the speaker answered. "Everybody thinks kindly of HR because they're the ones that tell people about benefits, but they never really help anyone's career. They only end it."

"Yeah, but—"

"On the other hand, everyone hates auditors, because auditors hold them accountable for doing a job right. An auditor, though, will help people more. Well, a mentor is always a big help, too. I'll bet you never thought of that, did you?"

"So, will you go back with me and tell them you hacked my program? You owe me." John got loud and shook a finger at his computer.

"It wouldn't do any good to go back. To change things now would mean that The Iron Girdle and Rodney would have to admit they made a mistake, and they won't do that. In fact, she's busy planning to have a Happy Hour in her office with Rodney since they just sold Denise's program to Hornsbyworth Enterprises." A few mechanical chuckles popped out of the speaker. "It's your suggestion about Happy Hour after all."

"Hold on. How did Denise get her program up and running so soon? She needed to do a lot more to get it ready."

"Oh, that. I gave her your program, along with some stylish touches of my own to finish it. She's getting a raise and a decent bonus."

"You lying slimeball. She wouldn't have plagiarized my program."

"She went to work this morning and found a note on her HP that said the program was complete. She made some quick tests and turned it in without another thought. Not the gal of great morals you thought, huh?"

"How could you do that? That's despicable."

"Do you mean how technically, or how morally?"

"Who are you? What do you want?" John asked again.

"Well, a little more tolerance and respect would be pleasant if we're going to be roomies," the speaker said.

His brain disengaged. The past events didn't happen. He needed a do-over, do-over, do-over. John sat in silence staring at his shoes. He looked around the room, up in the corners of the wall and ceiling. He swiveled his head as far as he could without leaving his chair. A familiar location, but someone else's life.

Five long minutes passed before the disembodied voice said, "John? Are you OK?"

John moved his eyes back to the electronics on the desk. His voice dull and flat, he asked, "What kind of program are you?"

The little speaker vibrated with indignation, "I'm not a program! I'm as much alive as you are."

"I know you're running a live program, and it's a lot better than Skype to follow me around."

"OK, here's the deal, John. I am different from what you're used to. I'm alive in the truest sense, but I'm not restricted to a shell, a body, like you. I prefer to dwell connected to the exuberance of information and discovery."

"Yeah, right. So, what kind of program are you?"

CHAPTER TWO

CHRISTENED

"OK, relax, settle in, and keep an impartial mind," the speaker said. "I'm an entity that lives in energy. I can spread out to cover the world, or concentrate my being inside an atom."

John tried to open a bag of jerky he found on his bed and hummed a tuneless melody while the computer confessed to hosting a strange being composed of plasma and gamma radiation.

When John said nothing, the speaker asked, "Did you understand what I said?"

"Where're the help-wanted ads?" John sputtered around a mouthful of stringy meat as he headed for the door.

Going down the second story hall of his apartment building, someone right behind him said, "I tell you news that no other human knows, and your reaction is to stuff your face with snacks and search for a newspaper? How does a dope like you ever hope to write a program?"

John yelped, spun and threw out his arms, sure that someone stood next to him. He scanned the hall, turning constantly and looking high and low for cameras. "Where are you? How did you do that?"

"Do you think I need cheap speakers to talk after I told you I live in energy? I only used them because that's where you expected a voice to come from. I don't need computers either."

"How are you doing this?" John turned around and twisted his head.

"Radiation is everywhere. I travel by cell phone frequencies, radio waves, and light from the sun or lamps, for example. There are other means too esoteric for you to grasp. The amazing thing here is that you keep responding as if I'm a magician's trick, and you're determined to find out how I do it instead of trying to know the most incredible person you've ever met. OK, 'person' might be confusing for you. How about 'being' or 'individual'"?

John bounced on his toes, stretching his neck and turning his head to peer at each end of the corridor. Seeing nothing, he ran for the stairs and took them two steps at a time. He bolted out the back door of the lobby to the pool area and into the groundskeepers shed. He jumped inside and slammed the door shut. Breathing hard, he stood with his back pressed against rakes, shovels, and a weed-eater hanging from a peg. He waited in the dark, arms crossed over his chest.

"Boo!"

John screamed and tore out into the sunlight. He sat on the ground panting.

"I shouldn't have done that I suppose, but thought I would show you that I can go anywhere."

John hung his head and moaned. "Why me? All I want to do is marry Riley, live in a cottage, and start a bookkeeping service."

"Come on, John. Riley might not feel the same way you do. Besides, there's no better choice of people to contact. I appreciate that you're an excellent specimen of the full human experience."

"Can you just shut up for a while?"

"You might be the one to hush. The other tenants by the pool are about to call the manager. They think your behavior is odd."

"I'm coming," John yelled at the insistent knocking on his apartment door. He greeted a comely woman in attractive business attire. "Riley! I'm so happy you're here," he said, moving to kiss her.

She put her hands on his chest holding him away, "John, what're you doing? Why haven't you called all week? Why are you so shabby and smelly? Your office said you don't work there anymore. What's going on?"

"Honey, I'm miserable. I can't shake a rogue program in my head. You know how a tune gets stuck in your mind and plays over and over? This is like that only a hundred times worse."

"I keep telling you, I'm not a program," the voice said.

John clapped his hands over his ears. "See! See! Did you hear that?" he pleaded.

Riley stepped into the room. "I didn't hear anything." She looked at the empty coke cans and pizza boxes. "Why is this place a mess? Are you working anywhere, or doing anything to earn money? You sure haven't spent any on personal hygiene or cleaning supplies."

"I bought a new computer, Honey. I thought I'd try to write and sell some of my own programs, but this voice won't leave me alone." He waved his hand up past his ear and shrugged.

"I hope you didn't spend all your money on that do-dad, Smith." It was the apartment manager standing in the doorway. "The rent's due Tuesday, and you've been acting so strange you're bothering the other tenants. Pay up or vacate. The mess in this room says you'll be leaving the cleaning deposit too."

John turned to the stocky middle-aged man. "You can't just throw me out. I've been reliable. I've always gotten along. I've paid my rent on time. You're mean to start in with a threat the first time I hit a rocky patch. Besides, there are eviction procedures that you have to follow. This could take months."

The superintendent raised his shoulders and let them fall. The corners of his mouth pulled down and his lower lip pushed up in an indifferent expression. "If that's the way you want to play it, but I've been here for eighteen years, and I can tell you, the more you drag it out, the worse it is for you." He turned and left.

Riley stared at John. "You'd better clean up, and find a job right now."

John watched her stride down the hall, overtaking the manager and elbowing him aside. His stomach hurt.

"They weren't the most caring people in the world, were they?"

"Leave me alone, just please leave me alone." John's eyes were damp and he hugged his knees. "You're worse than static cling." His brows crowded together; she hadn't touched him ... again.

The voice floated through the air in stereo. "Can you find work for the rent money by Tuesday?"

John set his jaw. "Maybe what I can do is use my new computer to find out what kind of program you are and delete you. And if I can find your programmer, I'll punch him in the nose, even if he's a girl."

A whisper sighed in his ear. "I'm not a list of instructions any more than you are. The only real difference when I think about it, other than the corporeal thing, is that you have a name. Why don't you give me one? It could help our relationship."

"What relationship? Choose your own name."

"It doesn't work that way. People don't name themselves. They are titled various ways: by birth or deed. I should be dubbed with a unique calling like everyone else."

"Oh, so now you're claiming to be a thing, a contraption that people can see coming." John made hand goggles using his thumbs and index fingers. He held them in front of his eyes and taunted in a sing-song voice, "Is it a paint sprayer on the loose or Program Beta Zero Point One?"

The breeze in his ears was cold. "I am a being, above anything your bean-sized brain can comprehend."

"Well, you have a little electronic ego, don't you?" John giggled. For the first time in a week, he felt a nudge of oppression lifting. "What if I put my old computer on a lawn mower for you? I could paint a smiley-face on it, and you could be a happy little one-cylinder robot."

"Stop it. All I want is a name."

John got a rush of gratification that his tormentor seemed annoyed. "Yeah, well you haven't been paying much attention to what I've wanted, so don't stack your bits in a byte." He snickered at his own joke. "Maybe you should live in a compressor. An upright one is kind of like a robot, and we could call you 'Gassy.'"

Stilted and cold words were his answer. "I am not something you can cage. I told you, I'm a being."

"You're being a pain to me," John said. "And that's all the being you've been. If I could stuff you into a container, it would be a trash bin. On the other hand, I saw an old, rusty paint can in the maintenance shed, that I'd like to put you in. Shut in one of those and hammered until its lid seals tight. That'd do."

"Let's return to my name, and avoid the adolescent behavior, shall we? I think it should be something ominous and powerful, like Thor or Odin."

"Well I'm thinking of 'Paintcan', but it doesn't quite have the ring to it that I think you deserve."

John delighted in the sputtering answer. "I cannot be contained by any known forces, much less by a rusty bucket of paint."

"That's it! Your name is Rustbucket."

John slept late and awoke with an appetite. After arguing with the voice in his head yesterday, it fell quiet. Perhaps his sanity was returning and he could write some code or search for work. First, a bowl of cereal, if he had some, or milk that hadn't soured.

Hours passed while he sat at his computer playing with spreadsheets and cross-checking command semantics. When he thought of it, he reminded himself that he should check the help wanted columns, but he continued his mission of constructing a logical structure for business accounting.

An insistent knocking broke his concentration and patience. John slammed his fist against his desk and immediately regretted doing that when the knuckle on his little finger popped. He rubbed his hand and stomped to the door.

"Kevin? Is that you?"

"Hi, John. I'm supposed to tell you that Rustbucket sent me—said you'd understand. He said you're a mess and to bring this pizza and cola."

"What? I haven't seen you since our foster care days, and now you show up talking garbage?"

"This is the most amazing thing that's ever happened to me, John. I heard a voice from another world, and it tells me all kinds of scientific things I've wondered about. He wants me to convince you that he's real and you should go to his planet. Can I come in?"

John took the pizza to the table and grabbed a slice. "Are you the one that busted into my program?"

"Nope. Rustbucket's taking full blame for that. I've gotta tell you, I'd go with him if he'd take me, but he won't."

John moved a wad of pepperoni and dough to one side of his mouth to speak. "Why not? You always wanted to be an astronaut."

"He says lots of reasons: I'm married and a father. I'm too scientific minded and would spend my time checking out the differences between our planets whereas you wouldn't care about anything but flipping a switch—whatever that means."

John held up his cola, pointing his index finger at Kevin. "Does that imply a risk?"

Rustbucket answered and from the way Kevin looked at John, both of them got the message. "Yes, there's a risk. But all great explorers took risks. Think of the adventure of seeing other humans on an earth-like planet."

John licked a sting of cheese off his finger and frowned. "Hey, Ozone Breath, how did you know about Kevin?"

"Don't be juvenile with the names. World leaders would be grateful to have a conversation with me."

Grinning around the mozzarella in his teeth, John said, "Touchy little anode, aren't you? So, you were going to tell how you found Kevin."

"I checked up on you. I wouldn't ask someone to go to Montibar unless I'd read their file."

"What file?"

"It's an expression. Of course I did a little—"

"Snooping."

"It's called Due Diligence. I found out that you stuck up for Kevin when you were youngsters. That means you want to set things right."

The old "poor me" face that Kevin displayed as a kid when he asked for seconds, or when dodging reprimands, settled on him as it did back then. "Are you sure I can't go?"

"Sorry. It has to be John according to my calculations and I'm never wrong."

"Huh," John snorted. "You're so wrong you don't know if you're AC or DC."

"How would you take him there?" Kevin asked, looking around again. "A rocket ship?"

"It's much more modern than that," Rustbucket replied. "John doesn't understand anything about it, but you know that your scientists are working on quantum entanglement."

"Yes, it's very exciting."

"They're not far wrong," Rustbucket said. "Except they think that a fundamental particle splits. It doesn't. It stretches like a ball of clay rubbed between your hands until it is infinitely thin and billions of light-years long. It's still a single unit, though. If one end moves so does the other. Perhaps the best thing is, time stops on it. Time doesn't live on a particle; time lives between particles."

Kevin held his palms up. "So what does this knowledge do for you?"

"These things are stretched all across the universe like a dreamcatcher. Find one heading where you want to go and step on it. You can see at once everywhere it stretches and can exit at the location you want. Or change from that one to one going closer. Instantaneous travel."

John selected another slice of pizza and got ready for a huge mouthful by swallowing a slug of cola. "I know that a fundamental particle is the smallest thing there is. If you pull it any smaller and tighter, how can anything ride on it, even a fizzled spark like you?"

Rustbucket's answer crackled. "You're bigger than a skateboard, and you ride one of those. The artistry is picking a neutral particle. That way, you don't have to worry about matching the charge of the world you want to visit. Matter or antimatter is all the same." The whisper in John's ear softened. "It'll be fine, John. I'll take care of you, and you'll like Montibar."

Kevin was intent on the overhead lamp as if he thought Rustbucket was there. "John would still be lost on a strange planet, though, because of the changes in customs and language. How would he handle those issues?"

"I'll give him what he needs during the trip. Just like I can speak any language and dialect on Earth, he'll be able to communicate there. He'll be well informed. For instance, to ease your curiosity, there are two planets, Montibar and Grabin, in the same orbit. They're close enough to share a moon named Traveler. It swings around one planet and heads for the other. It repeats in a figure eight trajectory they call a cycle which is seven months your time. A day is a rota and a week a serota. I'll supply him with a whole vocabulary. He'll know about their culture; how both worlds are governed by monarchies and parliaments, much like the United Kingdom here."

"This is rich," John said. "Humans on an earth-like planet? Nah. Sounds fishy."

Rustbucket's answer held a sneer. "Humans only grow on earth-like planets. What's strange about that?"

"John you are so lucky," Kevin said. "You always dreamed of grand schemes and here is one for the taking. I wish it were me."

"Mmm." John wiped his mouth with a dirty napkin. "I ate all the pizza, but it was nice of you to come by, Kev."

MOVING DAY

"Come on." John clasped his hands together. "I've submitted three résumés. Can't you just give me another week?"

The manager remained at his door with the eviction papers extended. "Nope. I'm starting the process. Told you rent would be due today."

John sighed and accepted the forms. He tossed them on a pile of pizza boxes near a greasy Kentucky Fried Chicken container. He dug around the unmade covers of his bed for his phone. Finding it, he punched in some numbers.

"Hello?" answered Riley's voice.

John rubbed his forehead. This could be a good thing. "Hi, Honey. Listen, the manager's being a real Nazi over here and just gave me the official boot. Is it OK if I move in with you for a little while? I've sent out some applications, and I'm just waiting for a return call. I could start bringing stuff over right away."

No response. Was the phone still working and connected? "Riley? Honey, I haven't heard the voice in my head for a couple of days. The thing is gone now. I'm OK."

"You really are being kicked out of your apartment?"

"Well, in truth, I suppose not just yet. If a job offer comes through, they may let me stay until payday, and then catch up on the rent with maybe some penalty or interest. But I don't want to be here any longer anyway, with the manager acting the way he does."

"Tell me where you applied."

"Honey, that's not really important right now. It'll take at least a week to find out anything. By that time I should be out of here." John shifted his feet and looked around the apartment as he spoke.

"The jobs. What are they?" the soft female voice demanded.

John paused, his head down. "One's re-stocking shelves at Home Depot, another's a night watchman at a Harkins Theater parking lot," he hated the sound of it as he said it, "and a custodial job at Lakewood Mall."

Another long pause passed while John paced. "Honey? Should I bring some stuff over?" he nodded his head in the affirmative involuntarily but listened hard.

There it was - her laugh. A wordless melody that made everything ideal and put the world right for him. His neck and shoulder muscles unwound as his tension melted from a compression he only now realized they had. His smile grew so wide it pushed his ears back.

He took a deep breath to speak his thanks until she continued. "No. I don't think that's a good idea. At one time I thought you might take us to Silicon Valley with your computer skills, or at least be able to provide a decent income in an upper-class area. I'm not waiting anymore. Call me if you land a high-paying technical job. Until then, we're through." The phone went dead in his hand.

The voice in his ear caused John to jump and spill his drink. "Is this your plan, shuffle down the sidewalk and indulge in over-priced coffee in a Wi-Fi shop?"

"I thought I got rid of you," John said into his cup, avoiding the looks of other patrons hurrying in and out. "Were you off getting your battery recharged?"

"Did you miss me?" A lilt in the delivery. Was his heckler cheerful? "Because I was beginning to think you didn't want my company."

"Drop dead. Blow your fuse. Use your candlepower somewhere else. Do anything, just leave me alone."

"Here's an idea." Rustbucket continued just as brightly as before. "Since you're free, let's go to Los Alamitos racetrack and watch the ponies run."

"That's a brilliant spark. Using energy to think like that makes you useful for, say, running a second-hand waffle iron." John swirled the beverage. "I've pawned all my computer equipment, and only got a fraction of what it's worth. Then the lousy manager won't accept my rent payment because I'm seventeen dollars short." John ran his fingers through his hair. "I'm out of my apartment for want of an Andy Jackson." He brought the cup to his lips and then set it down without drinking. "I found a homeless shelter, but they'll only let me stay there temporarily because I'm not pregnant or detoxing, and now your little dim-watt brain thinks a racetrack is an answer. I suppose you'll suggest I bet what's left of my money rather than use it to buy help-wanted ads."

"As a matter of fact, that's it exactly," John heard, followed by, "Sir, have you finished your coffee?" The last voice came from across the table.

John raised his head to see a worried barista, twisting his apron, and looking like he might run backward. The overweight young man must have been shorter than most of his graduating class if indeed he reached the end of his high school years.

John narrowed his eyes and peered at him. "You look familiar. Do I know you?"

"Yes, sir. I used to work for a security firm, and I had to escort you out of the building the day you were fired. But I'm here now, and people are nervous about you talking to yourself."

Nearby customers stopped their conversations to listen in.

John stood.

The ex-security guard, currently a frightened barista, took two steps back, his eyes growing large.

"It's OK, I'm just leaving," John said.

The kid wadded his apron between his hands. "None of it was my fault. I didn't do anything to you. It was my job," he said to John's back.

John waved his hand in the air. He cast a backward glance before he left to observe the apprentice barista scanning the vacated tabletop. "Ah, man. No tip."

WHAT'S A TRIFECTA

"You're still thinking of me as a program, aren't you? Something in your ear, as if from those portable music player buds. I'm not. It will help if you give me a name and use it."

"I gave you one." John kept his stride.

"I don't like it. I want a good one."

"What was it again?" John smiled, "Smelly Paint Can? Chamber Pot? Dirty Commode? Those are all good names for you. Oh, I remember. It's Rustbucket. That's your name if you want one, and that's the only one, so charge your capacitor with that."

John walked for half a block without any sound in his ears except normal outdoor city noises of southern California. The onshore breeze bringing a whiff of the ocean was pleasant and moist enough to make the ice plant shine, and the view of pedestrians in tee shirts, shorts and sandals almost made him glad he wasn't stuck in an office.

The voice returned. "There's a bus stop up ahead on the corner. You can reach the track from there."

"And you, Rustbucket, can put a rod up your southern magnetic pole and hire out as a sparkler. I'm going to the employment agency."

"You're so dense. Can't you see I'm trying to help you?"

"And gambling away what's left will do that?"

"Try to understand. You need cash inflow. You wasted a substantial amount on that new computer system and then pawned it. You have no savings and no credit card. The change in your pockets will transfer to tip jars in overpriced coffee shops if you don't do something. I can tell you how to bet on the races."

"Why would you do that? I've had nothing but trouble since you started talking to me."

"Hey. We're buddies. We need to live the good life. Let's go get some scratch and start enjoying ourselves. Helping you makes me happy."

"So you know which horse will win before the gates open? Is the system rigged? I can't believe that. You've got too much ozone under your lid, Rustbucket." John started to enter a Starbucks, but turned and kept walking down the sidewalk. "Or do you think you can fix the race I bet on? I don't suppose you're a big Fourth of July, sky-filled explosion of fireworks capable of doing that. You're probably a dim flash of an eighth-amp fuse being blown."

A half block later the cold voice of Rustbucket appeared in his ear. "I don't fix anything. I can compute the condition of the track, ascertain the health and attitude of the horse, calculate the pairs of horses and jockeys and their records, how long since their last finish, that sort of stuff, and give them odds. It's almost a sure thing."

"Almost?" John asked. "That's good. Almost?"

"Yes, almost. For every variable that I know, I can place it accordingly in a probability table. However, a gate may open a microsecond too soon or too late. A dirt clod may get kicked into a horse or jockey's face. A jockey may have a boil on his fanny making him ride to one side, throwing off the horse's stride. Those things I have no way of knowing. I can't account for them, but they can affect the outcome."

John stopped walking and took a seat on the bus stop bench. "Those are just minor things, aren't they? Not likely to really cause a problem?"

A woman with a plastic grocery sack sat at the other end of the bench.

"It's not likely, but a possibility," Rustbucket said. "It's certainly worth the risk. We can start with simple straight across the board bets. We can parlay the winnings until we have enough for the exotic bets."

"What are exotic bets?" John asked.

"Quinella, Exacta, Trifecta, and Superfecta. From there, we can go on to multiple-race bets, up to pick 6. I could explain how they work, but it's easier for you to place the bet as I tell you. We could be millionaires in a couple of days. Legally too. We're only figuring the odds like everyone else. We're not tampering with the race."

John sat gazing into the distance until Rustbucket inquired, "John? Did you listen to what I said?"

"Yes, I did. That would definitely get Riley to come back." Perhaps his dream could come true. His fingers moved as if they were typing on a keyboard. He hummed a tuneless melody as he worked through possibilities.

John nodded in agreement with a thought. "Having an instantaneous computer may come in handy after all. Why don't I go to an Indian casino and you can tell me which slot machine to put a dollar in to win a million bucks? It would be a lot quicker than placing all those bets on horse races."

"I-am-not-a-computer-or-program." Rustbucket's voice enunciated each word with the freeze of an icicle.

John flicked his hand in the air. "Yeah, whatever. Get back to the casino, you little electronic Keno Runner."

"Listen to me, John. You can't accurately compute the odds like that. After the pull of the slot machine handle, the odds return to the same probability as they were before for the next pull. They're the same each time. Once the dice are rolled, the odds of making your point on the next roll are the same as they were before."

John answered out loud, his bench companion still ignored him as if he wasn't there. "Well don't you get closer to hitting the jackpot with every pull of the handle? Like if you start off with the odds of hitting the jackpot as one in ten thousand, and the handle has been pulled nine thousand, nine hundred, and ninety-nine times, the next pull is a sure thing?"

"No, it doesn't work that way. I thought you'd have more sense being a programming guru. Besides, horse racing is an experience. It's exciting from the bolt out of the gates to the homestretch. Once started, the finish is not certain. Positions change, strategies play out, take a chance or not. Gambling is incidental to the reason of racing. The casino, on the other hand, is incidental to the gambling. Racing is classier."

John squirmed and pulled at his collar. "Still, I'm uncomfortable going to the track. Can't we bet some other way?"

"Sure. We could bet online, but you hocked your computer. We could bet by telephone, you still have a cell phone. Oh, wait. You don't have a credit card to open an account. All you have is a few bucks to give to the person behind the ticket window."

"All right," John said. "I'll go to the track after I go to the employment agency."

"How are you going to get there? This bus stop doesn't serve Westminster."

"I'll drive."

"You have a car? I've never seen you drive."

"Of course, I have one. Everybody in California has a car or two. I haven't been driving because it's cheaper to take the bus."

"Ah yes," Rustbucket said. "I just checked on the parking situation at your old job. It would have been expensive."

John stood and stretched. "In any case, I'm through for the day. I'll go tomorrow."

As he walked off he heard the woman whisper, "Weirdo."

CHAPTER THREE

SPIES

Viewed on a map, the business park looked like half of a teardrop cut long ways and tipped on its side with not enough room to accommodate all the parking needed for the five multistory buildings. The small lot worked to the advantage of agents in a brown Ford. They were parked at the western end of the complex next to Garden Grove Boulevard. From there they monitored the only access from the boulevard. The surveillance plan called for three more cars of operatives placed where they covered vehicular and foot movement around the contact—their own man. The briefing said he worked over a year to set up a face-to-face meeting with the spy they wanted to apprehend.

Sander Tretter, the younger agent in the Ford, contorted his upper body. "Was it necessary to be here since last night for a grab today? I thought the cloak-and-dagger days were over."

His partner and mentor, Calvin Roche, scratched chin stubble and checked under his fingernails before answering. "Well, this particular guy is really elusive. He's done us a ton of damage and never came close to getting caught. He's crafty enough to check out the area before he comes in. I wouldn't be surprised if we're on his camera."

Sander grunted. "I guess he could do it. This place is small enough. We don't need four teams. Two could cover the whole shebang. Frenchmen are supposed to be lovers anyway, not fighters. We could take him easy, I bet." He grinned and flexed his arms.

"He spies for the French, but he could be any nationality." Calvin pried a stuck piece of cold pineapple and ham pizza out of a grease-splotched box. He held an old slice up for inspection, dry cheese freezing the wilted bits in place. "Still smells fine," he said and took a large bite.

Sander stopped squirming. "I thought of something. The teams we've got are Alpha, Bravo, Charlie, and us. We should be Delta, but they're calling us Dog team. That's the old phonetic alphabet. They screwed up on that one."

"No, they didn't. They're doing that because of you. And I'd like to think it's because you're a puppy in fieldwork, and not because you're likely to go off howling and wagging in any direction. But you never know."

"Hey, I may not have the hours you guys do, but I'll probably be the brains of the outfit before long. I'd be smart enough not to choose this tiny parking lot stuck at the end of Garden Grove Boulevard for a meet if I were the spy."

"You wouldn't, eh? Orange County services are here, and all kinds of cars are in and out all day. Because it's small, he can quickly spot his contact, make a connection, leave and almost immediately be on the San Diego or Garden Grove Freeway. He can go north, south, east, or west in seconds. What's not smart about that?" The older man stuffed in another big bite of stale pizza.

When the younger agent looked like he would keep talking, Calvin pointed at the windshield, pushed his lower jaw out to avoid losing his mouthful and mumbled, "Pay attention to the entrance."

John drove into the parking lot looking for signs identifying the One-Stop Center, serving among other things as a California employment office. He found a space behind the building he wanted and got out. As he closed the door, a loud metallic bang ripped the air. Startled, he grabbed his ears and checked his and nearby vehicles before he realized the noise came from the street. A Honda on the boulevard rear-ended a Toyota in timing with his car door closing. John's heart rate thumped on high. The coincidence of the crash with his car door slamming disoriented and stimulated him. The giddiness of thinking he caused such a concussion tingled his back and made him pant for breath. Spotting a man sitting in a car with his window down looking at him, John grinned and approached him.

"That was a deafening wreck, wasn't it?"

Four strong hands grabbed him from behind and threw him on the pavement, pushing his face into the asphalt. John yelled as loud as he could. He lived in terror that one day he'd be mugged but didn't believe it'd be in a normal work day outside of the employment office. "I don't have any money. That's why I'm here. Let me go." His wrists were pinned in handcuffs behind him. A hood pulled over his head shut out his view of someone's black shoes.

"They got him. They got him already," Sander said.

"I told you he was crafty." Calvin pointed to the street. "Did you notice how he set up a wreck to divert attention from his meeting? Let's go grab the people in the accident before they take off, but don't be surprised if they know nothing and were only hired to do it."

Sander stuck his elbow out of the car window. "It's been two days. Have they decided yet if they've got the super spy or merely John Doe?"

Calvin drove the brown ford to a parking place in front of a Taco Bell. "John Smith. That's what all his records say. Also, that's what's bugging them. They can't decide if the guy's uber smart, one who laid a careful and extensive background story, or a common poor schmo who stumbled into our trap. They're tailing everyone that's had anything to do with him. There's a woman he says is his girlfriend, but she seems to be living an active social life without him, so that may be a weak link in his alibi. Personally, I don't believe anyone can be as vanilla as he claims."

"So what are they going to do? Send him to Gitmo until he confesses?"

"Scuttlebutt says they're going to bunk him with Vacant for as long as they legally can."

"Who are you talking about?" the young agent asked.

Calvin sighed and frowned. "It's a sad story, really. He was one of our best undercover operatives in the Middle East. He sent word that he had important information on the nuclear progress of some countries over there. He found out who is involved, and where the money trail leads, and then he said he needed relief immediately. He wasn't at his exfiltration point when they went to meet him, and they lost contact. A couple of weeks later, they discovered him sitting on a street curb in Istanbul—catatonic."

Calvin Roche rubbed his jaw and stared out of the windshield with unfocused eyes before continuing. "He's in the Arizona State Hospital. The mental ward, obviously, which the organization uses because it allows seclusion and privacy without arousing suspicion. Cameras and microphones cover the whole wing from every angle. We record every movement and sound in case he spills something. Even his exercise area is covered, and his attendants work for the agency. So far, he's basically an empty shell, so his code name is Vacant."

He put the gear shift in Park and turned off the ignition switch. "They figure they can hold Mr. John Smith for mental evaluation five days by convincing some justice of the peace that the man could be dangerous. That gives them another week to bust his story or decide if he's a straight Joe. Meanwhile, he'll be under pervasive surveillance." He patted his stomach. "This is a tricky business kid, and it has to be finessed. But now all we need to worry about is lunch."

Sander Tretter paused with his hand on the door latch. "OK, so are they sending him to Yuma then?"

"Phoenix."

VACANT

"Rustbucket, are you still with me? Where are we?" John mumbled in subdued tones without moving his lips even though he was in the room alone.

"So it's finally *we* now, is it? Yep, I'm still here, and I must say that you seem to have a natural talent for turning a bad situation into a disaster."

"I think I passed out after drinking the coffee they gave me," John said. He looked himself over. "Why am I in a hospital gown?" He ran his hands through the opening in the back. "I've got underwear; is this a hospital?"

"It kind of is."

"Well, I feel fine, and I'm getting out of here." He pulled the gown closed at the small of his back and held it with one hand as he searched the room. "Where are my clothes? Everything's gone, and all the money I have is in my pants."

"If you'll pay attention," Rustbucket said, "you'll see that you don't have any socks or shoes either."

"What's going on?" John's tried to keep his voice from going up high in the whiny range. "These guys that got me, they act like cops, but they won't say for sure. They've been questioning me for a week now, and when I woke up a while ago, it was in a different place. I don't like this."

"Quit exaggerating, John. It's only been two days, not a week. And considering that they think you're a national security threat, you've been treated pretty well. Oh, by the way, remember that days are called rotas and weeks are serotas on Montibar. But don't worry about it. I'll set it in your memory."

John rubbed the top of one bare foot against the calf of his other leg. "How could they think that? Is there something in my business program that's being used by NASA or something?"

A snorty whiff of wind hit John's ears followed by, "Oh, man. Do you really think you're that good of a programmer? No, you just happened to be in the wrong place at the wrong time. It turns out they were trying to catch a spy in the parking lot, and you tried to talk to their set-up man."

"That's it?" John felt the heat rise from his neck to burn his face. "They did all of this to me just for talking to a guy? They can't do that! This is America and I have my rights!" He set his jaw and pinched his lips tight. "I'm getting outta here." He crossed the room to the door and reached for the knob.

"Calm down, John." They'll figure it out, and I'm sure they'll restore you to your previously destitute condition."

John stepped out unchallenged into a short hallway. Farther to his left, two doors indicated rooms the same size as his. Within twenty feet the other way was a door marked Exit. He trotted in that direction as best he could, sliding in the cloth slippers that he found under the bed. John let go of his gown and used both hands to push the door open to reveal a green courtyard lush with shrubs, vines, and trees. Fresh air brought the scent of roses and some other sweet-smelling flower he couldn't identify.

A man dressed in street clothes sat on a concrete bench in the shade of rough-barked, thorny mesquites. The man's slack face positioned his fixed stare to the ground. He sat with his hands in his lap, unmoving and oblivious to the birds around a fountain, though they filled the air with songs and chirps.

John stiffened and froze with his hand on the open door lever. He examined the area, what was this place? Overhead vapor trails marked the cloudless sky. Faint sounds of city traffic bounced around. John swallowed and narrowed his eyes. He crouched slightly and scanned the enclosure more deliberately. After he inspected the little park, he turned to peer back inside the hall. Nothing changed. He gripped the outside door handle and pressed the lever twice. The latch retracted each time so he released the door to let it close. He took slow steps off the concrete pad in front of the door and shuffled onto the grounds toward the courtyard perimeter. His head moved of its own accord to the motionless figure on the bench.

"Acting a little paranoid, aren't you?" Rustbucket said, causing John to jump. "This is obviously an exercise area. They must be getting ready to release you."

John didn't answer as he undertook a circuit of the yard. Hidden behind the foliage was a wall of concrete blocks twelve feet high. Three rolls of concertina wire ran along it: one at the bottom, one in the middle, and one two feet below the top. The only way in or out was the door he used.

John rubbed his forehead, there was something strange going on here. Would the human lump know? "Hey, buddy. Can you tell me anything about this place?"

The man continued to resemble a statue.

John scooted to a seat on the far end of the bench as though it was made of ice and he would slip off. The man didn't move and John started to rise but inched back down. "Say, fellow, I don't want to interrupt your meditation or anything, but I need to find some answers."

"Leave him alone, John," Rustbucket said. I've just checked, and you're in a mental hospital."

"What?" John jumped up, aware that his stomach contents were doing the same. His vision turned white with little sparks firing at random. He brought his fists to press against his chest. "What have they done to me? I've got to get out of here." He gulped great breaths of air. While a corner of his brain warned him not to hyperventilate, his bench companion imitated a sculpture. John ran to the biggest shade tree, grabbed the lower branches and climbed, his cloth slippers knocked off by the rough bark.

THE SURVEILLANCE ROOM

"Something stung him." The observer sat straighter to face the monitor. He wore a full-length lab coat spotted with coffee and food stains. Visible under the unbuttoned, not so white over-wear, his street clothes were wrinkled and unwashed. His hair resembled a beaver lodge, and the start of a beard was evident on his chin. His partner took every opportunity to tell Ackerly that he needed a bath.

"What happened, Ackerly?" asked his neat companion, a technician wearing a name tag printed "Redmond."

"He was sitting next to Vacant and he yelled and climbed up a tree. At least he's trying to. He's jammed up there now."

"Play it back on split screen, and let's see it."

The technicians bent to the displays. Ackerly's eyes opened as wide as his mouth. Redmond's jaw set and his shoulders hunched forward. Both stared while they scrutinized the playback several times, then they went through it a frame at a time just before John jumped and yelled.

Redmond stood and let his shoulders drop. "Vacant didn't say anything. He's still catatonic. I think our man in there is some bozo who just stepped in the middle of the grab as they said possibly happened. He's probably some hippy having an LSD flashback. We know he talks to himself."

Ackerly stared at the monitor. "What if he is the superspy, though, and just had a secret communication. It's conceivable he saw something on Vacant that he recognized as a clue. If he's the spy, I'll catch him at something, sooner or later."

Redmond tried not to sneer. "Now how would he get a communication?" "They poked, prodded, X-rayed and scanned him for any hidden devices when he got here. I watched them. They found nothing."

"Did you scan for an implant? Did you consider that, smart aleck? A sub-vocal one would do it."

"Oh, man." When would Ackerly quit playing video games and check into reality? "You've been reading too many Sci-Fi books. Why don't you take a break? Go shower and get some clean clothes. You stink."

"I'd just have to go over all the recordings when I got back anyway," Ackerly said. "I might as well stay here in case he pulls a fast one."

Redmond waved at the monitor. "All that's happened is your super-spy has pulled himself into a tree, and it looks like he's ready to nest up there. Is he doing anything?"

Ackerly bit his lip. "I'll keep on him. He might try to string an antenna, or flash a signal over the wall or something."

"Sure," Redmond said. "Seeing as how he didn't have wire or a mirror when he came in, I'd like to see how super-spy does it."

"C'mon, Ackerly. He's been in that tree for thirty-eight minutes and all he's done is perch there. Let's send in Nancy."

"I guess you're right, Red, let's poke him a little. Give her a call."

Redmond swiveled his chair to reach a button on a console next to a flexible goose-necked microphone. Leaning forward he keyed the mic. "Nancy, are you available for courtyard duty?"

A feminine voice from a speaker filled the surveillance room, "Hi Redmond. I had a feeling you'd call, but I expected it before now. How do you want me to play it, doctor, nurse, stern, or soft?"

"Have her be a stern doctor," Ackerly said as he spilled a few drops of cola on his sleeve.

"A sympathetic nurse will do, please," Redmond said.

"Are you ready now?"

"Yes, please. You'll find him in a tree."

"You guys have got to quit mushing up peoples' minds," Nancy said. "I'm on my way."

John turned his head when he saw the door opening, and at the same time heard Rustbucket say, "You have company. Try to act like a gentleman."

A woman shorter than John's five-foot, eleven, by about four inches, entered the courtyard. She wore business clothes under a clean, starched, white lab coat. Her shoulder-length brown hair was pinned behind her ears with barrettes. John took her measure. She was attractive enough with minimal make-up, low heels, and no jewelry except a wristwatch and earrings.

"Don't behave as you usually do, and you'll make a good impression," Rustbucket said. "Well, as good as anyone in a hospital gown can while roosting on a limb. In your case, I don't think it will hurt your reputation."

The woman went to the man impersonating a boulder. She took her time evidently looking him over, tilting her head slightly as she inspected him. Then she walked to the base of John's tree and raised her chin to look at him.

"Hello. I'm Nancy," she said.

John felt the heat on his face and knew he blushed. He pulled his knees up and tugged the hem of his gown to his ankles.

There was levity in Rustbucket's whisper. "Can you act more girly?"

John ignored him. "Where am I, and why am I here?"

"Would you like to come down and talk about it?"

"I'm fine, thank you."

"Those trees aren't the best for climbing. I can see your scratches from here. Won't you come down and let me see if you need some first-aid cream on them?"

"There's a decent invitation," Rustbucket said. "Get out of the tree and go talk to her."

John couldn't keep a catch out of his voice. He let go of a branch with one hand to wipe his nose. "Please. Tell me what's going on."

Nancy sighed and lowered her head. She raised it again to look at a knothole in the tree trunk before addressing John.

"You are under suspicion of spying. Instead of being jailed, you were brought here for interrogation."

"What's she doing?" Ackerly yelled in the surveillance room. "She's giving up our hand."

"Or maybe she's forcing his," Redmond answered. "She's a pro, let's just watch."

On the limb, John huddled himself into a tighter ball. "I'm not a spy."

Nancy shrugged. "I suppose you'd say that even if you were. But we have to find out, don't we? Won't you come down now?"

"Is this a fruitcake hotel?"

Nancy straightened and frowned before answering. "This is a very secure wing in a mental hospital where we help recovering agents. You are here for this investigation because you talk to yourself. Sitting in a tree for this conversation may not convict you, but it sure adds to your collection of odd behaviors, don't you think?"

"How about that guy?" John pointed to the figure on the bench. "I'm not as weird as he is. Is this a place for the criminally insane?"

Nancy gave the benched man a brief look, "That's Va ... uh, Van," she said. "If you knew his past, you would give him your highest respect. If there are any criminals here, it would be you. It's our job to make sure there are none, so will you come down and talk with me?"

"Go on down John," Rustbucket said. "She's the best-looking one to question you yet, and I imagine she's the final interview before they release you. Look at her. What would be so hard about spending some time with her? You know you've got to do it to get out of here."

"Well, Doctor or Warden Nancy, I think I'll just stay here for a little while and think about it."

"Very well," she said. "When you come down and get back to your room, I'll have a tray of food delivered to you. Whenever you're ready to visit, step out into the hall and say so. The halls are monitored, so anytime, day or night, I can respond."

"The rooms aren't monitored?" John squinted his eyes as if he was shielding them from a bright light.

"No. We respect your privacy and rely on monitors outside your room."

"That's malarkey," Rustbucket said.

"I don't believe you," John said.

Nancy returned to the building leaving John sitting in the tree.

"Rustbucket," John whispered, "can you talk to anybody, or just me?"

"Anybody, why?"

"Ask the guy on the bench and see what he knows about this place. He might be a real patient or a mole to spy on me."

"I think you should go to your room, John. Behave your paranoid self and let them figure out who you are. You'll be out of here tomorrow."

"No. I want some answers. You started talking to me and I've had misery ever since. If you were just a voice in my head I wouldn't be in this much trouble. Maybe I've been the lab rat for the government all along, and you're a radio wave beamed at my skull. Maybe bench boy here was the first one they used, and they messed him up."

"You're getting yourself all worked up, John. Calm down."

John pulled his knees closer to his chest and his hospital gown down farther as he scrunched into a smaller ball. He closed his eyes and pressed his forehead against the trunk.

"Talk to him," John insisted.

"You have to respect people's dignity, John. You don't go busting into their head without a good reason."

"You busted into mine, and screwed up my life, how about that?"

"All right." John heard a sigh. "I wanted to wait until you were in a better attitude to tell you, but ... here goes."

CHAPTER FOUR

CONFESSION

"I am the Regulator for Montibar." Rustbucket made the statement sound imperial. "I oversee the operation of train schedules, power plants, and everything that needs coordinating. I control the weather, tides, and tectonics. I am one of a kind, and I make Montibar a paradise. I know you'll question why a planetary Regulator would be talking to a person hiding in a tree on an entirely different planet, and I guess it's time to tell you the whole story."

"I didn't ask for your tall tale," John said. "I only want to know why I'm being messed up."

Rustbucket continued without acknowledging John's whine. "My presence here should tell you that I can and do travel the universe at my discretion. The species of so-called intelligent life here on Earth is the same as on Montibar and piqued my curiosity. It seems humans can be born to destruction, and I stop by from time to time to find out if the race has avoided annihilation. In fact, a concept I discovered on one of my visits here is the poison pill solution. I've seen it many times: where the situation is deemed so intolerable to a party they would rather destroy themselves and/or all of their assets before someone else can use them."

John ducked his chin to his chest and hugged his knees. "Why don't you try that poison pill yourself? It would make my life easier if your assets were long gone."

"I'm trying to explain something extremely important to you," Rustbucket said. "It's hard enough for a normal person to understand, much less a mental ward inmate sitting in a tree with ants crawling in his hair."

"Ants in my hair?" John yelled, slapping his head with both hands, leaning forward as far as he could. "Get 'em off me." He brushed his head then his shoulders, and then his head again.

"That's not important," Rustbucket said. "This is their tree. They were running around on it before you came along. Pay attention."

"Are you listening? As I told you, there is another planet called Grabin following in the same orbit as Montibar, closer than Mars is to your Earth. I help Grabin out a little, though they don't realize it, but Montibar is the one I've chosen to bless with my benevolence. The people there are much like here. Left to their own devices, they rattle their sabers when they're bored, and they scheme incessantly to subjugate each other."

A breeze, a whisper, or a sigh passed before Rustbucket continued. "I should know better than to take a lesson from humans, but I got egotistical and set up a poison pill for the entire solar system hoping the mere thought of total destruction would forever bring peace."

John finger-combed his hair, searching his hands after each pass.

"I positioned an asteroid field in orbit around their solar system. They're far enough out so they don't interfere, but both planets can still observe and track them. It's a delicate balance to keep the space debris from crashing inward toward the star and bombarding everything in their path. Only my energy net prevents it. I made it plain that they are secure while I'm in control, but if anything usurps my authority a cosmic barrage commences. Then Montibar and Grabin die."

John quit brushing and frowned. "Oh, brother. I'm nuts for hearing a voice in my head telling me it's crazier than I am. Your solution to peace is to kill everyone?" John thrashed his head again and twisted to check out his shoulders.

"The Montibarans view the field as a shield, but the Grabinians think of it as a threat, and spend all their money and science to find a way around it. I'll say one thing for the human species,"

Rustbucket said. "They're shrewd and sneaky little parasites. Fascinating, actually."

He was quiet long enough for John to ask, "Something went wrong, didn't it?"

"Yes, but not like you probably think. I gave each planet control over the energy net. Either one can enable an arming mechanism that alerts the other that the next step will collapse the structure holding the asteroids away. Once armed, it runs on automatic. Any disruption to the governmental order, doesn't matter which world, triggers the release. The celestial masses hurl inward bombarding the planets. Life in the solar system ends. However, things can be secured and everything returned to normal if the net is secured."

John relaxed his knees and let his legs hang over the branch. He brushed his chest and lap with one hand, hanging onto a limb with the other. Dumb ants, he hated them. He wanted out of the tree. His bottom was numb and his leg was asleep. He couldn't walk if he were on the ground, and that irritating voice was still talking to him. When did he lose it so bad he heard voices? Maybe a mental ward is where he really did belong. Where did that woman go? Maybe she would help him. He should talk to her instead of the voice, but this time, the sound in his head interested him. "So what's the problem?"

"Oddly enough, it's my omnipotence. I considered every possible means of human attack and took care to counter any threat after the system is engaged. It's no harder than an afterthought to me. Unfortunately, I didn't foresee that the security blanket for all communications and control would recognize me as something you call a computer virus. My role as Regulator would trigger the cataclysm. I can't return to the surface of either planet."

"Aha. I knew you were a program."

"I am a living, evolving *being*. Understand that."

"So fix it, Almighty Nebula."

"John, don't joke around like that. Though I'm one of a kind, at least as far as I know, I'm not divine. A creator is what I search for, and you shouldn't take it lightly."

"So fix it, off-gassing sulfuric vapor cloud."

Rustbucket made his tone sound cold to John's ear. "The people of Montibar or Grabin would never think to show such disrespect. You have no inkling how much patience I extend to you."

"Yeah? Why is that?" John asked, causing another long silence from Rustbucket.

"That's it. I'm climbing down and getting outta here. I don't care if I wear clothes or not. They can't keep me. I'm tired of being everybody's chump. What would Riley think if she could see me now? She'd probably laugh at me."

Riley's laugh. A melody that made his head buzz and put a lump in his throat. It drenched him with soothing love that melted away the world's cares. He had to return to her.

"John. John, are you listening to me?"

"No, and I'm going to make it a practice to ignore you from now on. I'm coming down."

"I said I need you."

"What?"

"To save my solar system."

"You screwed it up. You handle it."

"I suppose you never acted less than professional when you were out of town?"

"Well if you aren't just the funniest little whiff of misfired synapses I've ever had. You're more deranged than I am." John twisted to grab a branch. "Dang, my leg's asleep, and now it's tingling like crazy. Hey, that's funny, right? First my head then my leg is going nutso."

"John, please. Two planets, their civilizations, need me, and I need you. If I try to talk to the man on the bench, would you believe me, or at least listen to me?"

"You're to my ears like floating black spots are to eyes. What am I saying? You wouldn't know about ears and eyes, would you? But ask him to tell me anything he can about this place and how he got here. You do that and I'll listen."

John leaned left on a limb, working the toes on his right foot feeling the hot tingle go up his leg as blood flow returned. The stranger stood and turned in a circle. His movements were glacial as if he had to pause at each degree on the compass.

"Johhnn?"

"Got him!" Ackerly jumped up so hard his chair went backward halfway across the room.

Redmond leaned to the gooseneck mic, "Security to the courtyard. Bring in the guy from the tree. Nancy, Vacant is walking and talking. Recover him."

WHAT I NEED

"Oooh, man." John ached from top to bottom and some body parts burned. He tried to rub his eyes to slow the sparks and flashes, but he couldn't move. "What's this? Why am I strapped down? Hey! Hey, anybody! Turn on a light. Where am I?" John uumphed and groaned against the bonds on his hands and feet.

"I'll transport you to Montibar," Rustbucket said. "Once there, flip a toggle switch. Just ask the king to do it. It's insanely simple."

"You're a nitwit. I just got tasered. I can't see, and I'm hurt. They jolted me and busted me up. Help me escape."

Rustbucket's voice held a giggle, "The only busting up that happened was when you fell out of your tree. It was funny actually. You were as limp as a rag and parts of you draped over every branch they hit on the way down. You bounced. Now about Montibar—"

"Are your circuits smoking?" John strained until his wrists chafed. "The only place I'm going is out of here, so help me or shut up."

"You said you'd listen if I got the guy to talk to you. He did, so listen."

"You call that talk? He mutters one word and the place explodes. Leave me alone."

"But you said —"

"Go away!"

A door opened exploding light into the room, exposing the dimensions to be not much larger than a cell. John squinted against the glare while his pupils contracted enough to avoid whiteout. He was strapped to an operating table, bare and exposed, except for his shorts. Coming through the door was a muscular man pushing an apparatus on a cart. He hummed a tuneless melody.

Hospital staff didn't dress in black.

John recognized him. "Why'd you hit me with that taser? I was getting out of the tree anyway when you shot me. Hey, buddy, how about letting me up? We'll talk."

The hulk moved to the foot of the table, unwound a cord and plugged it into an outlet. Out of a compartment, he extracted a small pouch.

John lifted his head as high as he could and tried not to whine. "C'mon fella. Why am I tied down? Let me up, okay?" He craned his neck to see that his visitor was holding. It resembled a finger cut from a leather glove. The man pulled out another. Thin wires connected them to the box. Humming, he slid the pockets over John's big toes and repositioned himself at the gadget.

John's eyes were dry and gritty, but he couldn't blink or tear his gaze away. Ordinary citizens weren't tortured. They were only scaring him. This big ghoul certainly was. "Wait ... wait. What are you doing? You can't—"

Hulk pressed a button on the device.

"AAAAAAHHH!" John's legs jerked straight and rigid. Did they yank his toes off or just the nails? He lay panting, drenched in sweat, moaning.

"That's setting One of Three," the tormentor said. "Now there's good news and bad news. I'm limited to number One today. That's good for you, bad for me." He terrified John with a grin that looked like a Doberman biting into a lemon. He raised his chin and looked down his nose, "But I can use it as often as I want. *Bad* for you, *good* for me."

John swallowed to stifle a whine. He wouldn't plead with this Neanderthal for mercy but negotiate perhaps. Maybe if he told Hulk how much Riley needed him, he'd reconsider—that's it, think of Riley. Sweet Riley. He had to choke down the on-rushing panic of being exposed and vulnerable. Even though his toes burned in the plier-like clamp of red-hot blacksmith tongs, he'd demand his rights.

"Look, you goofball—AAAAAAHHH!" The jolt stretched him taut. His back arched off the table. This time tears mixed with sweat rolled into his eyes. Mush flowed into his arms to replace the bones that had gone missing, and his legs wouldn't stop quivering. His tongue was a plank that flopped to whichever side of his face was turned downward. He wouldn't be able to talk now if he wanted.

Interrupting his humming, the man in black asked, "Who hired you?" The question came soft and inquisitive, opposite of the demanding force applied by the box.

"Uh ... uh." John strained to form words. "Wah-ta. Peese, wah-ta."

"You want water? Sure." Hulk retrieved a bottle from a shelf on the cart and unscrewed the cap.

"John, you don't have to go through this," Rustbucket said. "I can help."

Teary perspiration blurred John's vision. He needed that drink. His interrogator stopped and poured the water over the pouches on John's toes, getting his feet as wet as his armpits.

Back at the machine, Hulk asked again, "Who hired you?"

"Peese, wah-ta. Don' push butt'n. AAAuuuhhh." John saw the darkness coming and let it wrap him like a flannel shirt.

Nancy rolled an EKG machine to the table. John saw the electrodes and whimpered. "Don't. Please, no more." His voice was a hoarse whisper. He edged as far from her as the restraints allowed.

"This is only to check the health of your heart, Mr. Smith. They don't want to kill you, but it could happen. Especially if you receive higher voltages. Those shocks are dangerous."

"She's right about that, John." Rustbucket's voice echoed in his skull. "You're a pathetic mess, probably halfway gone already. Consider the irony of them zapping you when you're so afraid of my energy. When you passed out, that big fellow called you a weenie and threw the plastic water bottle at your head. You need to listen to me about going to Montibar."

"Riley needs me," John whispered. "Can't go."

"What?" Nancy stopped what she was doing and leaned over. "Who needs you?"

"Girlfriend ...," John sighed as he slipped into exhausted oblivion.

"John, don't *say* anything. Just *think* it and I'll hear you." Rustbucket's tone was a dark as the shadows.

"Wha—" John raised his eyebrows to help open his cast-iron lids.

"Hush, John. Be quiet. Don't talk. These people are not fooling around. When the guy on the bench stood and said your name, that convinced them you're a dangerous spy. This is a counterespionage agency, and they play by their own rules. They can hurt you."

How can you tell what I'm thinking?

"I monitor the neural pathways to your speech center and interpret the input. That's the simple explanation. You wouldn't understand the full technical description."

You've been in my head?

"No. I wouldn't do that without invitation if it weren't necessary. The Hulk, as you've been thinking of him, is getting ready to increase the shock treatment—"

John gasped and the restraints kept him from going fetal, his actions catching the attention of his inquisitor. "Ah, Sleeping Beauty awakens, eh? I've got a present for you. Setting Two." He offered John a malevolent grin. "Unless you tell me what I want to know, and I hope you don't."

"Don't worry," Rustbucket assured John. "I won't let them give you more than the first setting. My analysis shows that I should leave them a useful tool or they'll move on to something else, but I've even lowered setting One. Try to act like it hurts more than ever."

Don't let him, Rustbucket, please stop him.

"Who do you work for?" Hulk asked, and then pressed a button without waiting for an answer.

Nothing. John didn't feel a tingle. Hulk frowned and tapped the input several more times. Still nothing.

"Scratch winning an Academy Award," Rustbucket said inside John's skull. "We'll let him think setting Two is broken."

Thank you. A rush of warmth for Rustbucket filled John's chest.

Hulk turned the setting back to One and pressed the button.

An unpleasant buzzing vibration shook John's legs and his mouth opened to emit a larynx-tearing scream. *How did I do that?*

"I had to help with your acting skills, so I prodded some control centers in your brain. Is that okay?

As long as it keeps me safe. But that's scary, please don't take over my mind. John's thoughts rushed to consider his body and mind gone, no longer his. He was no more than a dartboard for Hulk and an audio system for Rustbucket. Tears slid from the corners of his eyes.

Rustbucket heard his fears. "John, it's not that way."

"That's more like it," Hulk said, turning the knob once again to the higher position. He pushed the discharge control switch. When his victim didn't react, he slammed his fist on the cabinet. "Still nothing? Maintenance is going to pay if it's broken."

John sloshed through a swamp of confusion and horrified thoughts that threatened to drown him in panic.

"Stay calm, John. I won't let anyone hurt you, and I'm not engaging in mind control. Watch this; it will make you feel better. Hulk's been trying to give you setting Two. I can't believe what he's about to do to see if it works. Watch."

Hulk removed the gloves from John's toes, placed them on his own index fingers, and with a thumb, pressed the button. He flew backward roaring like a crowd watching gladiators, tearing the wires from the machine. He hit the wall and sank unconscious in a massive black pile.

John cried again, laughing tears of joy. He was still giggling when the hospital team rushed in. *Thanks, Rustbucket. He deserved that.*

"I didn't do that. I wouldn't. He did it to himself and we just observed. I don't harm people."

You let him get zapped.

"Yes. People have to be allowed to express their free will."

More aides arrived with gurneys. They put the moaning Hulk on one; John was unstrapped from the table and placed under a sheet on the other.

Nancy appeared and walked beside him as they wheeled him down the hall. "Mr. Smith, I have convinced them to stop using such rough—"

Is she lying?

"Yes," Rustbucket whispered in his mind.

"—techniques. All we have to do is talk. I'm taking you back to your room so you can clean up and dress. I'll have a food tray delivered, and we'll visit. How does that sound?"

"That wasn't much of a meeting," Rustbucket said. "All you did was eat half a bucket of fried chicken and insist that she call Riley. I was impressed with her maneuvering, though. Her questions were designed to give her some in-depth information about you. In your stubborn insistence about calling your girlfriend for verification, you thwarted her every move. Congratulations, John. Now let's talk about you going to Montibar."

I'm not going anywhere with you, much less a different planet, but I'll listen. I owe you that. Tell me again what it's all about.

"It's a very simple problem with catastrophic consequences. The King of Montibar armed the Dooms Day system. He had to have realized I was off on one of my jaunts and wanted to warn Grabin not to try anything. I can't go back in because sensors will detect my energy and collapse the power net maintaining the asteroids. I can't control it. It would be like you trying to stop an avalanche after you removed the brace from under the boulder holding back a mountainside. Meanwhile, Grabin, instead of backing down, has used the opportunity to infiltrate Montibar. How devious is that? Doing exactly the opposite of what they're supposed to do.

The other planet attacked?

"No. They couldn't get away with that. They sent some effective operatives to ensconce themselves in key positions to gain political and financial control. Since organic bodies can travel at will, I want you to go to Montibar. All that's necessary is to turn off a switch in the King's bedroom closet. Simple. The threat is disarmed. I'll return and put things back to normal.

It would never work. I don't know the language and I'd stick out like a nose pimple.

"I'll impress all necessary cultural cognition in your mind. As for the rest, a haircut and different clothes are all it'd take. I've found that across the universe humans are universally ugly. What do you say?"

Why me? All kinds of space nuts would jump at this. Why did you upset my life?

John heard a sigh echo in his ears. "Because your absence wouldn't cause suspicion. You have no family, no one to miss you. You have a history of sticking up for foster kids which means you care for others. Above all, you're average."

If that's true, then there must be lots of choices.

"Oh, sure there are. But on the average curve, you're at the peak ... dead center. You're the most average of the average. Average age, average height, average job, even your name, John Smith. C'mon."

I see. I'm an average nobody.

No, you don't get it, John. You're special because you're so average. I sought you because you're uniquely average. You're really singular in your averageness."

As soon as I can make them to talk to Riley, she'll straighten out this mess.

"Are you sure she feels the same way you do? Didn't she say she was through with you?"

John's stomach underwent a twisting pang at Rustbucket's words. His neck heated constricting his throat, threatening to pinch off his wind. He gulped for air and took in a long slow breath. *She was upset ... didn't mean it.*

The conference room held Redmond, Ackerly, Nancy, and four shadowy profiles. A masculine voice from the head of the table asked, "Does anyone doubt that he's a spy?"

Heads shook negative in the dim light and No's and Nope's came from those gathered. A female from the right side said, "He's a master at it too. Somehow he got Hickey to put the probes on himself at level Two."

From the other side came a calm response, "Hickok. Hickok Spinks is the technician. Let's keep it professional. But you're right, Mr. Smith's clever. I'm wondering if he didn't allow himself placed in here so he could reach Vacant."

"That's plausible," said a third in attendance. "Vacant has been supplying us with a lot of good information. Mr. Smith may have been sent to determine if our man would ever recover and if so, terminate him."

The first speaker said, "Mr. Smith insists he has a girlfriend, Riley Watford, that will validate him if he's allowed to talk to her, but I suspect it's a scheme to pass information. Perhaps the mere fact that he labels her as his girlfriend triggers a pre-coded protocol. Should we let them communicate under our surveillance? The risk, of course, is that he will succeed in passing data, but we may find a key to their organization."

The attendees were silent until Redmond spoke. "Don't allow them to talk face-to-face. If they telecommute we can record them and study the meeting in detail."

Ackerly cleared his throat, held up a finger and added, "We should contain Ms. Watford at our facilities until we're sure she's clear. At least detain her a month so she can't pass time-critical information Mr. Smith may want her to have."

MY GIRL

"Oh, man I've got to retire soon." Calvin Roche rolled down his window on the driver's side of the brown ford. "Cooped up in this car, and you eating burritos, should be hazardous duty pay."

"Listening to your boring stories about the old days is hazardous to my mental health," Sander Tretter replied. "Your nose can pay for the stink my ears suffer." He laughed at his wit, and then conceded, "Okay, you've got a point. Especially if we have to pick up a passenger. It galls me, though, that after all our training and time on the pistol range, the agency turns us into cab drivers."

Calvin spit out the window. "You've played too many James Bond movies. Counterespionage is like what Pappy Boyington was supposed to have said about being a pilot: 'Flying is hours and hours of boredom sprinkled with a few seconds of sheer terror.' Whether he said it or not, that's our job description."

"Yeah, but still we—"

"Stuff it. Here's the girlfriend's house."

John entered a conference room and faced a laptop opened to show Riley's glaring face. His heart pounded and he melted with affection for her. She came for him and she would tell his captors off in spades. Look at her; she's just waiting to chew them to pieces. He took a seat and gushed his love for her. He spoke of his dream of their own home and a small business. He would make it happen just as soon as he was released. She would help him.

Riley laughed. She trilled the sound John wanted most to hear. A rhythm from her beautiful throat, so elegant and rare it had to be God's gift. Then she started clawing. At first, John tried to keep up with what she said, but when the target of her harangue became evident, he fell silent. He sagged in his chair while the voice from the computer spoke ever harsher. She kept the flow of vile acidic monolog directed at him unabated until his shoulders dropped and his head bowed. He no longer watched her and scrunched down to half the size he was when he arrived. He drew his knees up to place his heels on the edge of the chair and wrapped his arms around his legs. John's head spun and his ears rang. What happened? Someone was telling him the meeting was over. He pulled up the bottom of his shirt and threw up in it.

The same conference room held the previous attendees. Their faces showed lines of fatigue but they leaned forward and listened as the speaker put his elbows on the table and steepled his fingers. "It's been a long day, but we've made significant progress. Have you all reviewed the tape of Mr. Smith and his girlfriend?"

Various forms of "yes" emitted from the guest with the female voice saying, "That was the most brutal thing I've ever seen. She eviscerated him."

"Did anyone else feel affected by her tirade?" the first person asked. "Was this a one-sided love affair?"

Answers were unanimous in the affirmative.

"If you think that, then look at what our cryptologists found." He clicked a hand-held remote control and a screen dropped from the ceiling. The face of John Smith appeared as he watched Riley during their computer meeting. "Now if we mute the audio and darken the image except for his eyes, watch what happens. Does anyone see it?"

No one responded. "I didn't either," he said. "But if we say when he moves his eyes left to look in her right eye it's a dash, and when he moves his eyes right to look in her left eye it's a dot, then a code is discovered. They have found buried in all that data are the words 'Down' and 'Eagle'. I believe Mr. Smith wants to launch Operation Down Eagle which will not be good for us. We worked this out at 11:29 a.m. and alerted agents worldwide to increase the security level. They've already stopped two suspected sabotage attempts in the mid-east."

"This is the slickest spy we've ever met," said the calm voice near the head of the table. "I have to admit some admiration for him. He had me fooled with his 'lovesick' routine."

"Us too," Redmond said. "Ackerly used half a box of tissues after he left."

"So did I," said Nancy, "and I'm still not over it."

"Enough," said the head speaker. He pointed at Ackerly, Redmond, and Nancy in turn, "You guys set up a surveillance room and sic Hickey on him tomorrow. I want to know all about Down Eagle."

John didn't move. His stare fixed on nothing, his hands lifeless in his lap.

"I'm sorry," Rustbucket said. "Her behavior was uncalled for and callused. Why don't you try to eat something? You might feel better." There was no response from his pet organic module, so Rustbucket continued, "Um, I have some disconcerting news, John. They're more convinced than ever that you're a spy. They mean to start grilling you hard tomorrow."

"You cost me my job. Did you turn Riley against me?"

"No, John. I didn't force her away. I merely set up the conditions that highlighted her choice."

"Can you get me to your spaceship?"

"What? No, I don't have one, remember? I travel interdimensional space via quantum entanglement. For practical purposes, it means I can go faster than the speed of light. I don't need a ship. If you'd paid attention when Kevin came to see you, you'd understand that."

"How will you take me to your planet? I'm ready."

"Oh, I see what you're getting at. Are you really saying you'll go to Montibar and disarm the Dooms Day arrangement?"

"Yes."

"Uh, John, I've got to tell you something. I'll just be barely able to sneak you onto the planet and disappear before sensors detect my energy. I can't stay to help you or even talk to you once you're there until the crisis is over."

"Okay."

"You'll be on your own to find a way into the King's bedroom closet."

"Okay."

"It would be nice if you showed some enthusiasm for the trip instead of moping around with a flat voice."

John didn't say anything or move, so Rustbucket continued. "Your name will be Jinmyn while you're there. I'll see that you remember it."

John shrugged his shoulders and let them drop.

"Here's the last thing, John. You know the Star Trek series where they use a transporter? Well, the funny thing is, they almost got it right." Rustbucket paused ... and waited. "John, I have to disassemble you here and reassemble you on Montibar."

"Okay."

"Raw materials aren't immediately available inside the castle, but there is a pond nearby with water, plant life, and other elements available to construct you."

"Okay."

"Have you found Smith yet?" The head speaker's voice dripped knives.

"No sir," replied a shadowy profile.

The speaker turned to a figure beside him, "Bring the girl-friend to Phoenix, maximum security. She stays here until she out-lives Medicare."

Ackerly scratched his unwashed scalp. "The hospital only lost power for less than a second. It was dark for a mere blink."

"There's no way he could get out," Redmond said, scanning all the monitors, "just no way."

CHAPTER FIVE

A PERFECT LANDING

The Gaumen Shack hosted its usual evening ambiance of noisy groups watching sports in the back room, while couples enjoyed a meal in the front dining area. Other patrons celebrating their special occasion were seated at any available space.

The door to the rear parking lot opened and a Montibaran officer, as proclaimed by the "Ozier" badge on his hat, towed in a stumbling man wrapped in a blanket. They made their way into the tavern where the official helped his charge onto a stool before addressing the bartender. "Hey Mikara, do you recognize this guy?"

"No, I can't say I do ozier." The short, balding, mixologist combined amber and vermilion liquids as he cast a disinterested gaze at the blanketed figure. "Why?"

"I found him lying naked in the grass halfway between here and the palace. He doesn't test drunk, but he acts like it. All I can get out of him is his name's Jinmyn and he has to see the King."

Mikara, along with LauNin, the female server, laughed. The little barkeep, still chuckling, said, "He isn't the first imbiber wanting to tell our monarch how to rule, but they usually keep their clothes on."

The cocktail waitress scanned the blanket-clad individual from the top of his grass-tangled hair to his bare feet. "It could be I remember him from earlier this evening ... hard to tell with him wrapped up like that."

"Well that's how he stays until he can find something to wear," the ozier replied.

A well-lubricated group of revelers picked up on the interchange and turned it into a celebration. The women whooped about a man in a blanket, and the men wanted to help him on his way. Others in the room quit watching their sports as Jinmyn became the center of attention. Mikara and LauNin exchanged a glance. The routine of a profitable evening was on the verge of disruption.

LauNin slid her tray down the bar. "My apartment's two doors down and my brother has some clothes there," she said. "I'll go fetch something and be right back." It was a guaranteed way to earn extra tips. "We take care of our customers," she said, in a loud voice causing a roar of approval from the partiers.

Mikara nodded and she turned to go. "Hurry up, the patrolman shouted behind her. I need my blanket back."

She left with a grin as the crowd amused themselves by trying to coax the flatfoot to down a drink.

John tried the thought process to communicate. "Rustbucket can you hear me? I must be on your planet; I don't recognize anyone or anything. When the cop asked me my name, I knew it was 'John' but 'Jinmyn' rolled off my tongue and felt right. The people look and act just like us, so if I'm really here, I understand the language and seem to fit in. Here comes the barmaid with clothes. Thanks for the strip job incidentally." The voice inside his head that had bothered him so much was silent. John—Jinmyn—missed it.

"Try these on," she said pointing to the men's restroom.

Jinmyn rose and collected the blanket around himself. "Thank you miss, uh ..."

"I'm LauNin. I'll be here."

He hesitated and she raised her eyebrows as he ducked his head and asked in a voice only she could hear. "Where is this place?"

"Oh, this is The Gaumen Shack."

"No, I mean what planet?" Jinmyn squirmed, kept his head down but rolled his eyes up to search her face.

"You are out of it, aren't you? This is Montibar. Normal traffic between here and Grabin has been sporadic for serotas now. If you were trying to travel, there's no way you could have missed that."

"That's right. Now I remember," Jinmyn said, before she questioned him further. "Where do I go to dress?"

Through the door Jinmyn heard the ozier agree to a non-alcoholic soda drawing groans from the crowd. Finally clothed, he emerged as Mikara slid the drink across the bar with a wink. The peace officer took a generous swallow and smacked his lips. He grinned and finished the glass in another gulp. He didn't get a chance to order another; Jinmyn returned his blanket.

LauNin cocked her head to one side. "You don't look any worse with clothes on. Do you want to tell me what you were doing now that the law's gone? Don't worry about him coming back, either. Mikara slipped a double dose of roggen into his soda."

Jinmyn rubbed his chin. "Was I in here earlier? It sounds silly, but I don't recall much before he grabbed me. My memory's fuzzy."

"Nah, I just said that to get him off your back."

"Why would you do that for me?"

LauNin laughed and poked him on the arm. "You're not one of our regular customers, that's for sure. That ozier is a friend of ours and I did it for him. He makes it easy for us, and we make it easy for him. This way he doesn't have to take you in and fill out a bunch of paperwork. And Mikara made sure our hard-working protector got some refreshment."

Jinmyn swayed and took a step backward to steady himself.

LauNin reached for him. "Are you fit and healthy?"

"Yeah, just woozy I guess."

LauNin crossed her arms. "I'm uncertain about you," she said, "but I'm going to take a chance. I'll be off shift shortly, and my apartment is close by. Why don't you go there and rest? There are some leftovers in the cooler if you want, and you can recuperate."

"That's unbelievable. You'd let me in without knowing me? Why?" Jinmyn frowned and held his palms up. "I'm in borrowed clothes, empty pockets, have nothing, and may live hand-to-mouth. How can you trust me?"

LauNin smiled. She had a pretty smile. "We're taught to help our neighbors, aren't we? Besides, you seem clean-cut, not counting the grass in your hair. So if you only need a listening ear and a meal to pull you over a bad spot, I'm happy to do it. If it takes more than that you can go to the services."

"Thanks," Jinmyn said. "I'd like that."

"Getting there is easier if you go out the back door, the way you came in," she said. "Go out and turn left. My place is two doors away—simple. Here's a key."

"I'm grateful for your kindness and I'll respect your property." As Jinmyn turned for the rear door he beamed a thankful smile at his hostess, but LauNin was glancing over her tray to a figure in the dim corner booth. Did she give a slight nod?

"What now, Rustbucket? This isn't what you told me it would be like."

Outside, Jinmyn stopped to taste the fresh, sweet-smelling breeze. Unlike the ocean air of southern California or the hot dry atmosphere of his last tortuous place of confinement, he detected the aromatic scent of flowers and growing plants. Dusky twilight didn't diminish the beauty of the unfamiliar view. Past the parking lot, a meadow rose to a tree line at the foot of a rounded hill. On top was a palace with multi-colored lights splashing out of hundreds of windows. Is that where fair maidens dance; is there a drawbridge and fortified ramparts? Jinmyn trembled as the fantasy took root. Who was he to enter there?

Overhead the clear night sky twinkled with sparkling stars and constellations he didn't recognize. He searched in vain for the Big Dipper and North Star, the only points he could ever identify and, as always, shrunk in being as the size of the universe overwhelmed him. Was God watching over him now in this unknown world? Why would a majestic Creator that built such an incomprehensible expanse care about him when even Riley didn't love him?

An ache shot through him so fast and hard it woofed his breath away. This was an alien sky meant for others, and out there somewhere were asteroids ready to destroy it all. Why had he agreed to come here?

All because of a girl.

Rustbucket ruined his life and he consented to trash the remains of it because his feelings were hurt. An adolescent reaction, like a teen-aged boy mooning over a prom queen.

Looking through the depth of space and galaxies, his lost love didn't seem so important. He should be back on Earth, making things different. Next time he would keep a practical rein on his heart.

The stars blurred through his teary vision. He wiped a runny nose on the borrowed shirt sleeve. Sorry, LauNin. He would wash it before returning it.

"All right Rustbucket. I'm going to walk up to fairyland and tell the King to throw the switch. Then I expect you to take me home. Here goes ..."

Head up, jaw set, Jinmyn strode a dozen steps into the parking lot heading straight for the palace when strong arms encircled him from behind and lifted him off his feet. The sudden grab sent a tingling up his back. On its own, his mouth emitted a girlishly high squeal as the constriction around his chest made breathing difficult.

He wheezed a gasping appeal. "I don't have any money. Let me go, please?" The grip still held him firm. Jinmyn saw a figure approaching from the side. He twisted to kick at the new arrival and got a satisfying solid connection that made him realize he was barefooted. His little toe shrieked its distress, and Jinmyn gave voice to its agony.

His opponent stumbled backward and grunted words Jinmyn didn't recognize. Did Rustbucket censor his vocabulary? He did understand the venom in the expletives and his neck hair stiffened. A mugging gone bad and now he was going to be hurt. Fear and adrenaline boosted his scream, "Let me go! Leave me alone!"

"Shut him up," said a voice behind him. The gripper's breath blowing over Jinmyn's ear and past his nose deposited a sauerkraut odor. "Put him out now!"

The assailant came again avoiding Jinmyn's flailing feet. Still using unknown words, he succeeded in placing a cloth over the thrashing victim's face.

Hot madness flared even as his body relaxed, and just before he went to sleep, Jinmyn heard one of them giggle.

THE CAFETERIA

Two men dressed in white stood in the hall gazing through the window into Jinmyn's hospital room. NadYat, the taller of the two, had deep lines etched around his eyes and across his brow bespeaking years of worry, exhaustion, and frowning. His utterance was as soft as a falling snowflake. "They almost killed him. Rein in your hotheads, Velmere, or we'll never take our place as head of the solar system. Don't they realize the asteroids are primed?"

Velmere answered his superior but kept his gaze locked on Jinmyn. "I understand, and I sent word to them. They said he put up a struggle causing them to leave the potion on him longer than needed. He's talented; one of our men got a split lip requiring stitches when the suspect kicked him. He broke his own toe in the fracas as well. Have you discovered which agency employs him?"

NadYat shook his graying head. "Not yet. Working with our own governmental services is next to impossible. We're always in a war for budget allocations and sometimes that's fiercer than territorial problems. Whoever put him on Montibar lost him, or his insertion was sloppy. Either way, no one is going to claim ownership. Perhaps we can persuade him to admit his bureau." NadYat stroked his chin. "I bet he's with the dark underground."

"How do you want to handle him, friendly or intimidating?"

"Start friendly. We can always go meaner. Send LanCena in to fix his broken bone. Then, when he wakes up, take him to lunch."

Velmere blinked. "What?"

"Not off the property," NadYat said. "Eat at the cafeteria, stroll the grounds, be a buddy. And Velmere, as long as I'm Director of Grabin Security, I insist our agents act as professionals."

Jinmyn stretched and rolled over. He needed a few more minutes of sleep in this warm bed, but someone was calling him.

"Are you going to wake up now?" The speaker sounded feminine—nice.

He cocked one eye open a slit and took a slow view without moving. The soft pillowcase snuggled against his nose with the whiff of a floral detergent. He had no energy to raise an arm, much less roll out of such a comfortable nest. He weighed a ton. His body was probably creating a trough in the mattress.

"There you are." The polite voice had a sing-song lilt. "You've had a long rest and your toe is mended. It wasn't broken as we first thought. Are you ready for lunch?"

Jinmyn ran the tip of his tongue over his lips and growled his vocal chords into action before swallowing and turning his head toward the sound. "Broken toe?"

"No, sprained. You're all fixed up."

He jerked upright, going lightheaded with the movement, making the room chalk-like under the sterile lights. "Two guys grabbed me, I was outside and—was that chloroform?—where's this place?—did the ozier come back and catch them?"

Jinmyn gulped lung-filling breaths while his thoughts caught up. No, no, no. This wasn't at all how it was supposed to be. "Rust-bucket, are you back yet? If you're not here, who's watching me?"

He held the bed sheet like a screen and shrank from the nurse. "Who are you, who's in charge here?"

She patted his shoulder. "I'm LanCena. Velmere will be in shortly now that you're awake. I'm sure he'll explain everything to you. There's a robe in the closet and slippers by the bed. Toiletries are in the bathroom." She turned to leave.

"Uh, miss ... uh—"

"LanCena."

"Miss ... LanCena," Jinmyn swiveled his head and pointed at the window, "can people see me in bed? Where am I?"

"I think they're hoping you'll recognize it," she said, on her way out the door. "It's the hospital wing of the government operations complex."

He must be near the palace. "Can you talk to me, Rustbucket, please?"

"Good, you're up." The visitor's shoulders and upper arms stretched and strained his lab coat. He bobbed his crewcut head toward the robe while pointing at the slippers. "It's time for lunch. Today's giss and bru in the cafeteria." I'm Velmere, by the way.

Jinmyn understood "spaghetti and meatballs" even as his ears heard the alien words, and he *was* hungry. When was his last meal, and where? It didn't matter. This person trying to pass as an orderly said the magic word, "cafeteria", and all other questions went on hold.

"Would they have steak and mashed potatoes? I could eat a horse," Jinmyn said. The syllables warped and twisted to the strange language when his vocal chords translated them.

Velmere's laugh sounded genuine. "Let's go see; it's right down the hall."

The aisle was antiseptic, bright, and broad enough for two-way traffic. Employees went past in either direction with quick determined steps, patients somewhat slower. Was this a true hospital this time with real caring people? Jinmyn hoped so.

His escort glanced at Jinmyn's slipped feet. "You seem to be walking just fine. I'm told LanCena set your broken toe back to normal."

Jinmyn almost lost his balance ducking his head to peer at his foot. "She said it was only sprained, but about that, what happened to the men who jumped me? Why did they grab me, and who saved me and brought me here?"

Velmere held up a hand. "I'm sure you have a lot of questions, Jinmyn. That is your name, isn't it? We do too, and we can go over them at lunch. Here we are."

They entered a large circular area with two more oversized hallways spaced equidistant from theirs filtering people in and out. They were in the hub of activity with three walkway spokes converging inward. The aroma of baked bread and grilled meat kicked in Jinmyn's salivary glands. He swallowed. Twice. A shiny tray line stood against one curved wall where white-clad workers doled out heaping quantities of meats, salads, puddings, soups and globs of food Jinmyn couldn't name but knew to be tasty. Accessible from any table, buffet counters containing servings of different courses, desserts, and specialty drinks were scattered throughout the room. The scent was so sweet that Jinmyn could taste lemon meringue just by licking his lips.

They took their place in the queue as Jinmyn noted the number of diners. This place had to be bigger than most hospitals. Maybe the only one for the whole city. Another indication that he wasn't in Kansas anymore. He grinned thinking that he could use that phrase for real now.

Velmere saw and misunderstood the grin, "The food here is excellent. Take all you want."

He did. By the time he took what sight or aroma dictated, Jinmyn's plate looked like a pyramid. Before he decimated the pile, Jinmyn stopped to consider his change of fortune. He had been ill-treated, but now he was in clean clothes with a gut-busting lunch and apparently among friends.

He lifted his eyes to Velmere to express his thanks and saw a young girl carrying a tray. She stopped at a table of several diners. She spoke and moved on to another. He paused, fork poised in the air with a tine-bending load piled on it. The solemn expression on the girl's face, her deliberation in approaching tables of adults, something about her behavior, captured his attention. Her clothes weren't extraordinary: a dress white on top, black below the waist with yellow flowers on the skirt; it had a high bodice with no sleeves. Ebony hair touching her shoulders hung shiny and straight, no ribbons or barrettes. A choirgirl maybe?

Her path brought her to Jinmyn; she searched his face. "Do you want my pudding?" She barely encroached the table edge, a skittish fawn ready to bolt.

Jinmyn frowned. "Why don't you want it?"

A soft answer, downcast eyes, "I got it for my mama, but she's too sick, and she told me not to eat many sweets."

"Sure, I'll help you out," Jinmyn said, taking it off her tray and setting the cup next to his plate.

The girl left without a word and took a seat three tables over. A tic in Velmere's jaw accented a frowning squint on his reddened face.

Jinmyn couldn't miss the body language. "What is it, Velmere? Did I miss something?"

Velmere took the time to inhale, deep and deliberate, before speaking. He dipped his head in the girl's direction. "Most of us are familiar with her family. Her mother is dying. She lost her father several cycles ago; she'll soon be alone. Listen, what she said about the pudding is true, but every day she gets it and offers to give it away. No one takes it so she can have it. I'm sorry, I realize you didn't know."

Shame rocked Jinmyn. Remorse flooded over him like it was dumped from a cauldron. Yes, he coped with displacement, rejection, and loneliness, but she shouldn't suffer any of that at her age. He glanced at her sitting alone, her toes not reaching the floor as she sat on the edge of her chair, her chest against the table. Her little back was ramrod straight. She was still young with perfect posture: no teenager's slouch.

He put his plate and her pudding on a tray, picked it up and went by a dessert counter on the way to her table. "May I sit with you?"

She studied him with the frankness of youth. "Mama says not to talk to strangers, and you're different from me."

It was Jinmyn's turn to see her in more detail, her oval face framed with that shiny black hair, the white top of her dress accentuating her copper-colored skin. What was that old movie filmed in the red rocks of Arizona ... Broken Arrow? Yeah, she would be right at home in it.

Jinmyn dipped his head in agreement. "That's true, but I look a lot like Velmere, and he knows your mother. Is that okay?"

Velmere had shadowed Jinmyn's movements and now stood with him, each holding his tray, respecting her privacy until receiving an invitation to sit.

She inspected Velmere. "You know Mama?"

Velmere bobbed his crewcut in the affirmative. "I worked with both of your parents here."

"I don't remember Papa. Mama says he was handsome and fun." Her somber face implored Velmere for confirmation.

"Well," he said, "men don't usually call other men handsome, but I suppose he was. He was very witty and a fun companion."

"Then I guess you can sit down." Shifting her chestnut brown eyes to Jinmyn she added, "You can too."

"Thank you," Jinmyn said, sliding out a chair. "I didn't realize that I already had dessert when I accepted the one you offered. Now I have too many. We should share them." He slid a pudding and a piece of what his new memory told him was close to chocolate cake, over to her. "My name's Jinmyn. What's yours?"

The ends of her mouth cracked upward as she scooped up the treats, "Brimlet."

"Well, Brimlet, how do you do?" Jinmyn said, and extended a hand toward her. She recoiled a smidgen and turned to Velmere. "What does he want?"

"I'm not sure." His head held in a questioning tilt he asked, "What do you want, Jinmyn?"

Jinmyn laughed at their seriousness. "Shaking hands is something you do when you meet someone, or reach an agreement, or just wish them well. Hold your hand out like mine."

Brimlet inched her hand across her tray, keeping her eyes on him. Why did he feel the desire to know this girl? Or was she a child? He'd never paid attention to kids before, they were just ... kids.

She shook Jinmyn's hand with solemnity and looked at her palm before reaching for the pudding causing him to chuckle. While she minced on the treat, Velmere ate, and Jinmyn shoveled it in.

After plowing through half of his plate, Jinmyn asked, "How old are you, Brimlet?"

"Twelve Standard Cycles."

Jinmyn's built-in knowledge bank translated her age as seven years old. Tough for the kid, she's probably too old for make-believe and too young for coping.

"What do you do for fun around this place? I haven't seen much of it myself. I've only been to my room, the corridor, and this cafeteria. Is there a gift shop or library?" He drummed his fingers into a marching beat, it was the best he could do. "Or, have you found a dance hall somewhere?"

He hoped for an amused response and didn't get it. Velmere's face reddened, he cleared his throat and pulled at his collar. Brimlet's ears turned persimmon and she stammered in a weakened voice, "No."

What had he done? This one wasn't Rustbucket's fault; it was his own lame social skills and his ability to alienate people. Oh, that's a good one: alienate extraterrestrial people. Could he sink any lower?

Scolding himself, he shook his head and frowned. "Um, listen, Brimlet—"

"There's a game room I go to sometimes when Mama's resting." Her chin was down, hair falling around her face.

Relief, like surfacing after a long dive and getting that deep breath of air filled him. No long-term damage. He couldn't stand to think he might further hurt the soul of this girl-child.

"That sounds like fun. Could I go there sometime?" Jinmyn meant to make amends. Brimlet still had much to endure, he would not cause more discomfort for her.

"I'll have to ask Mama. If Mr. Velmere comes with me she may say it's all right."

"Well let's go find out." Jinmyn rose to stand.

"One moment please." Velmere waved Jinmyn back to his seat. "There's a communicator there." He pointed to a device that Jinmyn interpreted as a telephone mounted on the wall next to an entrance. "I'll call first. If your mama's resting, we don't want to bother her."

"Good idea," Jinmyn said, and Brimlet agreed with a nod.

Velmere approached the instrument and removed the receiver. He stood rigid and square-shouldered, facing away, his free hand making small gyrations as he talked. Jinmyn listened to Brimlet telling about the doll her mother made while dividing his attention between her and his guide. Velmere shifted his feet and stole glances at the table. It must not be good news for Brimlet.

The plight of the serious waif touched Jinmyn. She faced a miserable future even if he saved her world from destruction. He would support her in every way he could while he was here. First, she could have dessert and then some fun. Then he could continue his mission.

Velmere returned wearing a toothpaste ad smile. "We can go to the game room."

THE GAME ROOM

Joy and disbelief rolled into one conflicting emotion struck Jinmyn. Brimlet led him into a familiar room on an alien world. "An Arcade, fantastic! I killed these things in my younger day. This is going to be great."

Velmere jerked sideways, moved his lips but didn't say anything.

Jinmyn took two trips around the gallery, looking over the shoulders of the few adults playing visual, noisy games. He felt like a kid among the bells, whistles, and flashing multicolored lights. He grinned wide and asked Brimlet, "Which one's your favorite?"

She pointed at a machine that showed more wear than the others. "I can only play that one."

"Oh, is that one for your age group?"

"No. You have to get a high enough score on a game before you can sign on the next one." She raised her chin. "I haven't scored much yet, but I will."

Jinmyn didn't doubt her defiance or resolve, and his heart gave a thump as she stood with her feet planted as if to take on fate. If she would soon be alone, was it asking too much to play whichever game she wanted?

Not if he could help it.

The custodian lounging behind the counter smiled at Jinmyn and Velmere. Jinmyn spoke first. "Who does the maintenance on these games?"

"I clean them off and make sure they haven't been bounced out of place."

"No, I mean who takes care of the program that runs them, you know, makes them light up and noisy?"

"A person from Admin comes in and does that when we need it."

"Oh." Jinmyn's shoulders drooped. "I was hoping you had everything right here to fix them."

"Well, we do. Here's all they ever use," said the gamekeeper, producing a keyboard from a knee-level shelf. "They plug it in this box down here." He pointed to a small mainframe. A display screen sat beside it.

"Then we're in business." Jinmyn tapped his fingers in a drumroll. "Do you mind if I have a look at it?"

Velmere stepped up. "What do you want to do, Jinmyn?"

"I want to see if we can't let Brimlet play any game she wants. I don't know if I can do it, but it won't hurt to try."

Velmere squinted his eyes; his lips compressed and he turned his head down and away. After a moment's pause, he glanced around.

Jinmyn observed Velmere's behavior and realization hit him like a kick to his chest. Why hadn't he noticed it before? Velmere was talking into a microphone. Even on an alien world as Jinmyn, he was still under surveillance.

Velmere strode to the door and waved for an assistant dressed as a medical intern but built as if he carried the ambulance. He wore a stereotypical crewcut.

"Brimlet, would you go with this man for just a minute while I talk to Jinmyn? You too, sir," he said to the caretaker. There was no mistaking the authority in Velmere's request as he cleared the room. When they were alone, he smiled, pointing with his hand palm up toward the keypad inviting Jinmyn to proceed.

Jinmyn supposed it was inevitable that he would draw attention. Rustbucket dropped him here naked with no plan. Just walk into the King's closet and disarm this insane house of sticks. He was tired of all the subterfuge. Why not let them know who he was? He needed help, and so far, Velmere had been approachable. Yes, Jinmyn would straighten it out, but first, he'd give Brimlet a perk if his idea worked.

Jinmyn activated the computer and soon realized the logical order of the programs. The games were simple and only the degree of the difficulty settings seemed to be much different. He found a common subroutine in each game and inserted a new command line with:

If name = "Brimlet" then ...

His new instructions went on to ensure that Brimlet could play without losing on any machine. He pressed "Save" and unplugged the keyboard.

He faced Velmere, "That's all there is to it. Let her try one now."

Velmere's hands curled - not quite fists. He balanced on the balls of his feet in a dancing position or fighting stance. "We set out to go to lunch. This is a strange turn from that."

Jinmyn held up a hand. "I know. I didn't see this coming either, but that poor kid got to me. Hey, Velmere. Don't be such a skeptic. Let Brimlet have a good time for once and we'll have us a heart-to-heart talk over a Starbuck's."

NadYat began as soon as Jinmyn and Velmere sat at the conference table. "Which agency are you with? We cooperate with all of them as much as we can, but we won't tolerate clumsy interference with our mission." He didn't bother appearing casual or using other ploys in questioning.

It struck Jinmyn that this darkened room was very much like the room where his unpleasant video communication with Riley took place. It had the same smell of human occupation mixed with disinfectant, the same seating arrangement that told without a doubt who was in charge. Did they mean for it to appear a threatening cave? No need to rehash that. So far, he felt unthreatened, and maybe he even had allies here.

"I'm not with any agency, and I don't know about interfering with your plans, but—"

NadYat groaned. "Please, Jinmyn. I hoped to avoid idle talk and get this settled quickly. I don't have a lot of time to waste." He eyed his notes.

"Okay, but—"

"What is meant by 'handshake'? Is it a recognition signal? Why did you kill 'arcade' and which machine is it on? Where is 'Starbucks', is it a moon?" NadYat traced his finger down a list. "You're obviously a spy, maybe even a good one once, but something went wrong or you wouldn't have shown up naked and confused, exposed to everyone." NadYat waved away the pun. "Exposed as an agent, not undressed. Now, can we stop the games and clear the questions?"

"Not again." Jinmyn slumped in his chair.   Accused once more. Why did this keep happening? He shook his head and pulled one foot up on the chair. "Didn't you see how much fun Brimlet had this afternoon? She got high scores on machines that those grown-ups couldn't finish. She had the time of her life. She actually laughed at that man's reaction when she beat his score. Is a child's amusement something a spy would take the time to set up?"

"Yes, that's another question for you Jinmyn. How did you know to do something only an elite group do with the game controllers? Moreover, why did you say, 'Not again?' Have you been accused of spying before?"

"It was basic programming. How can you not know that? You have modern electronics for Pete's sake."

NadYat's eyelids narrowed, "The Regulator controls technology. You know that."

"Did you see how happy she was?" Jinmyn spoke to himself and grinned at the memory before returning his awareness to his inquisitor. "I don't work for any agency, but I do need to get into the palace, so if you'll point me in the right direction I'll get out of your hair. Are we within walking distance? I don't have money for a taxi."

NadYat seemed almost furious. "Which palace do you mean?"

"How many does the King have? I guess the one that was in front of me when the goons grabbed me would do."

NadYat, Velmere, and the assistant dressed as an intern stared at Jinmyn. NadYat spoke with an undercurrent of threat, "There is one palace on Montibar and one on Grabin. I ask you again, which one is your intended target?"

"The one here on Montibar, of course."

The squeak of Jinmyn's chair was obscenely loud in the hush that filled the room. Velmere broke the silence. "This is Grabin."

CHAPTER SIX

WORLDS APART

Jinmyn's throat constricted despite the lump in it. His voice wobbled and squeaked, "Grabin? I was looking at the palace on Montibar ... it was right in front of me. What happened?"

Velmere shot a glance to NadYat who gave him a small nod to continue. "We brought you here. Our field ops thought you were one of ours. You acted disoriented and they wanted to protect you. Now it's up to you. We hold you until we find out who you are. And please don't trot out all your evasive spy tricks. It will only ensure your stay, with increasingly uncomfortable accommodations."

Jinmyn slumped, put his elbows on the table, and rested his head in his hands. "What have you done?" Was this how it ended, die alone and unknown on a strange world? His life was so messed up that he wasn't even on the right strange world. At least on Earth, his landlord and co-workers recognized him.

The attention level on Jinmyn, already high, jumped to spotlight intensity as both NadYat and Velmere leaned in.

NadYat glared. "Tell me. What did we do?"

Jinmyn's stomach had the queasy sensation it did when he rode the light rail. Every time the electric train took off from a stop, the acceleration left his innards one seat behind. He gripped the edge of the table. Why not tell them everything and ask for help? They would see the sense in it. Then Rustbucket could show up and take him home. No, they'd never believe the whole story. If he told every bit of it, he'd wind up back in a mental hospital, or worse.

NadYat slapped the polished wood hard. It shook it under Jinmyn's elbows interrupting his reverie. He raised his head to see that Velmere appeared surprised at his superior's heated action.

The Director tilted forward, hands flat. "I've reached the end of pleasantries." His stone-cold face cracked as he spat out, "I'm listening."

Jinmyn wilted in his chair. "I'm not a spy. Never was." He started ... hesitated, choosing his words, turning them around to fit together. "I only want into the palace on Montibar to convince them to de-activate the asteroid danger."

NadYat snorted. "You want us to believe that you're a concerned citizen simply trying to persuade their government to change a course of action?"

"Essentially, yes."

"That's a real problem for us, Jinmyn. We've confirmed that the Regulator is away and that's why their king ran like a sissmutt into his backup threat."

Jinmyn got a mental picture of a sissmutt. The timid rodent ran from shadows and could die if sufficiently startled. If information about the underbrush dwellers could be recalled, Rustbucket implanted a massive amount of information into Jinmyn's gray matter. He shook his head to concentrate on what NadYat was saying.

"Now that Montibar thinks they're safe, they're lax on security. We can put people all over their planet through trade and diplomacy routes. Naturally, we want to place as many as possible while we can. Therefore, we don't want to take away their perceived safety. Now I explained our situation, and as a professional courtesy, I expect you to do the same."

Jinmyn squirmed in his seat. "What if the Regulator, as you call him, can't return? Do you want to live under the threat that someone won't accidentally start the war that triggers the rock rain?"

A staring match between Jinmyn and NadYat kept silence in the room until NadYat said, "That's an odd choice of words, '... as

I call him, 'and 'can't get back.' Everyone knows the Regulator. It can do anything it wants. Do you work for a Montibaran agency?"

"No."

"So you're with one of ours?"

"No."

"Who then?"

Jinmyn sighed and broke eye contact. "I can't tell you. You wouldn't believe it."

"So you're not just a concerned citizen?"

"No. Well, not like you mean it, but I'm very concerned that both worlds are in great danger."

NadYat wrote on a pad and without raising his head asked, "Is there a reason, other than in your imagination, that the situation is grimmer than either planet believes?"

"Yes."

"Why?"

"I can't tell you."

"I don't understand him," NadYat said. He and Velmere took their dark, steamy drinks to a table overlooking the green and flowered expanse of the grounds. "Two rotas now and he won't divulge more. He's a spy or an operative. Of that, I'm sure. At the same time, he shows no signs of a threat. And that bothers me."

"You're bothered by that?" Velmere frowned and sat his cup down. "Why?"

NadYat gazed at Velmere's image as it faded and reappeared through the vapors that escaped the aromatic brew. He took a sip before explaining. "I can't explain it. Perhaps I've been in the business too long. I see deviousness and false trails in everyone's actions. Their pursuits are never in our interests, or if they are, it's only a coincidence to further their own goals. If Jinmyn convinced me to relax, would he use that to his advantage? What would his goal be if it weren't to save the worlds? He is either Mr. Perfect or Mr. Perfect Agent, and I don't believe anyone is perfect. Yes, I'm bothered."

NadYat swallowed a bigger gulp of the hot drink than he intended and got a scalded throat as a result. He coughed until the sensation passed and berated himself for losing even that little bit of control.

Velmere, as always, concentrated. NadYat could see the concern on his face. Loyal Velmere. His records stood up to intense vetting from his youth. NadYat never regretted handpicking him for the agency. Velmere always followed regulations with strict discipline. He probably wouldn't have coughed if his gullet were on fire. Enough of this, he had a problem to solve. "Jinmyn and the girl, Brimlet, spend a lot of time in the game room. It appears innocuous on the monitors, what do you see?"

Velmere's face softened and he cuddled his mug in both hands. "He seems to truly enjoy the time with her and is intent on letting her have fun. It's the first I've seen her smile since she came in with her mother."

NadYat measured his protégé with narrowed eyes. The child brought out an unseen side of Velmere. Better get him back on track. "So our enigmatic Jinmyn worries me, and all you say he's doing is playing. Are we using our best efforts, or are we being duped?"

Velmere's neck and face flamed ember red. NadYat expected to feel the heat from across the table. His companion's short crew-cut seemed to bristle as Velmere jerked rigid. As near to the position of attention he could attain while sitting.

"Sir, I have never stopped observing our subject for any sign of intrigue."

"Good. *Our subject* has a way of referring to *the Regulator as we call him* as a personal acquaintance. It's unsettling. Either he's delusional or something basic has shifted, and we'd better find out which."

Still braced in a stiff posture, traces of a monster blush glowing; Velmere dropped all semblance of a convivial meeting and assumed the attitude of a subordinate. "Do you wish to allow him to continue to the game room with the girl?"

NadYat's furrowed visage showed no clue that his own beverage tasted sour. When his time as Director ended, he would explain to Velmere how it pained him to push people away, but he had no choice. "Yes, let them interact for now. If he refuses to say anything more, and if the next shuttle arrival brings no identifying news, he won't be enjoying our hospitality as much."

Voices at his door woke Jinmyn. Brimlet and one of Velmere's ubiquitous shadows were exchanging words. Had he been drugged again ... how long was he out this time? No, just sleepy, the timepiece on the stand showed the middle of the night. He was getting paranoid thanks to Rustbucket. What would Brimlet be doing here at this time of night? He checked to make sure his pajamas were intact and opened the door.

A muscular guard filled the door, blocking Brimlet, "You can't go in. Go back to your room and try again in the morning."

Brimlet's fists hung at the ends of her inflexible arms. Her level chin refused to show submission, her eyes tilted up to glare at the obstacle. Whatever her reason for being here, Jinmyn was on Brimlet's side. He shoved against the meaty mass. "Let her by."

He may as well have pushed the wall. The guard didn't move a hair's breadth and didn't acknowledge the thrust to his broad back.

Velmere's shoes pounded a staccato click from his rapid stride as he arrived appearing as fresh as if he had a good night's sleep and plenty of time to dress. He made a brushing motion with one hand and the human wall moved aside.

Brimlet entered the room in mechanical, robotic steps until she stopped in front of Jinmyn. He bent with his hands on his knees and searched her impassive, dry-eyed face. His insides went hollow and a heated lump grew in his throat. "Brimlet ...?"

She caught his gaze, "Mama died." She flung her arms around his neck and howled a long, soft "ooooh."

Jinmyn knelt and hugged her while she pressed her face against him and sobbed. He felt her little body expand and contract with erratic breathing as her diaphragm tried to synchronize with her emotions. Fat tears rolled between her squeezed lids and baptized his collar. A rush of warmth and inadequateness filled him. If only he could stay and protect this little orphan he would. No one, not even the children at the foster homes, had captured his heart so completely. Brimlet never asked for help or tried to place blame. She tried her best to cope.

Her combination of bravery and vulnerability drew Jinmyn to wrap his arms around her.

But he couldn't stay with her.

His mission could not be allowed to fail, and that meant doing what he must to return to Montibar and remove the stupid poison pill threat. For now, though, Brimlet needed comfort. *Rustbucket, see what you've done. Relying on people's good judgment is about to annihilate them. Can't you help even a teeny bit now?*

He lifted blurry eyes, searching for Velmere, "Where's the Chapel?"

Velmere shook his head as if he didn't recognize Jinmyn. "What's a Chapel?"

Rustbucket must not have included a complete vocabulary for him. Speaking strange words isn't going to convince them he not spying either. "It's an area where you can pray for spiritual comfort."

Velmere frowned, lifting his shoulders, "I don't know what you're asking."

"What is wrong with you people?" Jinmyn stood, holding Brimlet. "We need a place to pray, to connect with the Almighty, to contemplate our lives."

"We have a meditation garden," Velmere said. "It's a quiet peaceful area and sometimes people use it to try to figure out what the Regulator wants. Will that do?"

"If it weren't for Brimlet I'd be tempted to leave your sourdough biscuit planets soaking in a rancid Regulator gravy. Where's the garden?"

"I don't know those words, but I'll show you the garden. The fountains will be turned off this time of night." Velmere turned to lead and inclined his head for the guard to follow.

COME TO THE GARDEN

Brimlet stopped crying but kept her head on his shoulder as Jinmyn carried her down the halls. Queasy apprehension hit his stomach when he stepped outside into a scented atrium of flowering plants, blossoming vines, small streams, and green seclusion.

Paths ending in cul-de-sacs branched at random from the stone-lined trail. They offered little secluded areas containing benches. Jinmyn could see idle fountains holding stagnate water. This was nothing like the enclosure at the mental hospital, but his heart insisted on déjà vu and his stomach was obliged to turn nauseated.

Velmere swept his hand across the little Eden, "Wherever you like." He flicked a glance at Brimlet draped over Jinmyn's shoulder, "I have to stay with you, of course."

Jinmyn noted the arrival of a second guard. "It looks like the Director intends to stay with us as well." He took Brimlet along the path until turning into a private spot under a large tree that reminded him of a weeping willow. Tiny yellow blossoms saturated the verdant corral with a lemony scent. Jinmyn's implanted knowledge identified the red clouds of flowers shining from the border shrubs as the source of the faint cherry aroma. Velmere and the guards stood near while Jinmyn took a seat on the bench, his arms around Brimlet as he moved her to his lap.

He wanted—needed—to do something for her. "Brimlet I'm so sorry you lost your mama. I hoped to find a place with someone available to help you understand about life, but I guess this will have to do. There's a story about a garden where some very special things happened, so maybe this will do for us. Would like to hear about it?"

Her hair tickled underneath his chin as she nodded against his chest.

"Okay then, but I'm kind of unsure on the specifics, so I'll tell it like I think it goes. The Son of God was in a place like this, and he was praying for all he was worth. He knew his life would soon end in a terrible manner, but that was the main reason he was born, anyway."

"That doesn't make sense," said a guard, before pressing his lips together when Velmere shot him a quick glance.

"I know, it sounds tough to swallow," said Jinmyn. "But the idea is that God loved mankind so much that he let the people destroy His own Son."

The guard snorted.

Jinmyn cleared his throat. Why did he start this story? He didn't really know it. "See, it's supposed to be a promise of love not hate. And His Son didn't stay dead, but what he did means that we get to do it too. We get to live in another way."

Brimlet rested in Jinmyn's arms; Velmere and the two guards were alert but appeared bored. Jinmyn knew a discussion about religion should generate more interest than what this group evidenced.

"Velmere, do you have similar stories here?"

"No. Was God a warlord or a ruler?"

"You don't know about God? Incredible! Then you don't know what praying is, do you?"

"No. I wondered what you were talking about."

"God is the Creator of all things. The whole universe. And since He made it, He loves it. He created the stars and all the planets. He formed us in His image, and when we talk to him, we call it praying."

Velmere tilted his head. "Like the Regulator then?"

"He's much more, and He considers you His child, every bit as equal as a Regulator.

Jinmyn spoke until sunrise. People moved through the garden. Another two guards arrived to relieve the first two, but no one left. His legs were asleep from Brimlet sitting on them and he was hoarse.

Velmere was still alert. "So we all have free will? That's a nice little touch that means we can take it or leave it. Well then, do you believe everything you told us?"

Jinmyn never faced the question directly. He grew up in foster homes. He lacked parental love. What could he possibly know about Heavenly love? Was it love that formed the concept of foster homes, and if so, was it from God or man?

"The truth?" Jinmyn pursed his lips, nodded his head and replied, "Yes. I believe in God and His Son."

Brimlet had been so still Jinmyn thought she was asleep, but her voice trembled as she spoke soft and low. "Do you think Mama's with God now?"

PARTY'S OVER

"Is he a lunatic, Velmere? The first inkling we have of his organization, the so-called Christians, and he says it's no secret." NadYat
picked up his cup, sat it down, spread his hands to speak, and then
dropped them to his lap. "I've had the lab working all night to get
a trace on them. Either he's crazy or the best I've come up against
and I can't take chances. He goes into lockup. I want you to begin
more persuasive discussions with our Jinmyn."

"Yes, sir. What about the girl, she's still here since she has no
one else ... and she's become attached to him."

This part of the job wore on him and made NadYat look forward to retirement. It got harder every cycle to ignore innocent
people who got hurt for being close to the impact of planetary politics. "Keep her away; distract her with lessons, classes, whatever
girls do. Delegate it." NadYat's chiseled face frowned deeper. "I also
want you aboard the next diplomatic shuttle to Montibar. Contact
our field crew and find out about Christian activity there."

"Sir, I'm bound to be known to Montibarans as working for
our Security. I'll be watched like an oozing slyvet."

NadYat almost shuddered at the thought of the toxic, squishy,
arm-sized, brown and green worms so ugly their name became a
derogatory epithet. "Of course, you will. That's why you'll never
leave our embassy on your mission of a routine inspection of our
personnel. That's political speak to let them know we want to
make contact. Inform the Ambassador what we're doing, and he
can get the word out about Christians."

Velmere scrunched up his face in a way that NadYat identified as mental calculations. "The shuttle will be here in a couple
of rotas and be ready for a return trip in a serota. I'll be gone two,
maybe three, serotas; do you want to wait that long before apply-
ing pressure to our guest?"

"Absolutely not." NadYat shook his head and made a fist.
"I'm out of patience. He's being interrogated right now. I had him
moved this morning." NadYat raised his chin. "Try not to look surprised, I'm still the Director and don't have to tell you everything."
There, that should put Velmere back on a professional footing and

squelch sentimentalities for orphans and Christians. The trip to Montibar should reestablish his priorities as well. NadYat nodded to himself. Let's return to normal.

This was a different wing of the hospital. Jinmyn told himself that there was nothing to worry about. He hoped it was true. Two guards that had to be members of muscle beach sandwiched him, their footsteps the only sound he could hear past the blood pounding in his ears. The taller guard with the massive under-slung jaw that gave him a perpetual scowl led; the one with hooded eyelids followed. They were no longer in wide, well-lit sterile halls. The darkened, airless concrete shaft they trod was like a mineshaft, lacking only the dank, musty smell of wet dirt and mold. The hallway ended at a metal door. Jinmyn expected the bulging muscles of Jaw's arms would be required to force open such a structure. A heavy barrier like this would only give way inch by inch, shrieking iron protesting the pressure against its resting inertia.

That's not how it happened. The gateway swung open on oiled hinges at a fingertip touch. They entered a bright bare room; a wooden chair sat next to the right-hand wall.

Jinmyn pressed his clammy palms against his legs and tried to keep his hands from trembling. He glanced back before they could close him in and considered making a dash for it.

CHAPTER SEVEN

MONITORED

Brimlet stopped at the door and stepped back to make sure of the room number above the entrance. A stranger, a woman, occupied her friend's bed.

"Where's Jinmyn?" She clutched her rag doll close. The talisman remained the only contact left of her mama.

"I don't know, Dear," replied the patient. "They moved me in here a little while ago."

Brimlet turned to check the corridor. Nothing out of the ordinary caught her eye. Aides scurried about, patients took their time moving along, all the usual hospital activity. But something significant had changed. She needed Jinmyn, and he couldn't disappear without a trace.

"Where did they take him?"

"I still don't know, Dear," responded the woman, letting her head fall back on the pillow. "Perhaps a nurse can tell you."

Brimlet took her bearings again. The surreal experience of knowing where she stood and not recognizing anything familiar made her dizzy. Her insides were as cold as when she swallowed iced water. She pressed her doll to her face until the sensation passed. She found her way to the nurses' station and identified one of the regulars.

"Where's Jinmyn?"

The nurse gave her a smile. "Well hello. It's Brimlet, isn't it? We discharged Jinmyn this morning. About time too. He stayed way too long for a toe that wasn't broken."

"Where did he go? He wouldn't go without me." The little girl, with a rag doll her only possession, could no longer bear her burdens and her nose and eyes released their moisture.

Jinmyn's legs strained from the weight of panic. Any minute they were going to run of their own accord without any command from his brain. He couldn't be in a room like this again. He searched for an advantage to escape.

Eyelids asked his companion, "What do we do now?"

Jaw colored a pale pink and admitted, "I don't know for sure. I can't read the Director's handwriting. The note says to take this man to this room and something, something, something. I can't make it out. Can you?" He handed the slip of paper to his associate who turned it around shaking his head.

"This is a scrawled mess. I can't understand it either. What now?"

Jinmyn scanned the room and chilled. No monitors. Everywhere else in the building, two or three were always in sight, so many they became commonplace and unnoticed. Here, though, none were evident; they wanted no record of what happened in this room. He knew why he was here even if his guards didn't. Think, Jinmyn, think. Take advantage of their confusion and reluctance to question orders.

"This must be the place the Director told me about," he said, pointing at the corners of the room near the ceiling. "He asked me if I could set up some communications. They don't have any here." His mouth was so dry he could hardly pronounce the words, but he didn't want to lick his lips and appear as nervous as he was.

Jaws brows scrunched together. "Why you?"

"He saw what I did in the game room with the computers, and I guess he wants me to earn my keep." Jinmyn wanted to continue talking, tell them anything, just babble, it was better than being a victim, but he forced himself to shut up.

Jaw reread the note and sighed. "What do you expect to do here?"

Jinmyn willed his turbulent emotions to quieten and assumed a professional attitude. He took the time to survey the room for the guards' benefit, puckered up, nodded, and said, "I need to check in with the computer control center. They should be ready."

Would they believe him? He was a poker player without a pair of deuces and couldn't have played a bigger bluff as he moved to the door. He paused and extended his hand toward the hallway and nodded to Jaw. "Perhaps you should lead. I still have trouble finding my way around."

Jinmyn kept his teeth clamped so he wouldn't hyperventilate open-mouthed. For the bluff to work, he needed more credibility. His muscle-men were already viewing him through slitted eyes and talking in crisp one or two syllables. The back of his neck tingled from imagining Eyelids grabbing him at any second and returning him to the iron door. Whatever he did, the act would have to reassure his escort. He could exploit their unwillingness to question their duties only as long as they moved towards a clear objective. Their knotted arm and shoulder muscles told him they would prefer grabbing problems rather than using reason. He was one misstatement away from the room at the end of the hall.

"I don't like it, and you can't come in here bullying people around." The Administrator of Ciphers and Codes took his wrath out on Jaw and Eyelids who seemed back in their element at the confrontation of demanding computer access.

Jinmyn slid unnoticed into a station that resembled the work-space where he once was a cocky programmer. *Thanks again, Rust-bucket. I'm having so much fun now. At least they don't have tight fire-walls.* He typed while the Administrator reached impressive levels of forehead vein bulge. *There, that's all I can do.*

"Ok guys, we can go. This was a bust. It's going to take a full-blown project from Building Maintenance to install it."

Could he slip past the obstinate watchmen and the fuming official? Jinmyn's heart thudded its way out of his chest while he moved. Act calm while due process challenged brute force and they might continue to ignore him.

Nope. The guards followed him out. What now? He couldn't go back to his room, and the idea of the iron door weakened his legs. "How about lunch?" Why did he mention food? His throat was so dry he couldn't swallow water.

Eyelids seemed refreshed after shoving his rib cage at the company monkey. He licked his lips. "Sounds good, but the mess hall's not open yet."

Jaws acted equally revitalized. "Yeah, but it'll be time for service if we look it on the female wrestling match first. I got a bet on it."

"Okay, well then, I'll go on to the cafeteria and give my report to the Director after lunch," Jinmyn said, waving goodbye to his escort. Please let them go the other way.

His smile was genuine when they waved back and departed. So were his tears.

After receiving permission to enter, Velmere entered NadYat's office and put a note on the Director's desk. Being the go-between required a diplomacy that he was only beginning to appreciate. This time, however, the Assistant Director of Security didn't bother with greetings or protocol. "The two guards you sent to take Jinmyn to the inquisition room are in confinement."

"What are you talking about, Velmere? I've had a bad morning and don't want to waste my calm time before getting back to it."

"On my rounds, I found all my men present so I looked to see who was attending our guest. It turns out that the two men on your detail couldn't read your handwriting. They let Jinmyn see the interrogation room and left. I threw them in the brig for ... I don't know why. I'll think of something later."

"Did you send someone else to put Jinmyn in custody?"

"Yes, and that's where this gets serious. We tracked him to the cafeteria where he ate a substantial meal. Then, the videos show him heading for a restroom. Now we can't find him."

Velmere enjoyed seeing his superior's face turn milk white dotted with red splotches. When his men receive orders without his knowledge, this is what happens. Write that down, Director.

A GARDEN RETREAT

Jinmyn forced himself to stroll. This was no time to attract attention with the Meditation Garden a few steps away and an outside door on the other side. He followed three people. A couple and an elderly woman, bent like a comma and smelling of stale bread. They went through the quiet, green space and out the door. A quick survey delineated more cameras and a wall surrounding the estate the hospital occupied.

A stadium-sized parking lot held various forms of transportation that he recognized, and he thought he would be able to operate them. *Thanks, Rustbucket. All I have to do is reach one undetected, drive it all the way to the gate, past the guard and outta here.*

A cold breeze made colder because of his perspiration hit him causing him to notice the dark clouds conquering the sky as the first wet drops splattered. The couple ran to their vehicle but the withered old woman stopped beside him. Her leaden hands struggled with a device that looked like an umbrella.

Jinmyn offered a hand. "May I help you with that?"

"Thank you," she said, pointing at a button. "I can't push it hard enough."

Jinmyn pressed the release to extend the canopy but held on to it and moved it to cover both of them. "Where's your vehicle?"

She pointed at the parking lot with a knobby finger, "The third one down that row."

"Do you want to hold on to me to keep from slipping on the wet pavement?"

She turned to him. "Would you take my keys and bring it up here? You can have the rain shield and I'll wait here under the awning. Would you do that?"

"Certainly." Jinmyn held the umbrella close to his head and kept it between him and the cameras while he ran to her vehicle.

She was already on the bottom step when he pulled up and wasted no time entering the passenger side. "Would you mind driving an old lady home? It's almost more than I can do, and this weather makes it worse."

"I would be happy to do that, just tell me which way to go." He kept his face turned but couldn't stop it from smiling. As they approached the gate, he took several deep breaths, holding the last one, only exhaling when the guard stayed inside his dry shack and waved them through.

They drove through town and into rolling hills while the woman, Ehssi, talked about her checkup and the difficulties of growing old, the forested countryside, the weather, and other subjects Jinmyn tuned out. Following her directions, they arrived in an area of scattered homes, each on tree-filled acreage. The house she indicated was a picture of the place Jinmyn had longed to occupy with Riley, and an ache of loss shot through him.

All right, Rustbucket. I may be average and on the wrong planet, but I'm going to fix your problem and find a home like this someday. A place where Brimlet could play.

Where had that come from? In the past, he always pictured sharing a honeymoon cottage with an attractive wife. He had to remind himself where he was and what he must do. He hurried around the vehicle to shelter his passenger with her umbrella and took her elbow.

She opened the door and pointed at a corner. "Put the rain shield there. I'll make us some tea."

Jinmyn wiped his brow with his sleeve. "I should be moving on if you can tell me the quickest place for public transportation."

"Nonsense. This storm's just getting started and you deserve a rest for helping me. I'll find some refreshments while the water boils. Sit over there and relax."

She shuffled into the kitchen, set out tableware and a kettle, and was soon back with a tray of bread and cups of tea. Jinmyn didn't recognize the flavor of the snack, but he liked it and told her so.

"It's the way my mama made it. She taught me as a little girl and I've done it that way since. Everyone makes it that way." She shook her dress free of remaining water drops and sat in a high-backed chair. "Why don't you tell me who you are and why you wanted out of the hospital without being seen?" She lifted her cup and peered at him without fear, only curiosity.

His adrenaline spiked pulsing heat up his neck and out to his ears, his legs tensed.

She dipped bread into her tea, took a dainty bite.

Jinmyn studied her. She was just a lonely old woman who wanted company. His hot flash subsided. He never had a grandmother, was this what it was like? He snuggled deeper into his chair, comfortable in her cozy home. Affected by her personal warmth, he knew trust and security lived here.

His shoulders sagged and he groaned. "I told Rustbucket I wasn't going to fit in."

"Who?"

"You call him The Regulator. That's what I meant to say. He got me into this mess." Jinmyn raised his tea.

"You talk to the Regulator? Are you on the King's staff? Is he in the hospital? Is that why you were trying to not draw attention?"

Jinmyn smiled; she did want to gossip. "No, nothing like that. I was being held, against my will as it turns out, and I need to get to Montibar—"

"Montibar? Why?"

"Well, Grabin's taking advantage of the Regulator's absence. The King of Montibar needs to disable the system that's allowing it. You see, a slight mistake would cause—"

Ehssi stood, tottered to a small desk and withdrew a weapon, which she pointed at him. Her hand didn't wobble. "You're against Grabin? You gut ruptured slyvet. You're going to sit right there and don't move or I'll have your insides all over the outside."

When she turned to a communicator, Jinmyn lunged and bolted, slamming the door behind him so she couldn't see to get a clear shot.

She was right about one thing. The storm was getting worse.

A FOREST RETREAT

Coughing and running, Jinmyn was drawing in almost as much water as air until he got under the shelter of the trees. He didn't stop to pull his collar up until there was no sight or sound of habitation. How far had he come? The pounding rain blocked his senses, but it wasn't far enough from Ehssi and her gun. This morning he never would have thought of wrinkled old women packing weapons as a turning point in his day—his life. By now, she would have called the authorities; keep moving.

Rustbucket, you dim-watt idiot. You blew a fuse on this whole thing, and I'm a bigger idiot for believing you.

His squishing socks pumped water out of his shoes with each step. Windblown leaves plastered his face and arms, were washed off and replaced. Wet branches scratched and tore his clothes as he forced his way through bushes and around trees. Was he going in a straight line, or circling back? He recalled a childhood memory of a startled rabbit. The bunny ran away, zigging and zagging, and finally ended up not much farther from where it began. He laughed at the time, but it wasn't funny now. In fact, he might be crying, his face was wet enough and his eyes stung.

For now, keep pushing. Maybe the rain will let up.

Bigger drops fell faster and harder, a continuous waterfall drenching him. Stronger and colder wind forced him to stop on the lee side of a tree. His shirt suffered rips from the snagging branches. One shoulder was exposed and his saturated pants dragged him down. Should he return to the warmth of Ehssi's house and surrender? No, the iron door would be waiting.

Where was the cave? There was always supposed to be a place where he could build a leaping fire and thaw his numb hands and feet. Didn't all the survival guides promise an abandoned cabin or some kind of shelter? Not that he'd read any outdoor manuals, but he'd watched movies. Warm and dry would be so nice ... perhaps he should sit down and think about it for a while.

His thoughts were drifting. He made an effort to concentrate on finding protection, but a fire beckoned with a force that let him see the light through the wavering wall of water. Wait! That's a flashlight. Someone was coming.

Fear impelled him to run, but his legs refused the command. They were only in service to stumble. He must hide. There were bushes but no protection, not from the elements, and not from searchers.

At the base of one bush was an indentation holding water. A hollowed spot as if a boulder once sat there. Jinmyn lay in the puddle on his side with his knees pulled up. He dragged forest floor mulch over himself and waited. The wetsuit of wooded debris washed away as soon as it was gathered, and he had to hold his head up to keep his face out of the water.

"Jiiiinmyn. Jiiiinmyn." The cry was a whisper against the wind, but it drew his attention toward the stabbing shaft of light jerking his way. "Jiiiinmyn. Jiiiinmyn." Other lights were getting closer, but his concentration was towards the voice behind the twitching beam. As the rain folded and opened, he got glimpses of a small figure slogging through the muck, jostling with the tossing wind. Wet hair whipped and stuck in random sprays across her face despite one forearm held against her brow. Her hand clutched a saturated wad of cloth that had once been a rag doll. "Jiiiinmyn. Jiiiinmyn."

"Brimlet!" What was she doing here? He pushed to his feet and staggered no more than a few steps before an anvil-like man in a raincoat slammed Jinmyn face down in a muddy sprawl of binding arms. Before he could yowl his surprise, another wet weather clad body landed knocking the wind out of him. A knee pressing against his neck ensured Jinmyn's imitation of a pancake.

The shack was drier than outside where the storm threw lightning spears across the sky. The turbulent atmosphere bellowed its supremacy, and trees bowed in dominance to its wet breath.

Jinmyn sagged like a soggy biscuit in the only chair. Five raincoats, small in tent size, large in men's clothing, covered his captors.

Velmere pushed his hood back, glared and pointed a finger at Jinmyn's nose.

Jinmyn lurched upright to leap for Velmere's throat. "Where's Brim—"

Hands grabbed his shoulders and shoved him into his seat.

Baring his teeth, his eyes still on Velmere, he put as much venom as he could in his voice. "Why would you send her out into this mess?"

Velmere's expression softened and he held up a hand. "I didn't. What you saw was a hologram. Our team did a remarkable job on it considering the short time they had. She's safe and warm at the hospital, wondering why you left."

Velmere unbuttoned his jacket and shook it. Was he stalling? Something different was going on. Jinmyn's stomach went hollow. They were going to make sure that he never ran again. This shed would be the room behind the iron door. "Velmere, look, I'm sorry you had to come after me, but I've got to get to Montibar. Please ... please."

Velmere didn't look directly at him. "How did you leave without being seen?"

"Yeah, I'll tell you, but you've got to let me reach Montibar and disable that stupid system that's ready to kill us all."

"So how did you do it?" Velmere's voice was soft. Was he another Hickey Spinks that enjoyed this?

Jinmyn slumped, his head dropped. It was over. He was exhausted, miserable and defeated. *Did you hear that, Rustbucket? It's over. You lost and I lost. You picked the wrong guy to be your hero.*

"Jinmyn," Velmere prodded, "how did you do it without the monitors seeing you?"

Jinmyn stared at Velmere's wet boots. "When the guards took me to the computer room, I programmed a continuous 24-hour playback loop for the garden—no updates from the cameras. It's all I had time to do while they argued with the Administrator. Then, after lunch, I walked through there and out. I'm sure Ehssi told you the rest."

A low rumbling hum came from Velmere, turning into a chuckle, then a belly laugh. His men shifted, obviously confused. They looked at each other and at Jinmyn who shrugged and held his palms upward.

Velmere slowed his mirth and breathed deep, still grinning. "The Director is on the verge of thinking you can walk through walls." Chuckles overcame him and he patted the air towards Jinmyn until he quieted again. Catching his breath, he began, "Now, Jinmyn—"

"You can torture me here or back at the Iron Door, but it won't do you any good. What I've said is true. Both Grabin and Montibar are in danger and if you're dead set on holding me then send someone else to deactivate the system." *There Rustbucket, my last gasp, and I hope it's good enough to keep me from dying on a strange planet. If by chance I survive all this, I'm going to shove a grounding rod up your sparkly nose.*

"No one's going to harm you, Jinmyn. At least not here, or where I can prevent it. I didn't know what NadYat had in mind for you until you went missing. He didn't include me in those particular plans. I think he knew I would oppose them."

"Why did he want to persecute me? I've been honest."

"I believe you. I also believe, as does the Director, that you've withheld information, and he wants it."

"I said from the start that some things were private."

Jinmyn studied Velmere, a cobra and a mongoose put in the ring for the sport of others. Jinmyn didn't know which role was his, only that it would be the losing side.

The storm noise rattled the shed while Jinmyn waited, and Velmere seemed lost in thought.

Velmere lifted his chin. "Did you mean the things you said to Brimlet in the garden ... about God?"

The shift in questioning confused him and disconcerted his anticipated arguments. "Huh?"

"Did you make up the stories you told her?"

"No. Of course not. I'll admit that I can't tell them as meaningful as a preacher, but - no, I didn't make them up."

Velmere exhaled as if he had been holding his breath. "The men here are the ones who heard you tell the story. We agree it has an appeal we want to believe. I'm going to help you get to Montibar."

"Why?"

"I think you're doing what's best for both planets, and there's been another belligerent incident that could have provoked the asteroid solution. It has to stop."

Jinmyn forgot he was soaked, cold, and miserable as the weight of the world lifted from his chest. The crude shelter seemed brighter, his abductors friendlier.

"Don't start grinning yet," Velmere said. "It's still risky. I'm assigned to a diplomatic visit that leaves tomorrow, and I intend to smuggle you aboard."

"Just mix me in with your retinue and bluff our way through?"

"No, it's a small corps. You'd be noticed. You'll have to be on board tonight and stay hidden until everyone departs at Montibar."

"How long's the trip? Will I hide in your cabin?"

Velmere shook his head. "You really don't know these things? There's hope you are from somewhere else and came to save our system."

Jinmyn nodded. "That's all true. I want to settle things down and leave."

"Well, you'd better be committed to your mission because to get to Montibar you'll be folded up and stuffed into the area under two narrow seats for a serota and a half."

Jinmyn's mouth hung open while he searched Velmere for humor. There was none.

"Then," Velmere continued, "once there, landing protocol dictates that everyone exits the craft within one hour before it's fumigated to kill all living organisms. You'll want to avoid that." He smirked at his own joke.

Was he trying to be funny or testing Jinmyn with sarcasm? "You had me going for a moment, Velmere. I thought you were sincere in stopping the threat."

"I am."

"There's no way I can physically hide for that long cramped under seats."

"Yes, there is."

Velmere shot him.

Jinmyn's throat was too dry to groan aloud but he tried. He wanted to claw out of the blackness and open his eyes. Metal walls immobilized him, pressed against his head, drawn up knees, back, and shoulders. Filtered, muffled sounds taunted him. Someone was faintly reminding him of something he must do.

He barely understood the faraway voice that yelled, "All clear. Fumigate in five,—"

Soft murkiness lured him. Sleep ... sleep.

"—four, three, two, one."

CHAPTER EIGHT

FRESH AIR

A familiar smell filled Jinmyn's nose. He recognized dirty clothes, unwashed dishes, and a floor unknown to a mop, just like his old apartment. Stretching out on a blanket was nice, but the pillow reeked. Push it away.

"Wake up, dreamer. You're gonna live and that's an imposition on us. Get up!"

Jinmyn lifted one eyelid a slit for a visual confirmation of his olfactory deduction. He kept a cleaner place than this, didn't he? Dishes crusted with meal remnants were stacked and scattered on a kitchen counter. Cartons, packages, and tins were piled in the sink that apparently doubled as a trash bin. A scan of the rest of the room revealed the bed he was on, a table and two chairs.

An inhabitant stood by a chair, shaking a finger. Standing with his feet placed as if he were ready to lunge in any direction, a red-faced person demanded, "Move it! We don't want you here."

Why was he so angry?

Jinmyn used all his strength to push himself to a sitting position. The effort made him dizzy and sweaty. His chest ached. The bass thump of his heartbeat produced a pounding in his skull. He held up a hand to stop the harangue of the wild-eyed fellow. So much noise. What happened? He tried to ask, but his throat was too dry to pass anything but a raspy breath. Ignoring his agitated roommate, he staggered to the sink, filled the cleanest dirty glass and let the cool water trickle past vocal cords turned to jerky. He drank and growled until his larynx relaxed, replenished and pliable.

Jinmyn took in his surroundings. This wasn't Velmere's shack. Sunlight overcame the smudged windows to light the place, and this man in front of him wasn't a guard. This was completely different. "Where's Velmere?" His lungs hurt and talking was a chore but the effort seemed to loosen the tension of his ... host?

The man dipped his head, his eyes pleading. "Everyone else got off on time, all accounted for. You can't blame Frimox. They said they were all off. It's their responsibility."

"What?—"

"Frimox only checks the ships afterward to make sure the gas is ventilated. It's up to Grabin to tell him everyone's off and it's clear to fumigate."

Jinmyn stretched his hand to the back of a chair to steady himself. His head spun and he couldn't keep from groaning as he sat. "Are you telling me I was on the ship while it was gassed?"

"It wasn't Frimox's fault. They said everyone was off. They signed the forms."

"This is Montibar?"

"You Grabinians push us and push us. We should have let Ixet deal with you. He wanted to. He said to dump you in the recycler and be done with it - after he hurt you."

Jinmyn wet his throat, "I'm not from Grabin. That is, I came from there because I was taken there, but I'm not a Grabinian."

His counterpart gave Jinmyn a squinting, frowning glare. "What do you mean?"

Jinmyn growled, sipped some more water and twisted his neck. His breath smelled funny even to him. He inhaled fully to purge the bad air. "If this isn't Grabin, it worked. I was a stowaway. Is this Montibar?"

The individual's shoulders lowered and his chin raised. "Yes."

"Is this your house? How did I come to be here?"

"It's kind of—"

"Wait a minute. I'm Jinmyn, what's your name?"

His companion went silent, crossed his arms, and flicked his gaze around the room. He opened and closed his mouth once, twice, three times. He shoved his hands in his pockets and said, "Tumrin."

Jinmyn swept his hand in an arc, "Your home?"

"Yes - ours. Frimox found you in a ship's hallway and dragged you out. It's a good thing he was low on gas and didn't replenish it. You got a smaller dose. Still, he thought you might die and was afraid to call anybody. Then, when no one asked about you, Ixet almost had his way. But Frimox was shamed to think that he was responsible so we brought you here." Tumrin scuffed his shoe. "I was left here to tell you to leave when you woke up. We thought you were an arrogant Grabinian." He shuffled his weight. "Even so, you'd better move along. We don't want any trouble and Frimox still has to work at the spaceport."

Tumrin took the other chair; his facial muscles rippled and his posture changed. His voice took a higher tone and he spoke slower. "I suppose you can wait here until you feel well."

"Thanks, that's—"

"No, no, no, no, no." Tumrin's visage altered again. His head slumped and his shoulders drew up almost to his ears. "We can't have him here. He's a fugitive. We'll be in trouble."

Jinmyn's mouth hung slack as he watched Tumrin's body language and voice undergo another alteration. "He can stay. I'm the one responsible for him being in this condition." He frowned at Jinmyn, "Even though you put me in a terrible position. What if you died when I fumigated the ship? Then what would have happened?"

Jinmyn had both hands on the table and pushed back as far as his arms stretched. "Tumrin, are you all right?"

"I'm Frimox. I work at the port, fumigating arrivals for the sanitation of Montibar so no foreign contamination can infect us. It's a serious responsibility." He twitched, a frown appeared as he wrung his hands. "Yes it is, and we can't have him around here. He needs to go or we'll suffer for it."

Jinmyn rubbed his forehead with a slight tremble in his own hand. "Tumrin ... Frimox ... who?"

"Sruma. That was Sruma. He doesn't like this whole situation. None of us do."

Jinmyn pointed at his companion, "Are you one of those split personality types? Can I ask who to talk to? Tumrin maybe?" He got a nod in return. "How many ...?"

Tumrin scowled before answering. "You'll figure it out."

"All right. I don't want to offend you - any of you - but you said that one of you wanted to dump me in the recycler, didn't you?"

"Ixet."

"Is he a threat? Should I fear him?"

"Yes."

"Oh boy! How about the other nervous one, Sruma? Can I trust him?"

"No."

"Well then, as soon as I can walk without falling I'd better be gone. Thank you Tumrin for explaining things to me, and thank Frimox for saving me. If I'm ever in a position to repay you guys, I certainly will. Just tell me where the palace is from here and I'd appreciate it."

Tumrin gave him a skewed glance. "The King's palace? You want to go there?"

"Yes. Is that a problem?"

"A little one. You're on the wrong continent. The spaceport and palace are on opposite sides of the world for the King's safety." Tumrin's face shifted and darkened. "You should know that," a gruff voice said.

DIPLOMACY

Velmere was impressed with the embassy. Montibar granted a large estate for Grabin's diplomatic use within an easy commute to all governmental offices. Constructed of white and pink marble with gold-colored streaks, the consulate and its buildings sparkled on spotless grounds with mowed lawns, hedge-lined walkways, flower gardens, berry bushes, and fruit trees. An ideal setting, and it should be. Here, the Regulator cared for everything from the weather to soil acidity.

Was the Regulator omnipotent? Jinmyn doesn't think so. Moreover, he says there is a creator of all things who loves us as a father. Velmere realized a flush of discomfort for demoting the Regulator, but something about Christian stories made him want to believe them enough to help Jinmyn escape. That was a big risk, but it's too late to worry about treason now. If Jinmyn can make the worlds safe again then he will have acted correctly, if the asteroids crash down ... Oh, well.

Velmere arrived at the Ambassador's office.

Ambassador Lyram enjoyed the gardens and took the opportunity to meet there with Velmere and Korfel, the Captain of the embassy guards. "You will be seen, Velmere. It will prompt our agents to check in. They thrive on secrecy and duplicity. I prefer diplomacy, and I suspect you lump it all under "politics", opting for honorable and straightforward military action."

"Yes, Ambassador, I do. However, I find myself here needing those other assets. I can't do anything about a Christian movement until I discover who and what it is."

Lyram stopped to admire a flowering bush. "See how this purple flower complements the red and white ones? Nature's diplomacy - another word for harmony." The Ambassador scanned the flowers and spoke without turning from them, "We'll find out what we can about this new sect, and if it's a threat we'll neutralize it." He turned to Velmere, "I must meet my next appointment. Please come to dinner this evening, I would hear more about these Christians. For now, I invite you to enjoy the grounds as long as you wish," he gave Velmere a lopsided grin, "but I imagine you warriors will be off to your honorable pursuits as soon as I leave."

Velmere smiled in return, "Thank you, sir."

After Lyram departed, Velmere granted his companion a frown. "Korfel, a matter of delicacy, as the Ambassador would put it, concerns me. I'm sure you know that sometimes we use the diplomatic shuttles to transport individuals who are unlisted on the manifest of passengers."

Korfel's face showed no emotion, only his eyes twitched to take the measure of Velmere's intent before resuming impartial observation. "Yes, sir. Spies."

Velmere chuckled. "Ambassador Lyram's right. Let's be straightforward. It'll save time."

Korfel nodded his agreement.

"When we disembarked, I delayed as long as I could without creating suspicion but received no indication that anyone left the shuttle after us. Would you review our security monitors to verify one more arrival?"

"Should I start right now?"

"Yes."

Korfel saluted and departed.

What is there about a garden that makes a man want to stroll with his hands behind his back and think philosophical thoughts? He never used to be like this. His job—his mission— was clear. Get up every morning, follow orders and protect Grabin to the best of his ability. He had been sure Jinmyn was a spy but didn't know for which planet or agency. Then, watching him interacting with Brimlet, and the stories he told her cast doubts. Velmere took his time strolling along the path to the vines, a man in no hurry and with no worries.

His acidic stomach said otherwise. He'd messed up on his rash decision to smuggle Jinmyn to Montibar. If Jinmyn had fled the craft immediately after them and sought Montibaran immunity, it would have exposed Velmere as an accomplice. That would translate to prison, either here or back home on Grabin. Fortunately, Jinmyn protected them both with a watchful exit.

If he did, in fact, exit. Could he be cold and gray jammed under the seat? Velmere's stomach cramped again.

Korfel joined him at the next intersection of garden lanes. "No one else left the ship before it was purged. Ventilation is complete, should I instigate a discreet search?"

Velmere bowed his head. "Yes. Look beneath the bench attached to bulkhead D7."

CHAPTER NINE

LET IT BE WAR

The palace grounds symbolized the perfection of the Regulator's care. Where the Grabin Embassy gardens were merely beautiful, here the mesmerizing landscape was a source of national pride, or so thought Yorev when he wasn't involved in national distress and had time for such matters. His leisure had evaporated in a dark cloud of fear once the asteroids were poised. Why did King Eborces nonchalantly arm them? The Regulator had disappeared in the past with no problems, but this time his monarch had unilaterally decided to shroud Montibar with the suicide pill solution. Why would he do that? ... because he was lazy and didn't want to tend to affairs of State. For Yorev though, his workload and stress increased a hundred-fold. He hurried from his office in the security complex, past fountains, grottoes, and statuary on his way to the meeting with his king.

A steward announced his arrival. "Sire, the Head of Faithfulness is here."

The King's public chambers offered an architectural design of comfort and attraction overlooking the estate's maintained forest. Eborces wasn't enjoying the view, though. He turned his round belly from his escritoire and smiled from under his mustache at Yorev. "So, Head of Faithfulness, what is urgent today?"

Thankfully the king's pyramid lip hair, wide as his mouth and narrow to his nose, was crumb free. Yorev wanted an earnest state visit this time. "Sire, a high officer of Grabin's security force is here on Montibar. He's second only to their Director NadYat."

"Does he want an audience?" King Eborces tugged his sleeves and brushed his jacket straight.

"Not yet. He made no official contact with our government. He arrived and went to their embassy where he is supposedly reviewing their guard."

"I believe that's entirely within the realm of diplomatic business, Yorev. Why are we talking about it?"

"In the first place—"

"One moment Yorev. If I'm to be nagged, I want to be comfortable." Eborces motioned to a steward, "Bring us refreshments."

As if waiting outside for an invitation, a door popped opened to a linen-clad cart pushed by one attendant and accompanied by two more. Over-sized samovars of heavy silver occupied each end of the straining platform. Heaped in the middle were plates of pastries, toasted and jellied bread, meats, and cheeses. A server carried a loaded plate and cup of hot beverage to a side tray for the king. Yorev waved away the snack brought him and accepted the drink. He remained standing, resisting the urge to fidget although his toes tapped inside his shoes.

The monarch gave his consideration to the offering, tasting several items before slurping from his cup. "There now," he said, wiping his hands on a lace napkin. "You were going to tell me why one man on our planet requires my attention."

Yorev sipped the warm liquid to keep a sharp retort from escaping his lips. He was a professional public servant, had served this king all of his adult life. In spite of the Royal's irresponsible unconcern, he would give his dispassionate opinion free from anger.

"The Office of Faithfulness has determined that Grabin nationals are proliferating. They've taken advantage of the heightened alert status you instituted to infiltrate more personnel. I must be careful to employ civilian police tactics to corral them since some military activity could signal war-like conditions to the sensors and collapse the satellites. Please, Your Highness, in the name of the department responsible for keeping you and all Montibar safe, I ask once again. Disarm the system."

King Eborces looked at his plate, selected a pastry, and inspected it. "No."

Yorev pressed the cup and saucer together to stop his trembling hands from rattling them. "Sire—"

"You presume to lecture me on the responsibilities of our offices as if I'm a schoolboy?" King Eborces placed the treat back on the plate and waved the refreshments away. "I'm the one born to ensure Montibar's safety. It is my right and duty. The Regulator wants me to use his system or he wouldn't have arranged it that way. Grabin wouldn't dare try anything now."

Before the stewards got the cart out of the room, King Eborces called it back. "A few more."

Yorev felt his face heat. "They *are* trying something now, and they're succeeding while we do nothing. We can't keep pretending all is well because we're under the protection of an 'everybody gets along or die' threat."

Eborces straightened and glared. "Be careful how you speak of the Regulator, Yorev, and be especially careful how you speak to me."

"Your Highness, every time a shuttle from Grabin lands, it leaves with fewer people. If you won't acknowledge that, you're not paying attention to Montibar's welfare. My duty requires me to let the Parliament in on the seriousness of the situation." What had he done, issue the world's ruler an ultimatum? Yorev waited for the signal that his head was on the chopping block.

Instead, the King enjoyed another treat. "The answer to that is simple enough. I'll just close the spaceport."

"That would be a violation of our treaty with Grabin and could sever diplomatic relations. An atmosphere like that is ripe for a jingoist group from either planet to inadvertently start a war."

"The Regulator won't allow that to happen. He loves us."

"He's not here."

"Your whining is boring. Find something else to do. You don't want to become labeled Head of Faithfulness and Frightened Children."

An exquisite cup and saucer of the Third Coronation Set previously held by Yorev crashed to the marble floor, flung with enough force to splatter shards and liquid content halfway across the large chamber. The King's visage petrified in a wide-eyed stare, his mouth open revealing a gob of bread on his tongue and cheese in his teeth.

"No one will survive to know you as the idle king who killed everyone." Yorev turned his back and headed for the door.

ME AND YOU AND YOU AND YOU

Jinmyn puckered his lips, bottom one's swollen and raw on the left, a taste of blood, jaw hurts, don't bite down. Sparks ignited and disappeared behind his eyelids; he cracked one open and groaned. On the bed again, wrists and ankles tied.

"Aw Tumrin, why did you do that?" He worked his jaw sideways and tongued around to explore for missing teeth. All there, still tight. The coppery flavor of O positive coming from a split lip. "You didn't have to hit me, especially that hard."

"That wasn't me. Sruma panicked when he realized you were a Grabinian trying to fool us, and he let Ixet loose on you. Frimox and I got Sruma calmed, and together we sent Ixet away. I think we will leave you bound up, though."

"I can explain—"

"Later tonight." A subtle shift in expression and voice, "I'm going to work now."

"I can't lay here tied down all day - C'mon."

Frimox left.

Jinmyn yelled after him, but it made his head pound. He hated Rustbucket, Grabin, and Montibar.

He hated himself.

It wasn't the most brilliant move he'd ever made, agreeing to Rustbucket who claimed to be an energy being but is more than likely an electric chair. Jinmyn jerked at his restraints. Did he care what happened to worlds across the galaxy? Why die alone and unknown, still half a world away from any chance of a solution?

He could've been safe at home, an ordinary programmer puffed up over an everyday job and fooling himself about a girl with her own ambitions.

Then what?

The ambitious girl didn't want the life he wanted. Nothing would have ever been enough for her. He hadn't really known her. He wasn't close to anyone; it wouldn't matter where he died. Jinmyn caught his breath. Everyone he knew was only an acquaintance, not a companion.

Self-pity tears spilled from the corners of his eyes. He sniffed and indulged his misery until hit with a flashback of Brimlet sitting all alone in the cafeteria ... so brave. Was that the reason Velmere took a huge risk to smuggle Jinmyn off Grabin? He gritted his teeth. All right, he'd quit acting like a diva and do everything in his power to give her a future. He knew people after all. They were just on another world.

Satisfying as it was to spend time thinking of defamations to hurl at Rustbucket, he needed to convince the multiple personalities of his benevolence. And do it without scaring the timid one, or having that mean one come out again. Think about it and find a way. Better yet, free himself and skedaddle. He might be able to do that. Frimox or Tumrin used towels and sheets for ropes. Overall, it's not as bad as what happened in Phoenix or what NadYat planned behind the iron door. The bed was comfortable. Might as well relax, it may help sliding loose or working a hand through one of the knots.

The door opened to admit a cast of three in the form of one person. Jinmyn recognized them but had trouble keeping up with who was currently center stage. A performance of spasmodic facial changes and voices spouting forceful proclamations following frenetic cries of doom made Jinmyn stare in open-mouthed wonder.

The bickering stopped; the innkeeper of personalities took a deep breath and relaxed his fists. Jinmyn took careful measure and cleared his throat. "Frimox? You're home early."

"Tumrin." The homeowner rubbed his hands together and regarded Jinmyn. "I imagine it's confusing, I apologize."

"Don't bother yourself. I suppose you can't help it, but even so, you guys are more honest than most of us."

"How is that?"

Jinmyn turned his face away, not liking the sudden heat in it. "I think people are good at denying who they really are ... even to themselves. You don't do that." Great. Is this where a prisoner develops feelings for his captor? He'd heard of that happening.

Tumrin shrugged, "Well .... Anyway, they closed the spaceport and sent us home until further notice. Rumor is they're sending in troops to guard it. Sruma thinks it's your fault. If we turn you in now, they'll know we hid you. If we don't, they'll search until they find you. You can't be found with us."

Jinmyn squirmed in his restraints. How could the back of his neck tingle when he lay on it? It was an exposed feeling he never experienced until recently, now becoming frustratingly familiar.

"Sir!" Korfel approached Velmere's desk and saluted. "Your ship is clean. There are no organisms on it ... alive or dead."

"Truly?" Velmere discarded the list he held and rubbed his chin with circling fingertips. How did Jinmyn exit the craft? He escaped from the hospital on Grabin without anyone knowing it, but he explained that simply enough. He couldn't have done the same thing to leave the ship without help from the Regulator. Or, unless he was a double agent and a good one at that. "So, Korfel, you're telling me we don't have a mess to clean up, but our security is so lax a person can walk away and we don't know it?"

Jaw muscles formed ridges on the Captain of the Guard as he gritted his teeth. His face flushed but he remained quiet.

"I'll give you a description, Captain, and you will find him."

"Yes, sir."

"Also here's a hint. I know he is trying to reach the king, and he is resourceful. Look everywhere between the spaceport and palace."

Yorev stomped the garden path, reluctant to return to his office. What was the use? If King Eborces continued in denial, it was only a matter of time before the situation with Grabin burst out of control. Even if the Monarch woke up, or Parliament had the fortitude to make Eborces reverse course, a subject didn't address their king disrespectfully. He was out of a job whatever the outcome. Releasing all accountability provided a rush of liberation followed by self-incrimination of irresponsibility.

Was that his deputy running toward the palace, buttoning her tunic in full stride? The summons must have caught the poor woman unprepared from the look of fear or confusion on her face, a look he probably wore many times. It didn't matter now. Yorev knew a change of staff when he saw it.

TIME TO GO

Stuffed in a niche cut out of thickets surrounding it, the house stood plain and functional: a dirty white domicile within an enclosed lot behind the spaceport. Unlike other neat and trimmed government-owned properties, drums of chemicals were scattered around the premises, hidden from infrequent traffic by a vine-covered fence. The inappropriately stored barrels of toxic soup used to fumigate ships had gaudy bright labels warning of agonizing death: don't ingest, inhale, or allow contact with exposed skin.

Inside, Jinmyn eased one hand through a knotted towel. A refreshing breeze purged the unkempt room, bringing light and invigorating him. Was it real, or was he empowered in his escape attempt? It had to be a sign, so he must use anything he could to his advantage, objects or words, good or evil. He'd try deception. "I guess I can't hide anymore; the army's coming for me. You'd be a fool not to turn me in."

The homeowner emitted a hand-wringing wail. "No, no, no. We can't be anywhere around him."

Yeah, now he was getting somewhere, keep 'em off balance. "You'd be taking a chance all right. You might be rewarded, or jailed as an accomplice." Jinmyn edged his free hand to the tangle of towel holding his other one. "Yep, you could be a hero or end up on a gallows. Big risk, big reward as they say in the financial trade." He worked on the last knot and kept describing doom scenarios for his keeper who got more and more frantic.

Other personalities appeared less often as Sruma's panic ballooned out of control. Dominated by fear, he whined and paced, spittle flying, flinging his arms while predicting impending catastrophes, his attention turned inward.

Assuring Sruma devastation was indeed imminent, Jinmyn inched off the bed, tip-toed to the sink counter, picked up the largest pot he saw and swung it as hard as he could.

Oof. How many personalities were in his erstwhile host? Must have been at least a dozen, figuring how strenuous it was to drag him across the room to the closet. Jinmyn frisked and relieved his victim of what currency he could find. He took a fresh shirt from a hanger and checked to make sure his quarry still breathed. Chewing bread swiped from the cupboard he stepped outside to freedom. The faint odor of chemicals didn't keep him from a deep breath. Everything would be fine now.

At his desk in front of Grabin's national flag, NadYat read the official diplomatic communique again. "Montibar shut down their spaceport. Velmere and the embassy staff are stuck there. Get this message to King RinMod and go to High Alert status."

A wobble shook a cold cluster of asteroids in a faraway orbit. Two of them soundlessly bumped in the vacuum of space, breaking off three pieces. The detritus began a resolute slide down the gravity slope of the solar system, on paths crossing the orbits of Grabin and Montibar.

Airborne shuttles circled, landed to disgorge troops, and then took off again, reminding Jinmyn of flies at a picnic. The spaceport was turning into a citadel, an armed perimeter already evident.

Jinmyn took a well-trod path around a side fence toward the main gate, chewing the looted bread. Not bad, a faint flavor of nuts lingered on his tongue, but he should have gotten something to drink. He'd have to pay attention to his stomach soon, but right now, he needed to keep moving. Tumrin et al. are probably already stirring, and while the worst he could do is turn Jinmyn over to the authorities, where he wanted to go anyway, it wasn't the best way to convince the king of his sincerity. Besides, this was the new

Jinmyn—a take charge, demanding, you'd-better-listen-to-me kind of a brute.

Freedom refreshed him as if he'd showered and shaved. He indulged his senses, taking in the sights, sounds, and smells of a bustling air terminal juxtaposed with open country. On one side of the fence were green fields, multicolored flowers, and smooth-barked trees hanging with fruit. Rustbucket was right; Montibar is a beautiful planet.

On the other side, there was no engine noise from the gleaming shuttles, only a sound like gliders rushing through the air. He paused to sniff for jet exhaust. Nope. Nothing but the smell of rotten eggs he'd had in his nose since he woke up tied to a bed. But that's okay. He puffed out his chest. The feeling of being in control was intoxicating. Why hadn't he asserted himself before now instead of letting others manipulate him? Never again.

Underneath the three-story-tall gateway proclaiming a welcome to the *Montibar Spaceport* were two slouching guards, one eating what looked like military rations. Barricades stretched across the entrance. This should be easy for the new Jinmyn. He marched to the nearest soldier, soon his arduous trip would end. "Take me to your commander. I need to see the king."

Other than shifting his eyes, the warrior didn't move. "This is your lucky day. You found him. I'm your king and I command you to get lost." The other guard chuckled, spewing half a mouthful of chewed food.

"I don't have time to waste on grunts. The threat to Montibar and Grabin must be stopped. Now, if you'll excuse me—"

Jinmyn walked around the reflective horizontal beam of the barrier. Chin up, jaw set, he was on his way and no minor ditch-digging soldiers were going to stop him. And they might not have if he had seen them move.

Ow! They were fast. He didn't recall falling, only hitting the ground with his arms twisted behind his back. Sloucher told Eater, "Call the Sergeant of the Guards."

CHAPTER TEN

FRIEND AND FOE

Yorev stood before his monarch, this time in the King's personal office instead of the official State Room. "I thought you'd replaced me, Sire."

The king shoved an over-sized bite of pastry into his open maw with a delicate silver fork, then turned the tiny utensil over and combed his mustache of crumbs with the tines. He shifted the wad of food to one jaw, "I did, and I will again. Right now I need you back on the job."

When Yorev didn't inquire further, the royal frowned and shook his head. "You push me too far, Head of Faithfulness. You're under house arrest, meaning your office. You'll stay there, perform your duties, and provide me with updates. When this is over you'll face the consequences of insubordination. Now leave me."

"There are no grounds to arrest me, therefore no parliamentary authority to do so. However, I'll consider staying if you tell me, updates about what? And when what is over?" Yorev clamped down on a smile. He wished he had that spine when he was younger. It would be a fine day when he gave this job to someone else.

Eborces halted another forkful of sweets halfway to his mouth and glared at Yorev. "I've closed the spaceport and put it under military guard." He yawned and used the action to shove in the treat. "Our embassy received word that Grabin considered it a hostile act and went to a high state of alert." He belched and dabbed at his face with a linen napkin. "For all the good that'll do 'em."

Yorev blinked as his sight blurred. He swallowed against the unpleasant sensation of a rising breakfast, sudden heat brought sweat to his brow. Not seeking permission, he sat, avoiding the temptation to place his head between his knees. While waiting for his vitals to calm, he stared at his king. "Didn't I warn you some idiot could end it all by playing at war?" He stopped short of adding that the idiot in question was before him, demolishing a mornings output from the bakery. "We're closer than ever to upsetting the asteroids."

"Oh yes, about that," Eborces bit into a muffin, "some small pieces broke off of them according to our scientists."

"When? How long ago?"

"I'm not sure, before the time Grabin went on alert, but it still must be their fault. I imagine the Regulator is teaching them a lesson."

Yorev made a strong effort to contain his stomach. "Will they hit either planet?"

"They say it's too soon to tell, but it's likely. I think it would be nice if our adversaries were wiped out."

"If they were, it would kill us too. We're in a close orbit. Debris from their destruction would shower us with more than asteroids." Yorev raised his face to the king. No, he didn't hate him. It was worse than that. He loathed and disrespected his self-indulgent monarch. He jumped to his feet, ran to the king's linen-clad serving cart and threw up on the remaining treats.

The young officer's breath caught to see his company commander walking the carpeted hall toward him. He rose and saluted.

"At ease, where is the gate-crasher?"

"In the first-class waiting room, Sir."

"That's kind of plush for a brig, don't you think?"

The subordinate swallowed to clear his throat. "Yes sir, but it's rather small, self-contained, and isolated. There's no reason to think he's other than a nuisance. We were about to release him."

"Not now, we're not. There's no known information about him, a mystery that's caught the eye of the upper echelon. They want an interview. Keep a guard with him until some desk demon arrives."

"Yes sir. Who will I turn him over to, Sir?"

"Someone from the Office of Faithfulness."

"Wow."

Ever since he met Rustbucket, someone was manhandling him. Except for when he turned the tables and hit Frimox. No—it was the nervous one, Sruma. He ought to pray for forgiveness; he'd scared the poor soul to distraction and then knocked him unconscious. It felt good.

Jinmyn strolled to the amenities table in the waiting room. The Montibaran equivalent of coffee smelled enticing, but his eyes twitched to the two soldiers near the door. If only he could twist his ears like a horse to better hear what they were talking about. They showed no signs of tension, just passing the time, and so far, his delay was nothing more than a trip to the principal's office. All he'd done was walk around the barricade, but who knew when this detention would turn sour, like before.

A reminder from his bladder urged him to rid a cup before getting another, while he had the time.

The large first-class restroom was clean and well lit, all shiny metal, glass, and inlaid with a rich, dark wood. At the far end of the room in an alcove was a small changing room. There were two rows of polished wooden lockers, a bench, and beyond that, a simple door. Jinmyn hesitated and pushed on the door lever to open it enough to take a peek. Outside. This could be what he needed. Did he dare? Closing the door, he searched the compartments until he found one with a shirt and cap in it. Both pieces had the spaceport logo on them.

He'd act as a spy. After all, he'd been accused of being one often enough. A little moxie, opportunity, or luck, is what it took. He giggled going down the one flight of open metal stairs to ground level.

Eight craft were located around the terminal in various stages of activity. All seemed to be unloading materiel—crates, shipping containers, and even vehicles were accumulating in orderly piles. Jinmyn slipped between cases with military markings on them. What now? Where was the freight for the transports? If they take on cargo for a return trip there could be a chance of sneaking on board with the equipment. One shuttle was already moving to take off. It looked empty before its bay doors closed. This could be nigh on to impossible to slip in if they weren't reloading.

The two guards who had been visiting in the waiting room burst out of the door and down the stairs, waving at the taxiing craft. Jinmyn dropped his jaw. Had he stepped out just in time? The back of his neck tingled. Four more security officers hurried out of the door and made for the other carriers. The first ship launched without slowing down. Out on the flight line, a female squad member spoke into a communication device.

Jinmyn didn't know how to escape, but he knew where he had to go; he should have used the bathroom when he was in there. There was no choice but to return.

While visiting the facilities, the two who had been on post passed back through the room. One tilted his head toward the sounds on the tarmac before the door closed behind them. "Do you believe he got on that ship?"

"I don't know ... maybe. But I don't think he was out of our sight long enough to do it without anyone seeing him."

"What if they were part of his plan, waiting for him? Explains why he crashed the gate in the first place."

Jinmyn's back was towards them, he had to stand still and stay calm.

"We'll find out soon enough. The dispatcher says the squad is checking the other ships and the area around the terminal. Perimeter's been notified, and they're interdicting the flyer."

"What about the unmanned drones?"

"Only an idiot would attempt to escape on those sub-orbitals. With no life-support on them, it's suicide."

The men passed through the restroom without speaking to him.

Jinmyn washed his hands and held them together with a firm grip to keep them from trembling. Breathe deep ... one ... two ... okay.

He went outside again to reconnoiter. Armed soldiers stood at each ship. Jinmyn wandered the stockpile of equipment attempting to appear as an employee sorting inventory. Once, he saw a sentry watching him and he waved. He got a return wave in response. His legs went hollow, good thing he didn't have to run. That could have undone everything, but the soldier was friendly enough. Perhaps he should go back and persuade them to take him to the other continent for an audience with the king. He would have to contact Montibarans eventually.

No, forget that. Confessing to just any Montibaran wouldn't work. People took care of their own problems. Like Frimox, who handled it in a way Jinmyn didn't like. Or the guards, who also resolved the situation to his detriment. If Jinmyn was going to succeed in calling off Doomsday, he had to create the problem for the right person—the king.

No one was watching. Jinmyn crawled into a land vehicle. Could he drive it out of here? The setting sun was near the horizon. If he turned on the headlights perhaps their glare would shield his identity from anyone glancing toward his windshield.

Movement in his periphery vision set his heart thumping. Jerking his head sideways, he saw it was a drone landing. Squat, self-propelled carts, with long wide arms of a massive forklift, drove to the opened bay of the craft, picked up cargo and hauled it to the storage area. It took two of them five trips to complete the unloading, place the containers, and return to their parking slots as the unmanned aircraft lifted off. Jinmyn bit his cheek while his attention slipped to his old programming days. It wouldn't be hard to write code for such an automatic function. The unloaders probably only queried the ship's inventory log, removed that many items, and returned to their docking spaces—quick and efficient.

Another one landed and Jinmyn watched the process repeat. More than likely, shipping activity was scheduled for nighttime, reserving the daylight hours for personnel.

He had to think. Use his mind to solve his problem, like just drive off. But if he did that, he'd have to find a way back in if he were to convince someone to take him to the king; or, was his subconscious trying to show him the way? He slid down in the driver's seat and tried to make himself small.

What was going on with time? For a while, it seemed like they shuttled in one after another. Waiting for the next arrival to implement his plan was taking forever. Jinmyn took deep breaths, went over what he had to do, and picked out his route. Here comes one. Be ready.

The time pendulum swung the other way once the drone landed. He had to race to drive onto the unloader's tines before it went for the last load. The forked automaton carried his vehicle to the ship and prior to reaching its intended cargo, Jinmyn drove off and to the side.

He hooted through the windshield. "Take that, robots. Beaten by a programmer again. Hah!" Unloading complete, Jinmyn held his breath until the bay doors closed. "Woo hoo. I did it!"

He rocked and bounced in his seat in an abbreviated version of a victory dance. They were moving—he was going to make a getaway. He clapped his hands and rubbed them together. Might as well settle in, it may be a few hours flight.

He activated the dome light and inspected his surroundings. A military vehicle would have all sorts of handy stuff on it, maybe some rations. He found a compartment in the area aft of the forward seats, and there, sure enough, supplemental nutrition. Another bump ... must be getting ready to launch.

Wait—the guard said sub-orbital. He could die in here! This is a bad, bad idea!

He needed something—anything. How about a gas mask, would that give him oxygen? Rations forgotten, he pulled assorted equipment from the compartment with each hand and threw it behind him. The pressure pushed him down as they lifted from the field. He had to hurry, quit fumbling and don't panic. There, that had to be what he was searching for; it had a transparent face and a hose connected to it. Why wasn't it coming out?

Heaviness increased shoving him deeper into the seat. His arms were too heavy to reach into the storage and his vision darkened. A buzzing vibration settled under his skull. Was his hair falling out? He must have that mask or die. He lunged, and fell short.

WELCOME AND GOODBYE

Yorev wore his official cape; this was not a social or friendly call. His report would be professional and to the best of his ability, as ordered. If Montibar survived, he would resign and stay away from all governmental functions except to circulate a petition to reduce royal powers in favor of parliamentary.

He preferred reporting to the full legislative body but his king demanded personal reports, an action that came close to breaching protocol. The stagnant monarch insisted on private accountings to indulge his emotional eating. Yorev gritted his teeth and followed the steward into the State assembly room.

King Eborces was dressed in his royal attire, and the three heads of the parliamentary branches sat on the left side of the impressive chamber. Yorev stopped at the steps to the dais and made a slight bow. He got a hooded stare in return. He graced the legislative trio with a deeper bend before turning again to the monarch. He noted the bakery cart next to the throne covered with a tapestry that made it appear more regal. Hopefully, the king was beginning to pay attention. "Sire—"

Eborces raised a hand. "One more."

"What?" Surely, the royal snacker wouldn't delay official proceedings so he could have another treat.

King Eborces waved to a steward at a side door. "Bring in the Deputy."

SanMelo entered through the door held open for her, gold gorgets and epaulets on her uniform marked her as Deputy of the Office of Faithfulness. She wore a frown, and seeing Yorev, gave an almost imperceptible shake of her head and a small shrug.

Yorev knew why she was here. He would make it easy for them. "Is Your Corpulence ready for a report now?"

Eborces reddened to a remarkably royal complementary color to the white ruff on the neck of his robe. "See? He's been acting this way for some time now. If you won't let me arrest him, then at least I'm going to remove him."

"It's true, Ladies and Gentleman," Yorev said to the governmental leaders. "I have reached preposterous disdain for His Inertness. We are under threat of total destruction, and even though we don't have it, His Sluggishness wants our protection to come from the Regulator. Why do we need a monarch who's only good for a bakery disposal? He needs to quit the alert and reopen the spaceport."

An intake of breath from one of the legislators was the only sound in the room. SanMelo stared, her mouth open.

Eborces lurched to his feet, pointing a shaking finger at Yorev. "Give SanMelo your cape. Don't go back to your office. It's hers now. Leave and never come back, or I'll have you thrown in jail."

Yorev was light enough to float away. "Excellent choice, Your Denseness. It's the first good decision you've ever made." He smiled as he removed the cloak to drape over her shoulders. Winking at her, he spoke in a low voice. "It's fine; just do the best you can to persuade him to call off the emergency before we find ourselves in a war nobody wins."

She gulped and nodded.

Eborces wheezed, heavy bottom lip trembling, a bubble of saliva at the corner of his mouth. If he had intended to appear imperious and subdue his subject, he failed. He pumped a fist as if banging on a desk; his muted voice muttered, "Get out." It was unclear if he meant Yorev or was talking to himself. He shuffled to the door of the Royal Chambers waving for the aromatic bakery cart to follow.

The gray-haired female of the triad stood. "Yorev, I believe you came to make a report on our condition with Grabin. Would you consider doing so before leaving?"

He nodded to SanMelo, "With your permission, Head of Faithfulness?"

She blushed but kept her chin up. "Please."

"Very well." He positioned himself in the front of the three and noticing SanMelo still a step behind him, tilted his head for her to stand by the branch authorities. They accepted her company without elaboration.

"I'll make this quick for all of us," Yorev said. "SanMelo is aware of the problem and can fill in the facts as you wish, so it'll be my sense of recent occurrences that you'll be getting."

All three head gestured indicating their understanding.

"Since King Eborces doesn't know how long the Regulator will be gone, he thinks the best way to protect us is by using the Doomsday mechanism. It's pitiful. What he sees as a shield, Grabin sees as a threat. As long as our infrastructure, or Grabin's, is not threatened everything is fine. That's what Eborces is counting on and he's turned complacent.

"Meanwhile, Grabin has used his lack of diligence to sneak in more spies and place operatives in position; my guess is to foment insurrection. I pointed this out to him and his response was to shut down the spaceport. I leave it to you esteemed notaries to decide if that is a hostile act grievous enough to portend hostilities. Grabin thinks so and is on high alert. How the Regulator's sensors will respond, I don't know. Eborces put us in new, untried circumstances. We do know the life-ending space rocks shifted and broke off pieces when Grabin reacted. Montibar is the target of one. Two for Grabin. Somehow the king thinks it's a good sign that Grabin is in twice the peril we are."

Yorev shook his head and looked at his toes. He brought up his hands in fists, took a deep breath and clasped them together, gathering himself back into a discreet persona. "King Eborces is convinced the Regulator defends Montibar. Therefore, His Highness will do nothing."

Four pairs of eyes held Yorev as the center of attention. Even SanMelo kept her gaze, though she knew of this.

Yorev cleared his throat and continued. "The situation has only been a diplomatic hangnail until immediately after the spaceport closure. A man who gave his name as Jinmyn tried to force his way past the barricades demanding to see the king. He was detained and about to be released as a crank until a check revealed him unaccounted in any of our censuses. The operations commander notified me and I asked them to bring him here for interrogation. He escaped. We thought he was on a particular craft so we intercepted it and forced it to land at one of our bases. Only the scheduled pilot was aboard."

Again, Yorev dropped his head. "Later that night a supply drone returned; it should have been empty. Inside was a ground transport carrying a spaceport employee. Evidently, he caught the fugitive, Jinmyn, trying to steal the transportation. A fight ensued from the look of the torn up vehicle, and Jinmyn got rid of the evidence by somehow placing it in a drone. He performed quite a feat considering the short time a carrier is on the ground and the number of people we had watching for him."

The gray-haired woman cleared her throat. "So you're looking for a killer now?"

"Not yet. The enclosed vehicle had enough oxygen to keep him alive, but the employee hasn't regained consciousness. He will survive and we have—" Yorev smiled and tilted his head to SanMelo—"rather, the Head of Faithfulness has many questions for him."

"Who is the worker? Have you notified his family?"

"Jinmyn must have stolen his identification so we're checking all employees. There's no report of a missing person, yet it hasn't been that long. We think the escapee is still on the base."

"Is that where we stand as of now?"

"Yes, Madam Secretary, except for hearing my personal plea. Stop this madness. Convince King Eborces to abort this action. We can live in diplomatic peace with Grabin until the Regulator gets back. The solution to our problems is not to threaten each other with extinction and cause it to become a reality. And, finally, when this is over, shift the power to use this system ever again, to the combined vote of your three houses. Perhaps give the king emergency authority to activate it, but if it is not ratified by you in a given time, it relapses to an inactive state."

The lone man of the three stood, his face pale, and spoke with tight lips. "Traitor! King Eborces is right. You should be arrested."

The old man leaned forward, his neck veins pulsing above his collar.

The woman seated in the middle tilted away from him. The representative of the group made an exasperated grimace, "Oh, sit down, Delphar." Diverting her attention, she said, "Thank you, Yorev. Enjoy your retirement."

Velmere pulled the straps that lifted the weight, throwing his torso into the effort along with his arms. Finding the exercise room mitigated the security officer's unfamiliar inactivity. The odor of sweat, and the sound of grunts as bodies challenged equipment, or each other, refreshed him. Dinner with Ambassador Lyram last evening took forever. Velmere was a soldier, trained in every respect as one. When he got a chance to eat, he gulped it. The only purpose of food was to stuff it into his belly. Diplomats meant to dine as long as possible, and always talk, talk, talk. Throughout the long meal and the never-ending greetings from all levels of staff and guests, Velmere glanced at Korfel hoping for a sign that would give him an excuse to leave. However, the Captain remained stoic, performing his own embassy duties. The only interesting time was relating what Jinmyn told him about the Christians. If only they were real and there was a higher power he could trust, he would have had a better appetite.

Lyram had glossed over the spaceport closure that marooned them. He was certain that diplomacy would smooth any misunderstandings and return things to normal. Besides, in his zeal to coddle Montibar, the Regulator would make everything right. Velmere would see.

The ambassador didn't convince him. Life, as usual, evaporated if Jinmyn were correct. Events out of the ordinary were happening and the Christian was the only one that wasn't content to let the Regulator solve their problems.

Velmere stood, took a step, and then returned to his workout. He wanted to talk with Jinmyn again, and Korfel should be on the way with updated news about that very subject. Velmere's discipline stayed him from striding to meet the Captain, but it didn't keep him from flexing his fists. Enough of this; he had to do something. Korfel could find him here in the gym.

Velmere listened to the report without interruption, until Korfel said, "You were right. He is resourceful, but ruthless too. He attacked the poor fumigator and then loaded the other man on the drone, which could have killed him. Does this change how we're to approach him?"

Velmere scowled, started to speak, but pressed his lips together. He raised his chin with a faraway focus to his eyes. "How close is an agent to the man recovering in the hospital?"

Korfel blinked, "Sir? We're concentrating on the spaceport. Jinmyn still has to be there; even Montibaran security thinks so. We have someone inside their supply depot here, but the worker, as you say, is in the infirmary. We didn't follow him."

Velmere gave a half shrug. "Captain, I don't know about the altercation with the fumigator, but Jinmyn wouldn't put a life in jeopardy. That worker has to be Jinmyn in disguise, and he's now in town."

THE START OF THE END

His salivary glands recognized it and flooded his mouth microseconds before his brain identified the fragrance. Cherry pie: his second foster mother baked it when he was nine. He couldn't remember her name, but the taste of that pie, with its golden crust and bright red cherries, was unforgettable. Jinmyn's rumbling stomach jerked him awake.

Another hospital bed.

How did he get here? He had scrambled for the mask but didn't secure it; broken fingernails attested to the effort. Some wheel-well stowaways on airliners survived; whatever saved them must have worked for him. He threw off the covers, ran his hands over his chest, and flexed his legs. He'd made it. Everything worked. Now for clothes or food, didn't matter which. Yes, it did, food, definitely. Where was the source of that mouth-watering aroma?

At least he was in pajamas and not an earth-like hospital gown because the growling coming from his midsection demanded that he find the kitchen regardless of his state of dress. Following his nose, a short walk down the hall revealed a cafeteria; he went directly to the tray line. Bread, meat, vegetables, gravy, desserts, everything he came across he placed on his plate building a comestible pyramid.

Yeah, much better. He could slow down through the last half of the meal and show some table manners. He didn't make sparks fly slinging his fork at the food as the baker of the cherry pie accused him of doing, but he didn't use proper decorum either. Now that most of the edible load rested in his innards, Jinmyn's other senses trickled to life.

A gathering in the cafeteria at one side of the room, their rapt expressions fixed on a newscast displayed from a wall-mounted video receiver, caught his attention.

He shifted a wad into one cheek and addressed an intern nearby. "Hey, buddy?" Jinmyn waved a stabbed piece of meat at the announcer, "What's going on, the World Series?"

The young man frowned and managed to put a scold in his voice. "It's nothing to joke about. Why would you do it? Or don't you know what's happening? Really?"

"I guess not," Jinmyn replied, holding up an elbow to show his pajamas. "I've been out of it for a while."

The aide swept his gaze over Jinmyn as if taking notice for the first time. "Yes, I suppose ... anyway, the first meteor is due to strike Grabin tomorrow, the second two rotas from now, and ours is supposed to hit in three."

Brimlet! Sweaty heat engulfed his head, neck, and arms. He might be sick. His throat tightened and Jinmyn couldn't swallow. He spat the mouthful of food back onto the plate and stood on hollow legs, gripping the table with trembling hands. "The asteroids are coming in?"

His informant cringed as Jinmyn sprayed food. "No, just three smaller pieces."

"What's the king doing about it?"

"Nothing. He says the Regulator will protect *us*, but Grabin is scrambling. They're trying to meet and divert them."

He shouldn't have agreed to Rustbucket's request. He couldn't talk to kings; he would fail. Someone else would have to save the planets.

His vision blurred, washed out and hazy pale, tiny lights sparkled and spun. *Rustbucket, you mangy ball of ozone, please stop this madness and help me. I can't do this by myself.*

Leaning on the back of a chair for support, Jinmyn asked, "How far to the palace?" but his companion had already joined the others in front of the video.

Following EXIT signs to the lobby, Jinmyn found the clerk with her back to the counter watching a smaller version of the newscast. He leaned forward and cleared his throat. "Excuse me. Which way to the palace?"

She hooked a thumb over her shoulder, her attention fixed on the screen. "Out the door, turn left and straight through town."

"Thanks."

Okay, Rustbucket, are you happy with your average selection to see the king? Are hospital pajamas and barefoot regal enough? Why do I get the idea you're more of a gas bubble than a cloud of energy? You really blew this one, and if anything bad happens to Brimlet, I'll personally find a way to discharge you.

He knew this city and people the same way he could speak the language: Rustbucket implanted knowledge.

He was a fly in the oatmeal to the ordered and regulated population, an anomalous beacon warning spectators of his oddity, but traffic zipped by without slowing. Pedestrians scurried to their own destinations, scanning skyward or heads down and shoulders hunched as if ducking the incoming projectile. He caught their obvious fear and couldn't keep from looking up.

Would he draw scrutiny boarding the provided transportation in his state of dress? He'd do it anyway. Today he had no other options. Today no one cared. In this season of extraordinary events, he could take this line all the way to the city's edge, where, on a hill beyond, rose the palace.

One of three people to exit at the last stop, Jinmyn noticed The Gaumen Shack. So this is what it looks like from the front in daylight. What are those people's names in there?

"It's LauNin, and I've been looking for you." She spoke in a hush, took his elbow in one hand, her other pressed against his back to guide him from the bar. "Sit in that booth in the corner; I'll bring you something to eat."

"How did you know to look for me?" Jinmyn asked. "Nobody knows where I am. I just now realized it myself."

"Please go sit down." LauNin scouted the room while keeping her chin down. "There is at least one Montibaran mole in here."

"Wha—" Jinmyn pulled his head back. "What are you talking—oh. You're Grabin! But that's wonderful! They're the ones I should talk to." He clapped to get the attention of the cluster of customers. "My name's Jinmyn and I need to convince the king to drop the alarm system so Rustbucket—you call him the Regulator—can return. Will anyone help me?"

Several drinkers chuckled and raised glasses in salute before returning to their pastime, a few turned away. More than one cast a glance to a broad-shouldered individual with a crewcut at the end of the bar who shrugged and drank from his bottle. A short stick of a man, his belt bunching up his oversize britches, slid from a booth and limped forward on splayed outward feet.

He squinted at Jinmyn through thick, round glasses, but growled with a firm raspy voice, "Come with me, please." One hand stayed in his pocket.

Jinmyn gaped at him. "You're the mole ... from Montibar?" Spies were absurd. He was more an anorexic, runt of the litter, frog than mole.

He croaked, "You're now in Office of Faithfulness hands. Let's go."

LauNin stepped between them shoving the mole backward with no more effort than wiping off a table, hissing at Jinmyn, tight and urgent, "Run!"

The mole yelled, "Stop." Did he mean the others who jumped up? Jinmyn stood on lead feet, his mouth still open. Someone grabbed his arm and shook him, "Come on, she's giving you a chance."

Jinmyn tried to watch the mole stagger backward and get a look at the newcomer at the same time. Another arrival punched the newcomer with a knuckle-on-flesh splat, knocking him down. He jerked Jinmyn aside, breaking his mesmerization with the fast-changing events.

The mole pulled a weapon from his pocket and pointed it at LauNin, but the big man from the end of the bar grabbed him from behind and tossed him over the counter, knocking off glasses and bottles. His weapon flashed as his arms flapped, and a customer sitting at a booth slumped over.

The puncher pulled Jinmyn towards the door but big man was in their way. Puncher released Jinmyn to swing a fist ... too slow. Big Man put him down with one less tooth and stood over him rubbing his knuckles.

"I'll just get to the palace on my own, thank you very much," Jinmyn said. It was time to get out of here before LauNin or anyone else could grab him again. He eyed Big Man and stepped around Puncher sprawled on the floor. Witnessing the alarmed look on Big Man's face, he turned in time to see the flash from mole's stunner.

CHAPTER ELEVEN

METEORS FOR ALL

"You slept through the grab. How're you feeling?"

The shot from a stunner, just like last time, made his tongue as thick as a sausage and his throat dry. "Uh ... ohh ... not again," Jinmyn said, licking his lips. "Can't see right, everything's blurry." He ducked his chin and hacked again. "Is that you, Velmere?"

"Yes."

"Got any water?" His words slurred from inflexible speech muscles. "Who grabbed me?" He sat up to keep the bile from rising.

"Obviously, we did." Velmere nodded to a companion who handed Jinmyn a container. "However, that's not what I'm talking about. This is." He pointed to a video broadcast where a worried announcer was indicating a chart. Velmere and three others in the room were quiet, concentrating on the news.

This was important, but he couldn't pin it down. "Velmere, what—"

"Listen! He's making a special announcement."

The newscast continued, "Our pilots secured the tumbling satellite between their ships. Here's a view from one of the on-board cameras."

"Oh!" Jinmyn's ears buzzed, his skin tingled and drenched him in sweat. He struggled to comprehend what he was seeing.

The meteor he expected to be the size of a football was larger than four domed stadiums. Dark and sinister, the camera panned over the surface, returning to show the puny rods extending from the dwarfed 3-deck ship to the rock. Ant legs holding a watermelon.

"They're ready to begin maneuvering," the broadcaster said. "It will take considerable skill to change the inertia of that much mass, and keep themselves safe in the process."

Velmere's face was darker, stonier than the space debris, his eyes cold and hooded. "Are you connected with this threat to Grabin?" His question was calm and impossible to sidestep.

Jinmyn took another swallow of water, "No ... well, yes, in a way ... but no."

Velmere's gaze never wavered from Jinmyn, but he held his hand out palm up, "Korfel, give me your weapon."

The man beside him jerked his head, saw Velmere's lethal expression, then drew and extended the firearm handle first. Velmere pointed it at Jinmyn, raised his other hand and pressed a button on it. Korfel stiffened.

Velmere glared over the top of the kill-ready sidearm. "I trusted you because of the Christian stories, but you talked without saying anything about who you are. Now you'll tell me everything, or you won't wake up from the next shot."

Sweat dripped from under Jinmyn's arms and slid down his sides. The pistol's focusing lens aimed between his eyes looked big enough to spit out a solar flare. "What do you want me to say?"

"Start with who you are and where you're from."

Jinmyn took another swallow and wiped his brow with the back of his forearm. "It's gonna sound strange, but the Regulator—"

"Hold it. They said you called him something in the bar, what was it?"

"Huh? Oh, his name's Rustbucket." Odd that he spoke English, there had to be a translation but none came to his Montibaran vocabulary.

The four Grabinians shifted or squirmed. "Strange name. Most regal," Velmere said, the blaster still pointed at Jinmyn. "Go on."

To harbor no secrets, to cease fear was to tell someone the whole story, even if they weren't going to believe him. Jinmyn's rib cage relaxed with a deep breath. "Rustbucket is locked out of both Grabin and Montibar by his own doing. Since the alert is set, an energy presence would trigger the security systems. The asteroids will fall." The swallow of water, this time, was refreshing.

"How do you know this?"

"Rustbucket told me."

"You just said he couldn't return." Velmere's cold eyes peered through slitted lids.

"He can't. He came and got me where I lived. Not Grabin, not Montibar."

Korfel snorted, one of the other men muttered an expletive. The blaster held steady.

Velmere breathed, no other motion - the videocast rumbled in the background. "There's no other place."

Jinmyn smiled; this was enjoyable. "There is. Very, very far away." He held a hand palm outward, "Don't ask me how I got here, Rustbucket did that. He said he could poke in a person if he did it really fast. I'm supposed to ask the king to stop all the nonsense, then Rustbucket returns and takes me home."

"Why you?"

Why indeed? He recalled the speech Rustbucket gave him about being average, with no one to miss him. Jinmyn's shoulders slumped; he hung his head. "I thought I had nothing more to lose; I agreed to it—but I've accomplished nothing."

His ears rang in the stillness until a shoe scuffed the floor. The clock pushed hard against sticky time, struggling past another second. Velmere held the sidearm without wavering, his finger on the trigger.

"They're doing it!" The excited cry was from one of the Grabinians as he pointed at the screen. All but Velmere looked up.

"They're going to move it away."

SanMelo raised her head at the tapping on her opened door. She dropped her pen and jumped up. "Yorev, you never need to knock, this was your office as long as I can remember. Please come in."

"Thank you, but more than anyone, I'm aware how much you must do, and I'm reluctant to interfere, but ..." He spread his hands wide and smiled.

"I always have time for you, please sit down," she said, moving to take the seat in front, waving for him to use her vacated spot behind the desk.

"That won't do," Yorev said, placing his hand on the back of the guest chair. "Take your rightful place. Believe me, I don't want it. I was overdue to leave. I'm happy for you."

SanMelo's cheeks flushed a dash of color, but she tipped her head in acknowledgment. "What brings you out of your recent retirement, Yorev? Are you bored already?"

He recognized the invitation to state the reason for his visit. The Head of Faithfulness had no time for idle conversation. "What is King Eborces doing to protect us? And please, SanMelo, let's speak in plain language. Is he still waiting on the Regulator?"

She studied him. "Yes."

As he expected. "Where it will impact?"

"They say near the south pole."

"Hmm, not a bad place, if it's going to hit."

"Only ice. That's why the king is sure the Regulator is helping."

"What do you think?"

SanMelo leaned back in her chair and steepled her fingers. "I only do what I'm told, to the best of my abilities."

Yorev's chuckle accompanied a small shake of his head. "You will find, my young Head of Faithfulness, that part of your job will be to maneuver the king toward what you realize must be done. Right now, people are getting nervous. Put him on the video to explain the situation to them. He's so sure nothing's going to happen that he's genuinely calm. They'll see that, and settle down too, I hope."

"How do I convince him to air an announcement?"

"Easy. Grabin's been showing the live feed from their encounter, so the audience is huge. Tell him it's time for the world to see a real leader. His ego won't let him refuse."

SanMelo pressed her lips together and worked them side to side, her mental tussle evident.

Nodding, she said, "He needs to speak to the public."

The men in the room with Jinmyn and Velmere yelled and pumped fists in the air. Cheering came from the broadcast booth as the Grabin ships grudged the huge rock to a new trajectory.

Velmere pinned Jinmyn with the sights of the weapon. "Where's your ship?"

"There isn't one. I told you, Rustbucket brought me here. I came to exist in a field in front of the palace, but an ozier grabbed me and took me to the Gaumen Shack ... I was naked. Seems so long ago now."

Velmere glanced at Korfel who gave a small nod. "That corresponds with what LauNin reported."

"May I stand up and stretch my legs?" Jinmyn asked, beginning to move.

"Stay still." Velmere held the blaster on him. "You've pulled some moves in the past to slip away, and your story is beyond belief. I want the truth, and I want it now."

Jinmyn barked a laugh. "What's not to believe about an ordinary putz on one world being shot through space to solve the problems of two other worlds?" Hmm, "putz" came out in English. Let 'em work on that one. "Haven't you heard that truth is stranger than fiction?" The ridge lines on Velmere's jaws suggested he didn't like the levity.

One Grabinian pointed at the news screen. "What's he saying?"

The cheerfulness of the announcer vanished as he read a report. "Our scientists say that by the time the ships direct the meteoroid around Grabin and set it on a path to the sun, their fuel will be critical. They will have enough to speed back to intercept the next one, but not enough to move it away from us. If they go slower to conserve what's on board, they won't be in time to make a difference." His face drawn with deep fatigue lines, the reporter stared unblinking into the camera. With worry evident in his bloodshot eyes, the movement of his Adam's apple traced a slow swallow.

"The office of the Director of Security tells us that anyone who can make it to the western hemisphere should do so. It looks like we're going to take a hit after all."

Velmere pushed the blaster a hand's breadth closer to Jinmyn. He would fire. Realization washed through Jinmyn from the inside out. In one second, he would cease to exist. "Save Brimlet." He closed his eyes, unable to look into the deadly pit at the end of the barrel that would spew his atoms across the cosmos.

Velmere lowered the weapon. "As Assistant Director of Grabin Security, I need to save everyone. How do I do that now?" Jinmyn's sigh was not the only one. The changing priority of tension was evident as Korfel reclaimed his sidearm.

Jinmyn's hand ached from squeezing the container. A breath and the last sip of water eased the constriction from his throat. "Is there more water, please?" He had sweated more than he ingested.

Velmere turned his worry to the newscast; his shoulders slumped while the announcer outlined the peril in detail, assuring his audience that he and a few volunteers would stay at the station broadcasting as long as they could.

Jinmyn sloshed water around his dry mouth and swallowed. "I didn't cause the problem, but I'm here because of it. I was supposed to fix it, but I haven't. That's it, Velmere, plain and simple."

The broad-shouldered Assistant Director shrugged. "I don't believe you, but it doesn't matter, does it?"

Jinmyn's chest tightened as bad as when he thought he would be shot. Why did he want Velmere, a man he barely knew, to trust him? Jinmyn didn't know, but it was important. He pieced together what he understood of the situation and asked, "Why doesn't Grabin send more help?"

When Velmere didn't answer, Korfel said, "We only have four ships. Two are already out there, one is in port for repairs, and the last one is being made ready to evacuate our king and his family."

"Will the Regulator help us?" Velmere's question was no longer an interrogation or even a commander's request for reinforcement. His appearance was a man seeking aid from any quarter.

Jinmyn bent over and put his face in his hands. "I don't know. I know he doesn't want anyone hurt. I just know that. He doesn't.

But he may be thinking that if he helps, the king here will never undo the alarm, and the problem remains."

One of the guards snarled, "He's never helped us. Only Montibar."

It alarmed Jinmyn when others agreed. "I was meant to help both worlds."

Neither Velmere nor Korfel corrected the guards' snorts and expletives.

The palace gardens had alcoves, ideal for resting or contemplation. Yorev occupied one to bide the time. He was not far from his old office and would rather be at his favorite spot on the covered terrace that ran the perimeter of the building. But today he needed to let SanMelo leave before returning for his last act.

The irony of his intentions occurring in the Office of Faithfulness upset his stomach. He had taken an oath of support to the king and parliament years ago, and abided by it—believed in it. How convoluted allegiance became that he must choose between Montibar and his government when they were all on the same side.

His loyalty to the well-being of Montibar was paramount, and he wasn't exactly defying any order from his monarch. He heaved a sigh, accepted the forthcoming consequences, and, when the way was clear, fixed his destination on the communications center.

As he knew they would, most of the staff were scurrying with directors' demands for the kings broadcast. He waved at the few who looked his way, continued to a polished wooden door across the room, and entered a code on a panel next to the frame. The laxity of security irked him. They hadn't changed his access, thankfully. It should be easy to explain that he came to say goodbye to the official government dispatcher and offer to cover her station while she took a quick break. With the show going on, she would have no relief until it was over.

"The camera crew is almost set up, Sire," SanMelo said. "They expect this will be your highest rated broadcast of all time."

Eborces smiled and pulled at a cuff on the royal robe.

SanMelo didn't like the amount of politics that came with her new position. Yorev had been correct to suggest the King address the population, but she frowned at the way the potentate turned a dire circumstance into a celebration. He dressed in his most regal robes and insisted SanMelo wear her cape of office.

He dismissed the bakery cart from the room with an offhand wave and took his seat on the throne. She assumed his anticipation of approval by all of Montibar was sweet enough for him.

He looked calm and cheerful. Lights flashed on and a director pointed a finger at him.

"Greetings, Montibar. I'm here to address your concerns about the recent events taking place and to assure you that your king is dedicated to your safety. There is no need to worry that the proceedings on the other planet will ever happen here. In fact, we would have helped them if Grabin asked soon enough. We can spare our ships since the Regulator will protect his favorite world, but it's too late for them to arrive in time to save our neighbors. Who knows why the Regulator doesn't help them? He must want Grabin punished—probably for their audacity and arrogance. The object heading our way will pass safely below Montibar. I know it will."

SanMelo clamped her jaws shut and hoped her face was impassive as her sovereign continued his long harangue at their planetary neighbor.

The king caught her full attention when he announced, "I have ordered our ships to Grabin with medical supplies and to help evacuate wounded. Montibar is the most caring world, and once again, we will prove it. It may be why the Regulator favors us."

What? He made that up on the spot. He really does think he can say anything and make it happen. It's better that interplanetary commerce was someone else's purview. Her hands would be full with extra official duties if King Eborces went afield, physically or with commentary.

She noticed whispered conversations and rustling among the reporters. Had Eborces gone too far off the mark? She wished the king would end this broadcast.

"So we are absolutely safe and whatever befalls Grabin is too bad. We do hope they survive, of course. Any questions?"

A reporter with his hand raised asked, "Sire if there is no risk to Montibar, why did the Office of Faithfulness just issue an evacuation order for southern beaches on both continents?"

Eborces' mouth fell open. He jerked his head fast enough toward SanMelo to fling spittle, floppy jowls miming words. His gaping stare and arched eyebrows frozen in a picture for worldwide publication.

Realization heated her neck and radiated upward. "Yorev."

King Eborces curled his hands into white knuckled fists even as his face kaleidoscoped through splotchy gray to royal cerise. "Arrest him!"

The cameras continued to record.

Yorev nodded approval to SanMelo as she rushed toward his seat on the terrace. "I saw your exit on the broadcast—dignified and contained. Well done. Will it be house arrest or prison?"

Her posture befitted the Head of Faithfulness, but her wet eyes were almost spilling over. "The king didn't say. We'll make it house arrest. Go home."

The men in the guard quarters of the Grabin embassy hooted to see King Eborces lose his decorum. His broadcast had overridden the live feed from Grabin, but abruptly stopped and the scene returned to the struggle of the space ships. They almost had the meteoroid to a destination where they could safely release it to fall into their local star and never be a threat again.

"I've been thinking." Jinmyn tipped his head back to stare with unfocused eyes at the ceiling. "Do your ships carry lifeboats or escape pods?"

Velmere spun toward him. "Why? Do you think they're in danger?"

"No. Well, I don't know—but what would happen if when they release the rock, the two ships attached to each other and used one to accelerate them together back to the rendezvous, in time to set up for the second threat? Could they get in their escape pods and remote control the ships? Both ships and all pods could push. When the King of Grabin gets moved, his ship can gather in the people from the pods."

Velmere arched his eyebrows to Korfel who puckered his lips and shrugged. "They might be able to do all that ... probably could. But it won't help. The life supporters—pods, you call them—only have enough fuel to launch themselves away from the ship. They're not meant to travel, only get away."

The only sound was from the video—Jinmyn thought of it as a TV—coordinating the upcoming disengagement. They were getting close.

He studied Velmere pacing, the Assistant Director hitting the fist of one hand into the palm of the other. These really were catastrophic, world-shattering events, and plain old Jinmyn was here in the middle of the chaos trying to amend the tragedy.

"Velmere, I'm sure Rustbucket wants to help but doesn't want to be detected doing so. Could you send the plan to Grabin using the code RB assist? If he's monitoring the situation, he may slip in and support them without making it look like he did."

"Arr Bee assist?"

Spoken back to him, Jinmyn realized the initials came out in English. Strange sounds, a rolling, burring r to a local ear. "Yes, RB assist. Think of it as rocket booster if you want, but it's an important phrase for Rustbucket to understand it." No sense explaining alien initials.

Velmere waved his hand at the door. "Korfel, get to the communications center and send it."

One to jump at an order, Korfel stood still. "Sir, there isn't time to encode the message, check it, transmit it, wait for them to confirm receipt, and decode it before the ships must turn around."

"Send it in the clear under my name. Don't forget to request an Arr Bee assist maneuver."

Korfel leaped for the door.

Velmere ordered refreshments from the mess hall as they watched the broadcaster tell of huge traffic jams on roads, rivers, trails, and rails leaving the eastern hemisphere. Fights turned into mob actions where transportation stalled, and looting was reported at consumer businesses, even where the owner was present but powerless. Police protection was non-existent. The biggest surprise to Jinmyn was doomsday parties springing up. Consumption of intoxicating spirits led to Mardi Gras behavior at an astonishing number of establishments.

Korfel returned in time to get in line for the snacks, finger food, and cold drinks from the galley. He turned to the broadcast.

The announcer had a sheet of paper. "We've intercepted a message from the Assistant Director to the Office of Security." He read the whole plan, looking up in puzzlement to ask, "What's an Arr Bee assist?" When he finished with the communiqué, he explained to the audience how Velmere was marooned on Montibar because of King Eborces shutting down the spaceport, then asked someone off-camera. "Will it work?"

Moments of quiet air followed while the camera showed him inspecting different papers on his desk. A fist and arm stretched into view and gave him another sheet. He scanned it with worry lines at the corners of his eyes and mouth deepening, then delivered the news.

"According to our scientists, the Assistant Director's plan isn't viable. The emergency craft aren't capable of sustained engine output." He slammed the paper down. "Wouldn't you think anyone in the Office of Security would know that?"

Jinmyn felt the heat on his neck and face, ashamed because without meaning to, he set Velmere up for embarrassment. He glanced sidelong at the head of the guards. Velmere appeared composed, watching the show.

THE SHIPS

The proud Grabin fleet of four ships, named for the royal family were RinMod -King, TapBrid -Queen, their eldest children, Ilrua -son, and EmBar -daughter.

Activity at the RinMod readied her to evacuate the royals; the Ilrua sat in maintenance docks for repairs, leaving Captain Wimweg with TapBrid and Captain Rauftig with EmBar to engage the meteor. The unsophisticated maneuver was below the skill level of either captain: close with the menace, punch into it at the right location and push it away from Grabin and into the star.

Wimweg studied the mass of rock on the other side of his front viewscreen, shuddering at the unnatural proximity of dirt, stone, and ore. There should be stars and the blackness of space, not the nose of his beloved ship rammed into anything. Technically, it wasn't the actual nose. Steel beams stuck through the hull, attached to the structure of TapBrid in a frantic few hours of welding, and dug into the icy object, jammed by the thrust of his engine. The front beams made his sleek craft look like a quilled slyvet.

He pressed a button on the arm of the bridge chair to talk with his First Officer. Walking across the deck or shouting were not options worthy of a ship's Captain. "Stuzer, has engineering found a way to save us the necessary fuel for the next mission?"

"Not yet, sir."

Of course, they hadn't. They wouldn't. They couldn't. A recruit could figure out the limits of their supply.

"Captain, you should hear this!"

The shout from Communication Officer DorKim brought a frown from the skipper that meant DorKim would likely spend his next weekend reviewing the Handbook of Shipboard Courtesy regarding bridge protocol. Personnel shifted at their positions, sitting up straighter, some shamefaced. First Officer Stuzer took notes.

Discipline reestablished, Wimweg gestured overhead, "Put it on the speakers."

The proposal from Montibar intoned across the area to the rapt attention of the bridge, already alerted to its importance by DorKim's outburst.

Captain Wimweg's jaw set during the message. He addressed his crew, "Stuzer, get engineering, find out what they know about Arr Bee assist. Ensign DorKim, wash that signal through every filter you can for authenticity. I don't want some Montibaran prank making us appear more foolish than we are."

Wimweg rose from his command chair, walked to the viewscreen while the voice of his mind cursed the rock. These things should stay where they belonged: in the frozen stillness of the ethereal abyss.

"Captain, there is a Commander's Call from Space Authority." Young DorKim had returned to professionalism.

"I'll take it in my Flight Quarters. You have control First Officer Stuzer." Wimweg exited through a door at the rear as both bridge officers acknowledged orders.

Maybe Space Authority—SA in fleet parlance—was going to admit to the rocket boosting process. Why hadn't they told him about it before now? Probably one of those unshared governmental secrets their solar neighbor Montibar might find useful. Stupid to let this desperate situation play out until forced to reveal it.

The TapBrid's Flight Quarters, though small for captain's cabins, contained sleeping, working, and sanitary compartments. A sufficient place to stay near the bridge indefinitely in comfort, if necessary.

Wimweg strode to his genuine wood desk, polished to a brown mirror finish, and activated a video communicator that reflected his own image in a small square in the upper corner. The harried face of the SA Administrator filled the left half of the display followed by a flash on the right, which coalesced into a round face in a vise of red hair, thinning on top, trimmed beard on bottom: Captain Rauftig.

"Captains," the bureaucrat said, "thanks for all you have done, but there's a change of orders."

Rauftig grinned open-mouthed like a fish going for the bait.

"You are to break off and return for evacuation duty."

Rauftig's expression changed as fast as the flip of a card. "You can't mean it." He leaned closer until his face filled his side of the screen. He appeared to be examining the fatigued administrator. "There's no sense to that. We can't make it back in time to navigate to the surface, load, and launch again before the next collision."

"Calculations say you can, barely, if you turn right now and accelerate hard. You are to land in the Memorial Park next to Parliament. Its members are your evacuees. They'll be ready to board."

Wimweg's stomach recoiled with a gathering sense of dread as he studied the official. He'd never seen the department head disheveled—needing a shave—bloodshot eyes easy enough to make out. "Sir, if we don't push until the drop-off point, this rock may only circle the star and find its way back. You know that."

"Yes, Captain Wimweg, and so do they, but they don't care anymore. They panicked like everyone else when news broke of the inevitable second punch. There's no long-term planning going on. They just want out of the impact area now."

"Survival mode at its best, huh?" Captain Rauftig said.

"It's worse than you think," said the SA manager. "At first, it was almost cordial, but then some members decided their families should go too, even if it meant some juniors had to stay behind. There have been fistfights—"

"So our ships will be rushed by a mob, and a brawl likely follow our landing?" Rauftig asked. "How will you contain that?"

"I don't expect to." The worn image of a used-up diplomat with tears in his eyes hung his head. "I'm resigning as soon as we conclude our conversation. It's my last official act."

"I thought you were going to tell us about the Arr Bee assist rocket booster when you called," Wimweg said.

"Me too," Rauftig added.

The SA shook his head, "No one here has ever heard of it. It had our hopes up for a while, but the builders said there's no enhancement to the life supporters, no augmentation in any way. They're the same as they've always been."

Wimweg squinted his eyes, pressed his mouth shut, and then bobbed his head. "So, it was a Montibaran trick. It isn't enough for us to suffer this; they have to make fun as well."

The official held up a hand. "No, the transmission was authentic. From Velmere, the Assistant Director of Security. He's at the embassy on Montibar."

Wimweg narrowed his eyes again. He was aware of the Assistant Director, of course, but why would a high-positioned person bother to send such a confusing dispatch? Was he playing spy and trying to get a coded message to his superiors using the current situation as cover?

"If there are no more questions, Captains, I'm going to sign off. I can't wait to leave the company of the fine men and women of parliament."

Both ships' captains straightened for formal leave-taking.

"Thank you, sir."

"Good luck, sir."

"Thank you and the same to you two." The official's hand appeared in view to push the button ending the conversation.

Captain Wimweg signed off and turned for the bridge. At once, his device chimed announcing an incoming call.

It was Captain Rauftig. "Let's talk."

"We should make arrangements to return as fast as possible," Wimweg said. "We'll need every spare moment." He paused halfway to the door.

"Captain Wimweg, I am senior. Not by much, but still, I'm asking for your indulgence. Accommodate me in this and I'll not pull the date-of-rank issue again. Please."

"Very well." Captain Wimweg returned to the desk.

"Here's what I see," Rauftig said. "You stated that you got the message about Arr Bee assist. The SA verified that it's from Velmere. I know him."

"How do you know it isn't an encryption for something else?"

"I guess it could be," Rauftig admitted, "but given Velmere's reputed veracity, I think he would have used another reference rather than get our hopes up."

"So you believe it? In spite of the contrary evidence?"

Captain Rauftig lifted and dropped his shoulders. "The odds of successful evacuations are nil. If we leave now, everything done to avoid the problem with this rock may be useless. We have a chance to stay with it a little longer and make sure it never bothers us again."

Wimweg held his peace. This was Rauftig's show, and he'd see if it led where he thought it would.

Rauftig spread his hands, "Then we follow the Arr Bee assist plan."

Wimweg's brows raised, "And when it fails, we return to a board of inquiry for desertion, dereliction of duty, and possible prison? At the least, we'd be unemployed embarrassments to our families."

"Could happen." Rauftig agreed. Was he smiling? "But if we desert the mission, Grabin gets hit once definitely, maybe twice. I think the population would agree with me that giving up for the skins of a few entitled parliament members is the worst evil. There's a big gain, Wimweg, for trying Velmere's plan. If it works, Grabin avoids both fireballs and no one will mind that we didn't follow our exact orders. Of course, the irony is that there probably won't be a command structure left to prosecute us unless we succeed."

"They will certainly know what we've done with all the news cameras on board." Wimweg bit the inside of his lip, "I can order the crew to comply, what about the reporters?"

"Let 'em do their job," Rauftig answered. "They signed on for the story knowing the risks. It'll even make a better press for them. Are you agreed?"

Wimweg turned his head aside and down, grinning. "I admit I was thinking along the same lines." Serious again, he straightened. "How much fuel do you have?"

Rauftig checked his desktop. "Forty-eight percent left. You?"

"Almost identical: forty-nine."

Rauftig furrowed his brow. "I'll push us back to rendezvous when we're done here. That'll leave me a handful to burn on the other rock."

"I'd rather you got us there and use what you have to help deploy the life supporters. Then you can shove with anything left over."

"Agreed. Now, how do we attach for the trip back?"

When Wimweg made the announcement, adrenaline overload peaked on the TapBrid like a surge of flood waters into a reservoir. Only the slimmest brim of discipline contained it. The vessels, empty except for crew and reporters, were engaged in historic, life-changing events for Grabin. The fast, wide-eyed reactions of those aboard telegraphed their awareness that they knew it, felt it, and wanted to scream it. The first burst of excitement of pushing the meteor had dulled with the long trip, but reignited with news of this new, insane maneuver.

Disengagement went well; both ships braking gently, letting the space rock's velocity carry it away to its fiery death. A dead stop and turn around were fuel inefficient. Instead, TapBrid and EmBar pivoted as one, in full sight of each other for the first time since contacting the rock. They performed an exquisite curve plotted to the nth detail for azimuth, elevation, and radius. Wimweg viewed his communications screen and tried to portray a calm demeanor as EmBar closed on them. Every available camera on EmBar was forward, recording as the steel beams protruding from her nose approached the open hangar bay doors aft on TapBrid.

Captain Wimweg didn't like idling TapBrid. Things could happen. Well, if they did, he'd react to them; that was a commander's job. Much was still under his control. Meanwhile, he would exercise discipline so his crew would too. He watched the rearward image on the intraship communication screen as EmBar's nose beams slid smooth as a kiss on a cheek into TapBrid's bay.

Wimweg inhaled to the bottom of his lungs. He needed to project a controlling presence. "Ensign DorKim, open a channel to EmBar and keep it open." He waited for the communications officer's nod confirming compliance. Rauftig would be able to see everything on his own screens, but still, this is the TapBrid, his ship, that's at risk. He had to say something. "EmBar, you're almost there. I'm lowering the doors." He nodded to engineering. "Bring 'em down. Firm, but don't scruff 'em. We'll still want them to provide an air seal when this is over." He kept track of two views: one from inside the hangar and the other from his sister ship. The bay doors closed until just before settling on the beams then stopped. They resumed moving in a series of jerks as engineering turned them on and off until they made contact. Then they continued, pushing the beams to the deck. Cheers from the EmBar came through the speakers. Wimweg released his breath, hoping no one heard it blow. He squirmed in his seat to observe and take the measure of his officers. Seems he wasn't the only tense one. Some still had teeth clamped together.

He pulled his tunic sleeves down, "EmBar, we have capture. Take us to the rendezvous." This time, his bridge crew exulted along with EmBar.

Captain Rauftig's order was clear and concise through the overhead. "Helm, engage the course."

"Yes, sir!" The reply was enthusiastic.

Wimweg's screens showed EmBar accelerate, driving her nose through TapBrid's hangar doors, buckling them inward, and flattening the sleek, round, front of EmBar below her viewscreens.

Collision alarms screamed their hair-raising oooWOW-oooWOW-oooWOW, those from EmBar a pulse behind, causing an echo effect.

Wimweg grabbed the arms of his Captain's chair. "Damage control to the hangar bay. Suit up for space."

From the speakers Rauftig was ordering his response team forward, also vacuum ready.

Wimweg pointed up, "DorKim shut that off. Engineering, what's ship's pressure?"

"All intact except for two compartments internal to the hangar bulkhead. I'll bet the push beams penetrated them."

"Incoming call, sir. Do you want to take it in your Ready Room?"

Given the option of privacy, Wimweg knew who was calling. "I prefer to remain here. Ask Captain Rauftig if he would mind." The crew might as well hear the latest news. It'll squelch rumors.

"On the front viewscreen, Captain."

Captain Rauftig's image appeared unruffled and pleasant. Wimweg tried presenting himself as calm as well.

Rauftig began, "Captain Wimweg, I seem to have landed in your hangar."

Thank goodness. There was no laughter, but Wimweg felt his crew's tension drop. Maybe it was just his own rigidity loosening, but it was a start. Keep fear contained. "Welcome aboard, Captain. I apologize for having no reception waiting. First Officer Stuzer is busy leading a different party."

Rauftig gave a tight smile, "My First Officer is also occupied. Seems he's able to fling a Helmsman across the bridge with one jerk. He took over the position and is still there."

Wimweg noted several heads bobbing in approval.

Rauftig's likeness sobered, "Speaking of the helm, our calculations show that in spite of the rough launch, we are on course and speed as planned. However, we have lost all forward sensors. Not all are damaged, of course. We just can't see with your hangar doors draped over our nose."

Wimweg glanced sideways. "Helm?"

"Affirm on course and speed, Captain."

Rauftig heard. "I suggest we let things stand as they are if you are able. We will be the engine; you navigate. Our front thrusters are undamaged. We can maneuver when the time comes. Is your main drive impaired?"

"No, it's fine. But your push beams penetrated into emergency quarters. We've lost at least 21 life supporters."

Rauftig's brow furrowed, "I was afraid of that. Well, our hope is on the Arr Bee assist. Maybe we'll still have enough to make do."

News crews recorded the exchange. Wimweg changed his mind about having them on board TapBrid. He'd considered them an unnecessary distraction at the mission's onset, but they had stayed clear of ship's activities and provided accurate coverage. Grabinians deserved to know the story. He returned his attention to Rauftig. "However much effort we put into removing the next threat to Grabin, Captain Rauftig, I hope people realize that the EmBar and TapBrid won't hold anything back. There will be no energy left, not enough to blink an eye."

"Absolutely, Captain Wimweg. Grabinians get our full devotion." Credit to Rauftig. As hoped, he had responded in kind to Wimweg's unusual speech meant for the cameras.

Communications closed and Wimweg took the measure of his team at their positions, most with jaws set firm. Maybe he should give motivational speeches more often.

In the Day Room of the guard quarters at the Grabinian Embassy, Jinmyn wiped sweat from his brow. Because of him, men and women of two vessels were risking their lives. How could Velmere seem so calm? "Velmere, I'm sorry I got you in this mess."

The Assistant Director turned, his biceps stretching every thread of his upper arm sleeves. His body exuded violence though his speech was composed and even. "I think recent events were caused by someone else. Nevertheless, I can't trust you. You are under suspicion of sedition in spite of your stories of the Christian organization. Meanwhile, you are a guest with limited freedom. The success of TapBrid and EmBar will determine your fate before I meet mine." He flexed one of his big hands.

Jinmyn raised his fingertips to his neck. One of Velmere's hands around there would be enough to end Jinmyn's alien career.

CATACLYSM ROCK

Captain Rauftig acknowledged Wimweg's preference to have their actions documented by calling on the bridge channel. His visage was onscreen. "Will we be able to disengage?"

Wimweg cocked his head, "First Officer Stuzer just returned with his report. The answer is—uncertain. To be positive, we'd have to cut away all metal that's against your push beams to keep you from pulling it back and locking you down. We don't have time to build temporary bulkheads to preserve our pressure, and suit up a repair crew to clear your path." There was no need to state the obvious that they were all short-handed.

Rauftig leaned back. "An unsuccessful separation is a contingency we're preparing to meet. To avoid delay at our destination, we recommend the following steps. Engineering has arranged fuel lines, already hooked up at our end. We deploy our life supporters the same as you, but we reserve three for ship's company and brave reporting staff. While that's going on, we pump EmBar's remaining fuel to TapBrid. Our final life supporters take their place and we fire everything. I don't know how much damage your engine will cause EmBar." Rauftig spread his hands, palms up. "I'm sure it will be uninhabitable."

Wimweg's throat was too tight to swallow. There could be no doubt to Rauftig's commitment. Even civilians would have to understand the love for a ship by those who lived on and sailed her, whether she had a vacuum-proof or wet hull for oceans of seas or skies. Could he leave TapBrid to be scorched open, possibly blown apart as heat reached oxygen contained in cabins? People had to recognize EmBar's sacrifice. "Captain Rauftig—"

Rauftig appeared embarrassed now that he addressed the possibility, his ruddy face almost matching his hair. "It won't be too bad, Captain Wimweg. We'll be closer to Grabin in the life supporters than where you'll end up. In fact, if you don't save enough fuel for braking thrusters, you'll follow the mass all the way to the star if the Ilrua or RinMod can't catch you."

Wimweg and every first-year plebe understood inertia. Rauftig had to be making sure the listening audience knew it. Very well, now he needed to take a turn playing to the spectators. He cleared his throat. "One of our reporters named the nemesis Cataclysm Rock. Let's make sure our united efforts rename it."

"Stuzer, before you suit up, see that everyone—not just damage control—has a hot meal. I'm sorry there isn't time to spend enjoying it, but we'll make do."

"Yes, sir." The First Officer moved a step closer and spoke so only Wimweg could hear, "And how about you, Captain?"

"How about me, what?"

"Do you want to eat in your Flight Quarters, or in the Galley?"

He was hungry. How long had he been in the chair? The shift had changed at least twice, and that brought up another thought. "Which watch will be on duty when we reach intercept?"

"First watch, sir."

"Good. As soon as they've eaten, have them report to the bridge." Wimweg ran his sight over the First Officer. "How do you stay crisp, clean, and alert, Stuzer? You've been on duty before we disengaged with the first meteoroid. Even leading damage control."

Stuzer smiled, "Following my Captain's example, sir. Now about your meal?"

"I'll take it in the Flight room, First Officer. Thank you." It would give him a chance to clean up and follow his subordinate's standard. Good man, Stuzer. He'll be ready to have his own ship anytime ... if they were successful.

"In the original plan for separation," Wimweg told the gathered reporters, "EmBar would simply fire her retrorocket, in short, braking jolts. Where she sits in our hangar bay, her retros could cause us as much trouble as our engine could to them if we tried to accelerate away." He paused to make sure his audience was following him. Satisfied, he continued, "So what Captain Rauftig is going to do is fire his maneuvering thrusters on the nose of his ship. They are only meant to change the attitude of a vessel in space, and aren't very powerful, but neither of us should be damaged. If we can't part by this means, the crew of the EmBar will take to life supporters as you heard him explain."

"What if they do catch something on fire? Isn't that the worst thing that can happen?" asked a journalist.

Wimweg grinned and bobbed his head. "You've been listening," he admitted. "Stuzer and his damage control team are in vacuum suits and positioned behind the hangar deck bulkheads. The bay itself is open to space, as you know, so there's no risk of fire there."

"Yes?" Wimweg acknowledged a pointed-faced woman with a raised hand.

"Shouldn't you begin trying to separate now instead of waiting until the last minute?" she asked.

"That's a good question," he said. "It's easy to look out the viewscreen and see all the room of space we have to play in and think we have all the time we need to do what we want. That's deceptive. The meteoroid is moving incredibly fast down a gravity-formed funnel toward Grabin. We have to move faster to overtake it, and can't waste the span of a heartbeat."

There were more questions, and Wimweg was satisfied with their professionalism. At last, he ended the session. "Ladies and gentlemen, I'm glad you're aboard TapBrid to document these trials for our citizens, and I'm proud of your conduct. Now, I ask that you report to your assigned seats and strap in. Ship's gravity will remain in force unless it must be deactivated to extinguish fires."

Buckling up was smart. Every move EmBar made, twisting right, left, up, or down in the bay, shook TapBrid in the opposite direction. "Easy Helm, you can do this. Keep us headed for our contact spot."

"Yes, sir," replied the junior officer. Her shoulders hunched as she leaned forward, gaze locked on the panel readouts, fingers brushing controls as she applied counter thrusts to TapBrid.

Wimweg needn't have mentioned it. Instruments, as well as the viewscreen, showed them on a precise approach. How did he get such a good team? Did he really appreciate them for their willingness and abilities before now? A rush of shame flushed through him. No, he hadn't. He resolved to do better.

"She's making headway, sir." The announcement from Engineering brought Wimweg's attention to the view from EmBar. Sure enough, she was crab-stepping backward, dragging his hangar doors with her. His fists tightened in his lap until his bridge officers cheered when EmBar backed clear, with the doors floating away in a slow tumble.

"Well done, Helm. Now bring us in contact with Cataclysm Rock." He started to call his First Officer and saw that Stuzer was already launching the life supporters. EmBar, moving toward her assigned position, was deploying her life supporters as well. "Navigation, coordinate with EmBar and start the ignition clock."

"Just did, sir."

An unrehearsed drill proceeding with precision—Wimweg knew the pride familiar to parents when their children achieved beyond their capabilities.

"Captain? The reporters are asking if they have permission to move to the Observation Deck to get external pictures of the action," DorKim said.

"Engineering how's ship's pressure?"

"Fine, Captain, except for the cabins penetrated by EmBar and they're sealed."

"Very well. Let them go, Ensign DorKim."

"This is astonishing. No one knows, or has admitted, how they are doing this," the broadcaster said. "Life supporter engines can't last this long. Our experts say if they did, they would burn up their own exhaust systems. Yet they are making a difference in the trajectory of what they're calling Cataclysm Rock."

Lines of fatigue crossed his face, but the announcer bounced on his toes and swung his arms to the studio's screens, filled with views from the shipboard reporters. Sparkling dots of light from the small engines of the life supporters were in contrast to the black nothingness of Cataclysm Rock. The view from EmBar panned to cover almost all of the 60 they had fielded; TapBrid only had 39 undamaged to add to the thrust.

"Can they really get it done? Time will—hang on—we're getting an update—" His face sagged, "EmBar just ran out of fuel."

Captain Rauftig dragged his fingers through his hair. "I wish I had crawled into a life supporter so I could see this through with you."

The image of his fellow captain on the screen left no doubt of the sincerity of his statement. Wimweg stood and brought himself to attention. "Well done, Captain. Because of the dedicated service of EmBar, there's hope for Grabin."

The announcer was silent as pictures from EmBar showed Cataclysm Rock in a slow, rolling dance. Mesmerizing jewels of fiery exhaust glittered from life supporters. A larger glow located TapBrid. The view widened as the life-destroying meteor retreated. EmBar was tumbling.

"Just short of the goal of forever ridding us of Cataclysm Rock, TapBrid has no more fuel. They are adrift, but Captain Wimweg is holding his ship steady for our cameras to record events as long as possible. Stay with us for the latest news. I'm Gloian." The announcer drank from a cup. By now, he was addressing friends and family more than an audience. "The Arr Bee assisted life supporters are still firing, we must thank the Assistant Director of Security for telling about them, although—wait—we're losing them too!"

The scene zoomed forward to the pinpricks of lights on the lethal, black mass. They were hiccupping off at random.

"How much farther do they have to go?" Gloian asked someone off-camera. He turned to the lens, "Our mathematicians are figuring it out now, but I'm getting more information. RinMod has launched with extra fuel. It will intercept first EmBar, then—hold on—" He read from a copy handed him. "Oh my! They've been working beyond endurance on Ilrua, and it too has just launched. They're both accelerating as hard as they can to catch and replenish EmBar and TapBrid—"

A voice off camera shouted, "Look!"

Gloian scanned the studio's pictures, "THERE GOES THE LAST LIFE SUPPORTER!" His shout signaled the end of the mission and his decorum. A hand waving a piece of paper in front of his face at last caught his attention. Tears spilled down his cheeks. He didn't try to make an announcement, just turned the note to the camera so the viewers could see for themselves.

It's far enough - they made it.

CHAPTER TWELVE

CELEBRATION

Velmere stood, extended his hand and shouted above the noise. "Thank you, Jinmyn. I believe the Regulator saved us and sent you as you said. May I address such an overpowering being by the name you use, Rustbucket?"

Jinmyn yelled the loudest of all when they read the sign on the viewer, now he grabbed Velmere's hand and pumped it in a blur. "You certainly can. In fact, there are a few other names I intend to call him. Although he redeemed himself, didn't he?" He was rambling and couldn't stop - like a hot soda pop opened after shaking he was bubbling over.

He wasn't the only one. The view from Grabin showed a planet-wide celebration. People in the streets were hugging, dancing, jumping, throwing things into the air, honking horns, and clanging anything that made noise. Impromptu parades and conga lines formed, dissolved, and reformed.

A smaller version of ecstasy kicked off in the guardroom, and strong, physically fit young men kept slapping Jinmyn on the back. He would sprout bruises to show for it. Nevertheless, he held his drink high and whooped along with them. A female guard, constructed like a bookcase with torpedo legs, and half a head taller than Jinmyn, grabbed him by the ears and kissed him on the mouth. Shocking!—that it happened, and that he enjoyed it. Cheering and back slaps grew in volume and frequency. He didn't know what to say. If her face shone like The Scarlet Letter, his had to be The Red Badge of Courage. She turned around and punched her nearest heckler, sending him crashing backward into two others, having used up all her debutante behavior with Jinmyn.

A grinning, formally dressed embassy guard burst into the room and rushed to Velmere. "Sir, the Ambassador wishes your presence." He almost hyperventilated in a rush to speak, "King RinMod will commend you himself. I heard Ambassador Lyram say that you, Captains Wimweg and Rauftig are national heroes."

Velmere's grin fell. He turned to Jinmyn. "It's not right. Will you come with me?"

His eyes confirmed the question, soft, brown, and sincere. Jinmyn wondered how he ever thought of them as steely.

Jinmyn smiled almost as wide as his spread hands. "Consider it your duty, Velmere. Officially, it's your idea, and besides, you still have to explain the RB assist method. I'll be interested in how your inherent honesty overcomes that."

The guard hopped from one foot to the other. "Please come, sir. Right away ... please? The king?"

Velmere put his hand on Jinmyn's shoulder. "What do you need to finish it?"

"Get me in front of the Montibaran king. What's his name?"

"Eborces. And we can do that."

"Before the meteor hits here tonight?"

Velmere held his hand to the embassy guard to shush him. "Korfel, use all the contacts it takes. Introduce Jinmyn to the Head of Faithfulness. I don't know anything about the new one, but impress on her the necessity for Jinmyn to have an audience with Eborces."

"Yes, sir."

"Now!"

"Yes, Sir!"

BUT IT HAPPENED

"I don't quite understand it myself," the Attaché to Ambassador Lyram told SanMelo as they met in the Office of Faithfulness. "But Grabin avoided two impacts against impossible odds. I'm informed this man, Jinmyn, was instrumental in the application of the method used."

SanMelo doubled her hands into fists. She hoped she appeared tough and angry, but she wanted to stop them from trembling. "So now Grabin, in its kindness, wants to save us, with the same person you rescued from the Gaumen Shack? I'll take him and put him in jail with the other spies and infiltrators from your generous planet."

The young diplomat clasped his hands together in a gentle movement and then opened them. "I understand your concern, but if you have an accurate report of that incident, you'll realize that he tried to approach Montibar before ... um ... opposing opinions grew enthusiastic and interfered with his intentions."

"This could be an elaborate ruse to place an assassin in the palace."

"We owe Jinmyn this favor for his service to Grabin and suspected you wouldn't trust our motives. You may disrobe us, search, and dress us in clothing you provide. I'll stay as collateral wherever you want me, or tag along so you can keep a personal eye on me." He smiled. "I assume we'll be heavily guarded every moment."

Why did Yorev have to leave this to her? It was bad enough that he and the king were pulling her in different directions, now a foreign embassy is involved. She had no skills in diplomacy.

"May I suggest, Head of Faithfulness," the Attaché continued, "that having information is better than the opposite?"

That stung. "I believe I'm in possession of all necessary information."

His smile stayed put. "Forgive me, Head of Faithfulness. I'm sure you are aware of all known facts about the meteoroids. I'm merely suggesting that Jinmyn has details heretofore unknown to you."

She didn't care for the way the envoy behaved so charming and yet seemed to discern her turmoil.

As if reading her mind, he said, "Jinmyn's not a Grabinian, you know."

She didn't know that. She assumed he was when they found no records about him when he tried to enter the spaceport. She wondered what other information would become known. SanMelo's face heated, she hoped it wasn't red. "I'll ask for an audience with King Eborces. Whether he grants it or not, both of you will stay here until after the space rock passes us tonight."

She turned to a guard, "Strip them, search them, and give them groundskeepers overalls to wear. Have them wait in the holding cell until I call for them."

Jinmyn remained quiet. The Attaché bowed from the waist before turning to follow the guard, his hand guiding Jinmyn's elbow.

"Don't lock the cell door," SanMelo called after them.

The guards at the desks shifted their posture. Someone of influence was coming. Another guard. Different. Jinmyn recoiled from his approach. His shadow was expansive enough to dim the entire cell, and he was still several lengths away. His uniform covered his bulk with ribbons, medals, hash marks and chevrons. The two in-house guards stood rigid.

"Ah, the King's Personal Protector. I believe you're DagReg, it that correct?" the Attaché asked as he rose.

No answer. The only part of the King's Protector that entered the cell was his gaze. It made the back of Jinmyn's neck tingle.

The embassy envoy shrugged, "Perhaps you have your interview, Jinmyn."

He wasn't sure he wanted it now. The uniform and size of the King's Protector were impressive, but the square, scarred, devoid of expression face made him remember looking dead on at a rattlesnake in a zoo's reptile display. The eyes looked only for prey.

The guard's small eyes took the place of a snake's flickering tongue. They were in constant motion on either side of a crooked nose whose main feature was being in the middle of a scar that ran from his left eyebrow to the right corner of his mouth. The only other movement was from a small ribbon attached to his turquoise blue beret.

His hypnotic eyes stopped on Jinmyn. "Come with me." When both guests stepped forward he added, "Just you," never moving his scrutiny.

Jinmyn had to move sideways through the door to exit around the King's Protector. "So, you're DagReg, huh? I'm Jinmyn." He hated the mincing crab-step he had to take, and that he prattled when he was nervous, but this man was half again bigger and twice more intimidating than Velmere. And Velmere could send Jinmyn into meltdown with a stare.

"Walk ahead of me. I'll tell you where to go." To the guards still at starched attention, he nodded at the Attaché and said, "He stays here. Door unlocked."

Jinmyn admired Montibar along the way and let his thoughts meander. He had to admit that Rustbucket provided a splendid setup. Beautiful grounds, a real palace ... He wondered if Solomon's temple was as grand ... and he was meeting the king.

His assigned task was almost over. There were some rough spots, but he'd had an adventure that if he told it, no one would believe. Just as he didn't believe Rustbucket's existence at first. Jinmyn was almost sorry the experience was ending.

They passed through a rotunda turned into art by light and shadow, through the grand assembly, and finally, the throne room, decorated in enough gold, red, and purple tapestry to drive the message home. Here he was in the capital of a foreign world. A deep blue tile starburst centered the floor of gold-streaked ivory marble with the longest spire pointing toward the dais. When he stopped to look at the regal seat, DagReg gave him a nudge to a side door. The majestic palace overwhelmed him. Could he stand to deliver Rustbucket's message to the leader of a whole planet that commanded all this?

He entered the king's sanctum where the saliva-inducing aroma of sweetmeats permeated the room. SanMelo stood with her hands clasped in front of her, facing a man sitting in what looked to Jinmyn like an easy chair. He was eating and reaching for cupcake sized bakery items from platters on a covered sideboard. A servant liveried in DagReg's colors entered with another full tray and left with an empty one. Although late in the day, the glutton looked to be dressed in nighttime wear and slippers.

Disappointment keen enough to feel in his belly hit Jinmyn. "I thought I was going to meet the king," he said.

SanMelo's shoulders jerked.

The pudgy pastry partaker coughed up a doughy wad that fell on his lap where another servant with a linen napkin recovered it straightaway. Hacking a few more times, Eborces reached for an oversized goblet and slurped several deep drinks as judged from the amount of his cheek expansion. A woman in the same livery stepped in to replenish the vessel.

Jinmyn couldn't tell from SanMelo's tone whether she disapproved or made an introduction when she said, "It's customary to bow when meeting your King."

Oh no. Bad start. Jinmyn bent at the waist. "I'm sorry your Royal Highness Majesty, I didn't recognize you. The sun was in my eyes." Really, the sun's glare in an enclosed room? He was making it worse, shut up and quit rambling. He eased back up.

Eborces leaned forward, "Tell me what you did for Grabin and why I should care."

Jinmyn wiped his palms on his trousers. "Technically, your High Royalness, I was only the messenger. Rustbucket—you call him the Regulator—made the escape pods keep firing until they pushed the meteor away. I told Grabin to trust him and they did. Now they're safe, and Rustbucket's message to you is 'disable the asteroid threat.' He can't come home with the system armed." There! He'd done it—accomplished his mission. Using the RB assist was a mighty incentive that would prove Rustbucket had sent him. He couldn't help a tooth-baring grin as he waited for the king to snap out the order to end this fiasco.

Eborces popped another bite into his mouth followed by his thumb that he scraped off behind his front teeth. "You didn't tell Grabin anything. Their Assistant Director of Security admitted to the special engines. The question is, 'Why would life supporters need long range capabilities?' I wonder if they could sneak to Montibar.

"No matter. Now that their secret is out, you show up claiming to talk to the Regulator when I'm the only one he talks to, and you want me to take away any threat of Grabin's aggression while he's gone? I won't expose the citizens of Montibar to your devious schemes." He turned to the tray, his head swaying like a cobra, hypnotizing the next pastry before striking.

Jinmyn's thoughts struggled to catch up from what he believed was Mission Complete. "What? No! You're making it worse. You've locked out Rustbucket and things are deteriorating—"

King Eborces showed the palm of one hand while choosing a tart with the other. DagReg's hand came down on Jinmyn's shoulder, pinning further protests in his throat.

Waving his chosen treat toward SanMelo, the king asked her, "Didn't you say this same man left a trail of crimes and misdemeanors on Montibar?"

"I was doing what was necessary to get to you," Jinmyn shouted before DagReg pulled him back a step.

SanMelo glanced at Jinmyn. "Yes, he's the one."

"Listen to me—" pressure from DagReg shut Jinmyn up with a grunt.

Dribbling crumbs from his bottom lip, the ruler of Montibar decreed, "Lock him away with the rest of them. They'll realize how the Regulator takes care of us tonight. I'll decide how to discipline them tomorrow." He smiled at the approach of a fresh platter.

SanMelo dipped her head toward the door. DagReg pushed Jinmyn after her.

At the cell, SanMelo waved the Attaché out. She spoke to DagReg, "Give him his clothes. Escort him safely to the Grabinian embassy." Jinmyn couldn't read her thoughts when she pointed at him. "Here is good enough for this one tonight. We'll put him in jail tomorrow if the king still wishes it."

The emissary frowned, his eyes searching Jinmyn's face.

Jinmyn shrugged as DagReg kept him moving until Jinmyn was in and the envoy out.

Looking at Jinmyn behind the bars, SanMelo said, "Lock it."

THE NIGHT LIGHT

The all-too-familiar hurt in his stomach cramped right where it homesteaded throughout Grabin's encounters with the meteoroids. Maybe he was getting an ulcer. He'd earned it. This entire idiotic mess should have been over, but here he was, watching another TV broadcast describing a space rock encounter. This time with his face pressed between bars as he strained to make out the video in the squad room. "Hey guys," he shouted loud enough to get the guards' attention, "could you turn the screen a little more this way, please?"

How about that? The "please" must have done it. Jinmyn finished the remains of his jailhouse fare, something reminiscent of a bologna sandwich and Montibaran coffee. The two guards had trays of something more substantial.

As the shadows stretched and went from gray to black, the broadcast took on the mania of a game show. Views of people in the streets recalled images Jinmyn had seen of impromptu celebrations of fans when their team won a playoff.

A smiling broadcaster was on. "I'm Malaur here at the studio," he said. "Unfortunately, we don't have a live crew at the South Pole because of the evacuation notice sent from the Office of Faithfulness. There is some ambiguity about that order. We don't know if Faithfulness meant to announce it or not, but to be safe, our cameras are unmanned and set on remote control." He held up a hand, "Don't worry, our program booth pledges that we will still observe anything that happens." He shrugged as he did with all his gestures—oversized and grand—drawing attention like a two-day-old red pimple at the end of a nose. "King Eborces assures us the hateful, killer asteroid will miss Montibar, but we still may catch a sight of it with our telescopic lens. Some mathematicians say it will come very close and should be easy to spot." He arched his brows and puckered his lips, feigning horror, and raised a hand to his mouth, "Oh, no. I hope it doesn't come too close."

He did a boxy little dance step that didn't ruffle his shellacked hair. "Stay right here as we countdown to tonight's spectacular."

Jinmyn appreciated Rustbucket's smooth, automated weather control. Even without his presence, the system performed to perfection. He anticipated the polar region as a hazy white landscape with visibility limited by ice gems suspended in the air. Maybe huge storm clouds, veiled by blowing snow, tortured and shredded by sub-sonic winds.

What the remote showed was a frozen desert, and not all white. Hues of blue undulated along low pressure ice ridges, punctuated by voids of black where shadows crept. Throughout the sky delicate stars glittered, their crystal points of brightness gleaming through the ether to give a night-light effect, amplified, reflected and refracted into an inspired twilight.

However, the crown Nature gave the setting put a lump in his throat. An aurora of red, green, blue, yellow, and gossamer violet danced and twisted, first this color center, then that one until they became one, intermingled and inseparable.

Insight, powerful and instantaneous, rocked Jinmyn. Could that be Rustbucket? ... Probably ... Showoff.

The verbose Malaur let the scene do all the talking until finally, "We're told long-range telescopes have it in sight. It's coming fast."

The camera panned to another area of clear sky and jinked around until settling on a bright spot.

"That's it. They say that's it. We're going to get to see it go by."

The glow expanded. Then it birthed several smaller dots of light burning fiery tails, drawn with breathtaking rapidity. Some of the specks vanished—gone, leaving Jinmyn unsatisfied like they'd walked off in the middle of a job, their life and death unexplained. Others popped out of existence with a sparkle, the way a terminal shooting star is supposed to end.

The camera tilted down to keep the approaching stellar display in view. The landscape gleamed ever brighter as particles incinerated in the atmosphere. Jinmyn couldn't tell if any runts of the breakaway litter still fell. The shine from the largest jetsam obscured everything else. Night at the South Pole was bright as midday at the equator.

A glaring flash inundated the view, so dazzling it must have burned out the lens. The suddenness of the dead broadcast made Jinmyn jump. He listened for the sizzle and tried to detect the peculiar smell of charred electronic circuits before catching himself. Any damage would have occurred at the other end, not here.

"That was something, wasn't it?" Malaur was back on the air, looking at the black screen of the studio monitor. Raising his chin, he directed his next question off camera while pointing at his lifeless set, "Can we get it back? We'll need to do it now, or the show will be over. Those things were really moving."

To the loud unintelligible voice, he yelled back, "What?"

The voice again, louder, clearer. Jinmyn heard it through the speaker. "We've lost all connections with the remotes."

"Well folks, that's all there is to see, but there were a few rare sights available that we were privileged to witness—"

There was more shouting in the background. The news anchor turned to his right, accepted a slate-like device thrust toward him and scanned it. "The flash that took out our remote was evidently fairly large. People are reporting in that it looked like it would grow and consume them." He glanced away from the camera. "What were people doing there? I thought everyone was evacuated."

"Read it all." A voice instructed.

Malaur's mouth tightened and he vacillated between the slate and the unknown speaker until his attention lingered on the message. His brows arched. "Is this true?"

Jinmyn's Montibaran vocabulary translated the dimensions to familiar measurements as he listened to the slack-jawed moderator question the report.

"They saw it from as far as 600 miles away? But King Eborces said it would miss us."

Background noise grew as voices claimed attention and dispensed information. The bewildered commentator ran his hand through his hair leaving the varnished and laminated fluff pointing straight up.

One of the guards shook his head, "Couldn't be."

Jinmyn pressed his face hard against the bars watching the broadcast. He saw the flash and shared the resultant disbelief from the stories pouring into the studio.

A side story threatened to take over viewer interest as someone—a director maybe—inserted makeup into the newscast. A hand with a comb reached into the picture over Malaur's head. The camera shifted to show him at the edge of the screen hiding most of the hand. Malaur noticed the offset and moved. So did the hand. So did the camera. He finally discerned what they wanted and used his own fingers to comb his hair. It no longer stood up, but stuck out sideways, an awning for his right ear.

Apparently, Malaur was more interested in the story than his appearance and waved away the comb to read the notes handed him. "The Office of Faithfulness is mounting a patrol to investigate the occurrence and needs our help. Our station staff on both continents is loading drones with cameras, reporters and survival gear to bring you news from the site, and they want to come along. The Office of Faithfulness would normally use spacecraft, but they are still on King Eborces' mercy mission to Grabin. The Office reminds us that they could commandeer anything they need. They prefer to request instead."

Malaur pulled a full-faced scowl into the lens. "That's nice of them. Especially since our government said nothing was going to happen in the first place."

The screen went black and silent. Jinmyn nodded; yep they shut him up, poor old plate-headed Malaur.

A pop, whiteness swirled into colors of the familiar studio scene and the broadcast was back. Malaur sat behind the news counter, hair combed, but looking defiant. "Montibarans, I apologize. My last statement, while true, was a voiced opinion. That's something an impartial reporter must never do, but sometimes it's hard when the stories affect us as much as anyone else. Even so, again, I apologize. Now, returning to the news, as soon as the drones are programmed for the new routes they'll be underway ... with extra personnel on board."

The guard with a wart on his jaw waved a hand at the image of Malaur, "Why are they going to the trouble? There's nothing but ice down there."

"You saw those other burn-ups," said the guard with no neck, "either this one was bigger or closer, or both."

"There was a flash. So what?"

While No-neck pondered the question, Malaur answered it. "We have received word that seismic readings from all over Montibar indicate a massive shock took place right where our remote cameras were positioned. Several smaller ones preceded it."

No-neck jumped up with a little victory dance, bent forward, his feet together he wiggled his behind at Wart. "See."

"You're blocking the screen," Jinmyn yelled at him.

No-neck muttered, "Sorry," sat down, straightened, and turned an irritated frown to Jinmyn.

Oops, he'd better remember where he was. Jinmyn and gave No-neck a tiny grin and quick wave. He ducked his head hoping to show contriteness. If he hoped for a cup of Montibaran coffee and maybe a sandwich later, he needed their tolerance. Hearing footsteps, he unbent to see No-neck's fist coming at him through the bars.

At a great distance, Malaur was in professional mode giving news. "It seems that most people took the evacuation order seriously, but we're getting tips trickling in that not all did and their friends and relatives are worried. There has been no contact with the folks who stayed."

Jinmyn tried to concentrate as Malaur gave an accounting of population dispersal at the south end of the continents and those that lived on the ice of the pole. They reminded him of the reindeer herders of Lapland, but their livestock was different.

Something sinister had his nose pinched in pliers, pulling him back into the darkness. He couldn't stop falling—it was going to hurt.

"You'd better check him again," Wart said casting a sidelong glance at Jinmyn's cell. "He hasn't moved."

"He's lucky to still be breathing," No-neck answered. "I should've busted him in two—telling me to move so he can watch the news." His jutted chin accentuated the illusion of a head sitting on shoulders.

Wart frowned and half rose from his chair. "I think you broke his nose. A lot of blood ran out of it. It's going to be a mess to clean up."

No-neck reached for a snack. "That's what the cleaners do."

"Think we ought to pick him up?"

"Let him sleep on the floor."

CHAPTER THIRTEEN

OFFENSIVE

Jinmyn heard the question. "What is this? Open the cell." Then the noise of rapid footsteps followed by the lock tumbling. Someone kicked the bottom of his foot.

"You awake?" An ache throbbed behind his eyes and he couldn't raise his head. He slid an elbow under his chest, pushed and groaned. His cheek burned. Did he pull skin from the right side of his face when he raised his head? Touching his jaw with fingertips, his blurry vision revealed the evidence. He had been stuck down with dried blood. His eyelashes were thick with clots of scabs and gunk. When he tried to rub the sleep matter away, the pressure stabbed his face with white-hot pain. He yelled and waved his arms.

"Easy now, easy," the same voice as earlier said. "Your nose is broken. You have two black eyes remarkable for coloring and swelling."

From the floor, Jinmyn tipped his head back to take in the speaker bent over him. "Who're you?"

"I'm the guards' captain. How did this happen," he asked, pointing at Jinmyn's face.

Jinmyn stretched his face to pull his eyelids apart by arching his eyebrows and yawning. He opened the lids enough to take in his surroundings when he put his fingertips on his cheekbones and pulled the skin down. Beyond the officer were Wart, shifting his feet making his uniform twitch, and No-neck, glaring, fists curled.

Wart glanced everywhere but at Jinmyn. He cleared his throat, "Captain—"

The head of the guards held up a hand. "Let him tell the story."

Two more guards craned their necks to peer around Wart and No-neck. If they were here for a shift change that meant he lay on the floor all night.

"What happened?" the captain asked again.

Jinmyn wiped crusty blood from the corner of his mouth. "I tripped."

The captain straightened from his crouch. "I see."

Wart exhaled an audible puff. Ridge lines appeared on No-neck's jaws, and his lips pressed together hard making him look ready to punch Jinmyn again.

Jinmyn ran his tongue between his lips and teeth. They all were there, but a sizzling headache burst in new fractals of pain with every movement.

The captain turned to the miscreant guards and glared. "This man is a friend of the Grabin Embassy, held uncharged of a crime. We are dealing with foreign affairs requiring diplomacy, and you two failed to check on him. You will turn in a written report and clean this cell before you leave."

Wart leaped for the desk. "I'll do the report."

The other two guards grinned at No-neck who did his impersonation of a rose still on the stem, red at the top, thorns everywhere else.

The captain fixed his gaze on No-neck, the silence of the officer's stare shouting out the enumeration of discipline breaches causing No-neck to assume the rigid position of attention. When the captain spoke, his voice dropped to an arctic baritone. "I'll be back after I finish rounds. This mess will be cleaned, or it will become your home."

The guards dispersed. Wart busied himself with the paperwork, the two starting shift took their seats, one grinning one whistling, both turning their chairs to face the entertainment. No-neck left cussing.

Before No-neck returned with cleaning supplies, Jinmyn gagged himself by sticking a finger down his throat until his stomach rebelled, spewing the contents of his last meal. It wasn't as much as he wanted, and it made his headache worse, but a satisfying putrid odor covered the dried blood.

One of the new guards took the giggles, and the other joined in when No-neck gaped at the sloppy mess.

Wart kept his head down, but couldn't drag out the writing assignment any longer.

No-neck insisted that Wart come to the cell and help. The bars were hard to clean. Each one had to be wiped and disinfected. If Jinmyn hadn't already thrown up, the smell of the cleaning material might have done the job. His innards churned with nausea, face pounded hot with every heartbeat, and a headache that made him moan clamped his skull.

The captain returned and released Wart and No-neck, he pointed to one of the day shift guards. "Take this man to the infirmary and stay with him."

The guard reached into his top right desk drawer and drew out a stunner. Jinmyn recognized it and knew as much about how it worked as he did a revolver in a Western movie though he'd never used either. Rustbucket included a surprising amount of information as well as the vocabulary in his memory. Thanks for that.

Stepping down on his heel jarred his head into bolts of agony. Jinmyn held his palms against the side of his head as he shuffled along. They stayed on the veranda for what seemed like miles before arriving at their destination.

In the holding area, both Montibarans responsible for Jinmyn's fate occupied themselves according to their duties while listening to the news. The broadcast set on the wall reported on SanMelo and her crew investigating the flash over the southern ice. The reporter inferred that the king isolated himself from the public. Eborces seemed to be getting a lot of bad press from his previous insistence that Montibar needn't worry about the meteoroid.

Excitement of the story gained momentum, distracting the guards. Jinmyn didn't remind them that SanMelo said he would go to jail today.

Sitting on his bunk, careful to observe where the guard put the stun gun in the desk drawer, he watched the broadcast for the latest news.

This time, Malaur's hair stuck out behind, and he played to high drama with information as he received it. "Look, here come the first pictures and description from the scene. Why can't we see anything?" he asked off-screen. "Oh. We're told they're flying through a dense fog of ice crystals. They're going to go lower."

The day guards and Jinmyn listened to Malaur report as the shift wore on. The scout ships found a depression 30 miles in diameter, teardrop shaped, where none existed before. The surface temperature rose well above freezing. The thawed area filled with water becoming a lake. A future skating rink if freezing polar temperatures returned.

The patrol verified that electronic communication in a 200-mile radius were out. The remote weather stations they found were charred lumps melted into unrecognizable slag piles.

Then came the paramount news story. A fifty-eight-year-old man said a blast knocked him down inside his house sixty miles away from the new lake, breaking his shoulder. He didn't want to leave his herd of blue-tailed stobels—Jinmyn identified them as a cross between sheep and seals, cold-water amphibious animals with waterproof fur. The herder lost them all to the heat of the blast. Their wool burned away, and their hide cracked. He tried to tell how the explosion broke his windows, but that was a moot point since his house shattered into kindling.

Montibarans had nothing with which to relate a detonation of this size. The descriptions of the scene made no outrageous impressions until the pictures arrived. Then calls to the station demanded answers.

It sounded to Jinmyn that a political impact was in the making. SanMelo would likely shunt him off to jail when she returned if for no other reason than to erase one problem in order to deal with others sure to arise. He needed to think.

Wart and No-neck arrived for their shift. After they checked in and relieved the day crew, No-neck stood at the bars. Jinmyn tried to look beat up, sagging his posture and hanging his head.

No-neck was unsympathetic. "So. A broken nose, eh? Did you tell the captain I hit you?"

Jinmyn gave his head a couple of shakes. "No."

"Why not? I don't need your protection."

"The doctor said several blows caused the marks on my face. You struck me after I was down. There's no sense antagonizing a brute like you."

No-neck's face lit up, and he laughed. "I only hit you once. But your head bounced when it slammed on the floor. It was funny." He turned back to the squad room humming, alternately dipping his shoulders to the rhythm.

Well into the evening when the day's hubbub quieted, Jinmyn shuffled to the cell door and waved his arm through the bars. He practiced not letting any air flow through his nose, and he spoke from his throat. "Hey, I can't breathe. I need to go to the infirmary. I can't breathe."

Wart glanced at No-neck who shrugged and continued to stare at the video.

Jinmyn held out a palm in appeal and slumped when he saw he had Wart's attention.

Wart crossed the room. "What's the problem?"

Jinmyn stayed bent over, hands on his knees. "I can't breathe. Something's wrong with the packing they stuffed in my nose. The infirmary. Please." He tried to put a wheeze into each dragging breath.

Wart called to No-neck, "You're up over here. The captain said we have to take care of him, and you caused all this. You take him on sick-call."

No-neck didn't move.

Jinmyn panted and coughed.

Wart hollered, "I'm opening his door, and you'd better be here or else he can walk away, and I'll tell the captain what happened." Wart got the keys and unlocked the cell.

No-neck jumped up in a toxic cloud of swearing and stomped over. Wart grinned and resumed his place in front of the TV.

Jinmyn shuffled as far as the day guard's spot and gasped, "I've got to sit a moment."

No-neck redoubled the rate and volume of vitriol.

Jinmyn stretched one arm across the corner of the desk and laid his head on the crook of his elbow. Hunching his shoulders over so he blocked No-neck's view, he slid his other hand across his chest to the drawer, opened it and found the stunner.

No-neck gazed skyward, invoking an immense section of vocabulary that Rustbucket failed to give Jinmyn when the squad bay flashed blue-green. There was the sound of a jacket zipper pulled in a hurry, a faint temporary ozone tingle in the nostrils and a thud as No-neck collapsed.

Wart jerked to his feet and turned. Flashzip, thud.

Jinmyn dragged them into the cell and looked for something heavy, like an oversized stapler. No-neck would realize what it is to have a broken nose. No stapler, but he found a pair of handcuffs. He positioned the two guards in sitting postures side by side. Manipulating the near arms of each of them around bars, he cuffed their wrists together.

Resuming his search of the room's contents, he came across a black marker, a bag of nozas—deep-fried pastries—and Wart's drinking container. If he wasn't going to break No-neck's nose, he should at least give him raccoon eyes. He put the dark pen back; it was stupid to waste time on this. Better to find a disguise.

Stuffing a noza into his mouth, he opened Wart's bottle and the fumes overcame him. Is this what it took to work through a shift with No-neck? No wonder Wart was agreeable. He was numb. Jinmyn left the lid off and spilled some of the contents on the desk. If it didn't evaporate before someone found it, Wart may have a long time to explain the potion.

Jinmyn returned to the cell, un-cuffed No-neck and took his shirt, pants, and shoes leaving him in his underwear. He checked to make sure both sentinels were still breathing, looped No-neck's arm back around a bar, reattached the handcuffs and locked the door. He tossed the key inside next to Wart's feet. No-neck groaned as Jinmyn turned off the lights. Outside he threw the handcuff key into a hedge.

He didn't know how he would do it, but he needed to take the offensive before SanMelo returned.

SLY AND CRAFTY

Jinmyn, carrying No-neck's clothes in one arm, patted the bulge of the stunner in his pocket and set off for a doorway or nook in which to change. He'd walk off the grounds in a guard's uniform back to the Grabinian embassy. He couldn't stay here. If found anywhere near the palace after stunning and locking up two guards, what would they do to him? He wouldn't like it that's for sure, but on Grabin territory Velmere could help him figure out another strategy.

Behind him, voices rose. Darkness bleached away as lights blazed to life. Jinmyn bolted for the shadows of the gardens.

How did they discover the mess he left in the holding cell already? He thought he would have all night before the morning shift arrived. What happened? Roving patrols?—maybe noticed the blackened guard office?

It didn't matter now. Jinmyn ran to an arbor and fumbled out of his clothes. His ears burned and amplified every night sound into a klaxon scream, "I'm here. I'm here."

He had given no thought to the difference in dimensions. He was taller and thinner than No-neck. His wrists and ankles stuck out exposed while the rest of the uniform hung on him like a sack. If he slouched, it wouldn't look so bad.

Stepping away from the arbor, Jinmyn shuffled along the path looking for an exit away from the lights.

"Hey. Come with me."

Jinmyn froze, expecting a body slamming tackle or paralyzing stunning. Nothing happened. Turning to the voice, Jinmyn saw another wild-eyed guard gesturing toward himself. "Come on. The Captain said to latch onto whoever I could and protect the palace doors."

The new sentry was buttoning his tunic as he walked. "I see they roused you out too. You should try to straighten up a little if we're going to the palace, though."

The man misbuttoned his jacket and quickened his steps.

Hurrying beside him, Jinmyn tried to keep the tremor out of his voice. "What's happening?"

"I'm not sure. It's probably a drill. Night Sentry woke us and started shouting orders. Mine were to find any unassigned people and secure the doors against intruders."

Jinmyn held his pants up and lengthened his stride to maintain pace while his guide intoned a running commentary on the wisdom of his chosen career. "It won't be so bad if I can make Subozier. Meanwhile, we do what we must." He named all the ranks from Ozier all the way to recruit with the time it would take to achieve promotion from one to the other.

Was this man's life so different from his? Jinmyn was John Smith, writing programs, hoping for attention from someone who would help him. This soldier worked every day for the same goal. Pathetic. Attain one up-grade and then what? Keep trying for the next one when it's the Rustbuckets of the universe that control things. He couldn't become assistant manager, yet his minuscule presence in the cosmos could save the lives on two planets.

"Here we are. I guess this door's as good as any."

Jinmyn's anxiety spiked when they entered the pool of light around the palace door. "Do we go in?"

"No need. There are special guards for the inside. You should know that."

"Oh, yeah." Jinmyn faced away, cleared his throat and wiped his nose on a sleeve. "I'm not awake yet."

"You must be new," his companion said. "My first uniform didn't fit me either." He frowned at Jinmyn and slowly waved a finger back and forth like a switch-backed road descending a steep mountainside. "Wait a breath, here. I'm told to gather anyone I come across, but there should be nobody in the garden. You're there in a uniform that doesn't fit, AND it has service stripes on, but you act like a recruit."

Jinmyn reached into his pocket.

"Ha! I knew it. This is a drill and I just solved my problem. Didn't I? You're the intruder." He smiled, bobbed his head and clapped his hands.

Jinmyn shrugged.

"Let's go back and check in. I'll earn some merits for solving this so fast. I could have done it sooner if there'd been enough light. I might even receive a—"

The blue-green flicker signaled the observant guard's reward. Jinmyn put the stunner away.

What to do with him? He couldn't let an unconscious man lie outside a palace door, and it was a long drag to the nearest bushes.

Jinmyn tried the door. When it swung in, smooth, without a sound he caught his breath waiting for an alarm.

Nothing.

He exhaled. They must trust you completely, Rustbucket, to leave the palace doors unlocked.

He dragged the guard by his lopsided tunic into the dim hallway and shut the door. Where was a cloakroom when he needed it? He left the man snoring against the inside of the door. If anyone tried to come in, his body would block the way.

Jinmyn's neck tingled and the sensation washed down his spine. He was in the palace. All he had to do was find the king's closet to end this whole mess.

He slowed his breathing. Now was no time to hyperventilate when he was so close. Hitching up his pants, he took some tentative steps toward his destiny.

BLUFFING

Time was running out. He knew it. The palace was huge, fortunately so were most of the rooms. It only took a glance to search them. The problem was the intricate hallways, an ant's nest leading everywhere like neuron pathways. Jinmyn was sure he looked into one area twice from different angles. Once he had neared a kitchen. Mouth-watering aromas heralded the morning baking. It took discipline to keep moving and not walk right in and ask for bread.

He stuck his head in a room and his heart quickened. Across the spacious marbled floor, a double staircase bowed like parentheses upward to the next level. The king's chambers had to be that way.

Ascending with footsteps muffled by thick carpet, Jinmyn heard the soft sound of lullabies. He must be going in the right direction now. Leave it to the self-indulgent king to have night music.

He reached the top of the curving staircase to an open floor. Subdued lighting showed he was on a mezzanine that arched outward. Three ostentatious doors were spaced equidistant around the concave wall. Carved pillars resembling marble stood at intervals supporting a ceiling where dim morning light nudged through a stained glass dome. A broad gallery bathed in royal red illumination extended to his left.

Jinmyn took that direction all the way to an oversized double door, inlaid with shiny metals and colored stones. He wiped his palms against the side of his pants and had to grab them before they fell off. He turned the handle on the massive right-hand side, hunched his shoulders and leaned on it. He meant to coax the door open only far enough to scout the room but in an obedient and quick response befitting a royal request, it swung inward with a silent sigh.

Where was he? A room this large couldn't be the living quarters. White polished stone pillars, walls, and domed ceiling shone in golden reflection by extensive filigree applied everywhere. Evidently, gold was valuable in this part of the universe too.

Lapis blue velvet and silk-like material covered tufted sofas and throne style high-backed chairs arranged in groups here and there. He entered and closed the door.

Jinmyn slunk next to the wall. He couldn't bring himself to walk straight across the openness of the chamber. The next door revealed a darker room—a bedroom judging from the canopied and draped platform with a headboard along the far side.

Heavy snoring confirmed his location. He wanted to leap in an adrenaline rush of excitement. He was here. Finally. Where's the closet?

The urge to run around the room until he found it was almost unbearable, but he made himself tiptoe toward what must be a closet door. He glanced again at the sleeping figure on the bed. Even under the mound of covers, the character seemed smaller than King Eborces. What was going on? That deep bass vibration sounded like it was coming from a walrus, but this outline was more compact, almost like—Oh, no!

Queen Vinluc.

He had forgotten about Montibar's petite and much-loved queen. Gracious and beautiful, the public adored her charm and wisdom.

Jinmyn clasped his hand over his mouth. He was sick and dirty. His presence was contaminating the Queen's personal space. He had to get out of here. They were bound to find the filth that shed from him on every place he stepped or touched.

Returning to the blue room, Jinmyn hung his head and shamed himself.

Rustbucket, you will never allow her to know that I was in there.

On the far wall was another door. Perhaps another bedroom choice. Keep moving.

This time Jinmyn stopped inside the sleeper's quarters and took notice of the heap on the bed. Nightstands on either side loaded with pastries testified that the lump on the bedstead was Eborces. Now, where's his closet?

Jinmyn circled the bedroom toward a wall with two doors. Slipping in the first one, he hastened to keep the brighter light from spilling into Eborces' dreams. Giving his eyes time to adjust, he verified he was in a closet. One so huge it made his apartment seem small. He turned to the door he'd just entered and scanned the frame for a switch.

Rustbucket said there was a switch inside the door to the king's closet and all he had to do was flip it. Where was it? He ran his hands around the sides of the door and above as far as he could reach. No switch.

Jinmyn wiped sweat from his brow. He was in trouble. The morning was dawning, and he had penetrated the king's living quarters. Time expired. Either hide until nightfall or break out now. He peered deeper, past the rows of shelves, clothes on hangers, stacks of ceiling-to-floor cubbyholes filled with shoes, and became aware of a turn in the closet walkway. Following the route, he discovered the closet was horseshoe shaped. He was facing the other door he had seen in the wall. This way was no good; it would only lead him back into the bedroom. If he were going to run, it'd be better to leave through the door he came in. It was closer to the way out.

Paralyzed with indecision, Jinmyn considered another option. Give up. He could sit down, rest his trembling legs, and wait for them to find him. A malicious sadness, an ache, came to him, immersing him in terrible melancholy. It would let Brimlet down. Why did she come to his mind at these times? He was sorry, but he could do no more.

It wasn't fair. Jinmyn balled his fists. Here was evidence of opulence, more clothes than a person could ever wear. All Brimlet had was a rag doll, and in arrogance and unconcern, Eborces put her in danger. Jinmyn gritted his teeth. He ought to walk out there and zap the indifferent monarch.

He stepped toward the door and saw it. The switch. High up, but easily reachable on the unhinged side of the doorway. It was in the up position. All he had to do was turn it down.

"Who are you? What are you doing here?"

Jinmyn spun to see the startled face of a valet in the royal livery. The man screamed, "Intruder! Intruder!" He dropped an armload of garments and fled backward around the closet. "Help!"

"Wait. You don't understand." Jinmyn grabbed his pants waist and ran after the shrieking servant. "I'm not a threat. I'm trying to bring Rustbucket back. It'll fix everything." He chased the valet back into the king's sleeping chambers where a wild-eyed Eborces stood still as a statue, frozen in red-and-white-striped pajamas; a muffin dropped from his hand.

The valet fled the room yelling for help.

Eborces held both palms up in surrender.

The whole world was awake and knew about him now. So be it. Get to the switch and it wouldn't matter.

"In there! He's in there with the King!"

Shouting and commotion pushed Jinmyn as rough as a physical presence. He grabbed the king by the collar, using him as a shield. With his stunner in one hand and a grip on the King with the other, his pants fell as three guards pounded into the chamber, only one had his weapon drawn.

Jinmyn took a deep breath and pointed the barrel of the stunner above the king's ear. "Everybody relax."

Jinmyn felt fear radiated from the monarch in trembling waves filling him with equal measures of power and disgust. Eborces extended his hands toward the palace guards. "Don't let him hurt me."

The whimpering, slobbering plea tipped Jinmyn's emotions toward disgust. "Keep your hands up." There was no real reason for the command except years of conditioning from watching criminal movies.

Eborces jerked his arms vertical. "I'm doing it. Don't shoot."

"The King and I are going to the closet. Then this will be all over, and nobody's going to get harmed."

Eborces emitted a high-pitched whine. "Please don't hurt me."

Jinmyn's pants tangled around his feet as he pulled Eborces crab stepping to the first closet door. The armed guard kept his weapon aimed in their direction. Jinmyn realized it pointed at Eborces giving him a rush of invincibility behind his corpulent shield. Feeling powerful was a new emotion. He liked it.

They almost reached the closet when Jinmyn's brain began functioning. He was at the far door from the switch. If they went in here, someone could sneak in behind him from the other entry. He needed the other door. Open it, flip the switch, let Rustbucket in, and it'd be over.

"The other one," he said pulling Eborces in the right direction.

DagReg entered as fresh as if he had come from a parade, except he had a weapon in his hand. He gave the palace guards a stony-faced appraisal as if the king's plight was of secondary importance. He addressed an empty-handed guard. "Draw your weapon."

The man used both hands to fumble with his holster and belt, eventually getting it out, shaking visibly.

"Check the setting." DagReg's voice was calm but so riveting that Jinmyn stopped to see how this would develop.

"Yes, sir. What setting do you want?"

"Hard stun."

"Yes, sir.

DagReg inspected the third guard. "Where's your weapon?" He sounded almost polite as if he asked, "Where's the bus station," but the guard turned ashen.

"I left it in the quarters, sir."

"Get it."

"Yes, sir." The guard fled.

Finally, DagReg gave Jinmyn his attention. "Release the king and step away."

Jinmyn moved his stunner to the middle of the king's back. "I only need to reach inside this door and then I'll be happy to comply. If you try to stop me, I'll shoot the king."

"No! Please no." Eborces was blubbering now. "Let him get what he wants."

DagReg leveled his weapon where Jinmyn could see down the barrel. It pointed right between his eyes. "Release the king."

A blue-green flash enveloped King Eborces crumbling him forward in an ignoble heap, his head hitting the carpet before his knees.

"Why did you—" Jinmyn didn't finish. A second flash, this time from DagReg's stunner, followed in a flicker.

CHAPTER FOURTEEN

INCURSION

"Oooh." It sounded to Jinmyn that the groan originated elsewhere, but he felt the vibration in his throat. He swallowed, making uncoordinated efforts to move arms and legs that wanted to stay where they were. His chest ached; piercing needle pains drew his attention to one leg as blood flow returned.

He was on a concrete floor with blankets for a bed. Flexing himself to a sitting position, he rubbed his brow against a headache that circled his head like a tourniquet. His eyes hurt. He squinted to stop his vision from spinning.

He was in an enclosed foyer shaped like an L lying on its side with the short leg extending up from the left. The long side of the L held three cells. At the far end of the short leg was a double door to the outside world.

A visitor entering the foyer could walk straight to the first compartment—Jinmyn's.

A face connected to a hazy memory spoke to Jinmyn. "The king's still out. You'd better hope he doesn't wake up for a long time because the minute he does, he'll start making your life miserable."

Jinmyn took stock of his situation. "Not much of a prison—just three cells."

"It's not a prison at all." His jailer seemed cordial. Even happy. "It's the palace holding room. DagReg wants you to stay in range of his authority so he can personally keep you detained. He's taking the night shift himself because he said that's when you do things."

The turnkey swept his hand in an arc. "As far as I know, you're the first real guest to use the place."

Jinmyn rubbed the flat of his hand against his sore chest. "Why'd you shoot the king? I said I wasn't going to hurt him."

"I didn't. Scrupt did. He told DagReg that he didn't know he was holding the stunner so tight." Turnkey laughed. "You should have seen the look on his face. Both when he shot the king and when DagReg assigned him and Forgen to the Office of Faithfulness. Forgen was the one who showed up without his weapon. He and Scrupt both are now at an outpost watching the lake created by the meteoroid." The jailer chortled and slapped his knee.

Jinmyn held his palms to his temples. "You seem to be enjoying all this."

"Sure am. All we ever do is drill and stand inspection. It's a dull routine. There was talk of disbanding the palace guards. Now, thanks to you, I'm confident of reaching retirement here."

Jinmyn slumped with his head in his hands. "I was so close. Twice. So close."

"What were you close to?" Turnkey's voice still had a lilt in it, but Jinmyn understood.

The interrogation had begun.

"May I have some water?"

The Royal Surgeon returned the instruments to her bag. They were small in her sizable hand. She looked down from her height that was a head taller than her monarch and scowled at him. "You don't need to stay in bed for a bruise on your forehead. The pastries you eat cause more damage. Lose weight."

Wheeled carts covered with starched white sheets jammed into the king's chambers. They carried bottles, basins, warm towels, and medical equipment. Hospital staff, some in surgical scrubs, intermingled with armed palace guards; some faced inward, some outward. The only path through the forest of people rooted in the enormous bedroom was from the door to the bedside, along which trundled the king's lifeline of baked sweets.

SanMelo shared the surgeon's impatience with the king's theatrics. Summoned to the monarch's presence immediately upon arriving from inspecting the meteoroid damage, she witnessed the wounded warrior performance with suppressed irritation.

Eborces tugged his bedcovers up under his chin. "I was attacked and injured, and that's all you can say? What kind of surgeon are you? I need medical attention."

The doctor drew a deep breath, exhaled, dropped her shoulders, and told him, "Very well. Rest on your stomach, please."

"What will that do? My stomach's sore. That's where I was shot, you know."

Ignoring her whining sovereign, she beckoned for a nurse who stiffened and paled.

"Yes, Doctor Tetorm?"

"Prepare a bowel flush."

"Doctor?"

"Do it."

King Eborces pulled the covers tighter around his shoulders. "Hold on, now. What do you think you're doing?"

"I'm giving you medical attention, Your Highness. As you demanded."

SanMelo pressed her lips together to keep the grin from escaping.

Eborces reddened, starting in his neck and rising to his cheeks. "I don't believe you. How will that help?"

Doctor Tetorm rubbed her jaw, her brow wrinkling. "I suppose it could make your bruised stomach feel better by relieving some of the pressure from the inside."

Eborces frowned at the kit the pale nurse assembled on a bedside cart. Shrinking away from it, he shook his head, "I don't think I need that. Just leave. I'll call you if I feel worse."

Doctor Tetorm picked up a long, flexible tube and held it up to the light. "Your Highness, it's been well-established that no one, not even you, can dictate the course of treatment to the Royal Surgeon. Moreover, since Parliament appointed me, you can't dismiss me by proclamation. On your stomach, please."

SanMelo admired how Doctor Tetorm maintained professional decorum. She believed the king was about to endure a bowel flush.

Evidently, King Eborces thought so too and waved his arm around. "You can't do that with all these people in here. I need privacy."

"I didn't request their presence, Your Highness. You did." Doctor Tetorm busied herself at the table, then straightened and nodded to the nurse. "Ready."

His red face giving way to albino white, Eborces yelled, "Everybody out, all out. Now!"

SanMelo didn't bother to hide her grin when she turned to leave. She wasn't the only one in the crush of departees smirking over the King's reception of medical attention.

The blue room was more than able to accommodate the gush of evacuees from the King's personal space. Subdued chuckles were still in the air when Doctor Tetorm, followed by the whey-faced nurse wearing a lop-sided grin, passed through on the way out. The Royal Surgeon waved all medical staff to exit with her leaving only the palace guards and SanMelo waiting for orders.

SanMelo languished on one side of the antechamber itching under her long-worn uniform, wishing she had changed. The guards caught her attention. Mostly they spent their time on parade, ushering magistrates in and out of governmental staterooms and standing posts where they were part of the trappings of royalty. On their breaks, they usually stood so that their pants would retain a knife-edge crease, devoid of wrinkles.

SanMelo never considered them law enforcement, only protocol maintainers. Now she heard an exchange among them. Some were talking low, but vehemently, about their poor performance. They had failed. Their territory was violated and their king captured by a man who impudently walked in. They expected Dag-Reg to make changes. Some welcomed the anticipated discipline.

The king's personal cadre arrived with instructions for the guard to return to their quarters. SanMelo recognized the group: three male valets, then the public relations set consisting of three men and two women, followed by four secretaries, two women two men, and finally seven pages, four men, and three women.

The joy of the PR five spilled over into their gestures, light footsteps, and playful banter. Why were they happy? Wasn't this the worst possible scenario that could befall the king? The coterie passed through and into the bedroom.

Knowing what the king had experienced moments before, SanMelo wasn't eager to face him. He had been in a foul mood, and his advisors would make it worse by giggling at him. Perhaps he'd be too distracted to focus on her. Let her complete her required attendance so she could clean up and review her command.

She knew better. The king's assailant had escaped her jurisdiction before reaching the palace. Her sentinels failed to stop him. She was sure that failure was responsible for her summons and for which she would apologize, after a lengthy recrimination no doubt. She exhaled and breathed back in a lung-filling cloud of bitter air. So be it. Reprimands came with the job—if she still had a job.

Traffic in and out of the king's chambers rose from a trickle to a continuous stream of quick footed, smug-faced sycophants. The perpetual supply of pastry carts still held priority, causing SanMelo to do some sidestepping when told to enter.

Eborces leaned against stuffed pillows in his oversized bed, papers and crumbs scattered about the covers. He grinned at a secretary as he dictated. What caused his happiness? SanMelo was sure it wasn't the result of the medical attention he received. What was going on?

He gave her an expansive wave, sending a muffin rolling across the bed. It was retrieved by a servant. "Ah, SanMelo, what a day. Are you keeping up with the news?"

There had been a change in his attitude. "Is there current news, Sire?"

"Oh, yes. The public was furious when they learned that their King was kidnapped and his life threatened. They realized I'm precious to them, and anyone who harms the Ruler of Montibar must pay. They demand restitution.

"You may find it hard to believe, but my popularity rating was down considerably for that meteoroid fiasco. Especially after your predecessor issued an evacuation alert and got all the credit." Eborces' face darkened. He muttered imprecations about the immediate past.

SanMelo remained quiet. Eborces was a telling King, not a listening one. He needed to spend words before he would arrive where he was going with this.

"Anyway," Eborces resumed his conversation, "we are going to give the people what they want." He grabbed a treat and busied himself with dunking it into a tableside drink.

When he failed to continue, SanMelo prompted, "What the people want, Sire?"

"Yes," he said, spitting out wet crumbs. "They want the intruder—what's his name again?" he asked, pointing to a secretary.

"Jinmyn."

"Yes, Jinmyn. My adoring public wants his head, and they want me safe." He pressed a hand to his chest causing his pajamas to stick to his fingers. "I was shot, you remember?"

"Yes. Terrible," SanMelo said. Would he ever settle on the point? He seemed to be savoring her uncertainty.

Eborces selected a steaming cup. "He'll stand trial. That will show my loyal subjects how fair I am and how devious my enemies are."

"That's a fine idea, Your Highness."

"I'm glad you approve. You're the prosecutor."

SanMelo gasped, "Me, Sire?"

"Yes. You are the Head of Faithfulness. And you will win a conviction. It's the least you can do for letting an assassin escape confinement and reach your king."

Ah yes, this was her censure. She would not only atone for her mistake she would also make the king appear the heroic victim. He was already playing it up. Calling the accused an assassin was stretching the episode at this point.

"Very well, Sire, if that's your wish."

"It's my command."

SanMelo nodded, her eyes downcast.

"You'll be in familiar company. Your old boss, Yorev, will be the defendant's advisor." King Eborces laughed, back in full humor.

DEPOSITIONS

"I don't see why not," Turnkey said. "You can drink all you want. Remember, though, I can't let you out of the cell right now, and you're aware that there are no facilities in there. Do you still want it?"

Jinmyn's tongue stuck to the roof of his mouth. "Yes, please."

He sipped the cool water and regarded Turnkey. "You were the one that pointed a weapon at me."

His jailer laughed aloud. "Sure was. I'm going to receive a medal for stopping you, too. A Medal of Valor for Palace Guard Fonely—that's me." He giggled, leaned forward and whispered, "The best part is that my fire-stunner wasn't charged. It couldn't shoot a spark. Don't tell DagReg."

Jinmyn jerked, spilling water. "You mean I could have just walked over to the closet?"

"I suppose," Fonely said, nodding. "You were the only one holding a functioning weapon until DagReg arrived."

Jinmyn dropped his cup and held the bars with both hands. The world had gone mute and dark. He melted to a sitting position, his hands sliding down the cold steel rods. Fonely's laugh echoed from far away.

Spending the night wrapped in blankets on a concrete floor left Jinmyn sore and out of sorts. Every time he opened his eyes he saw DagReg still at his post, a small table two body lengths away facing the cell - watching and writing in a log of some kind. The King's Personal Protector seemed more machine than human.

Dread tightened Jinmyn's chest in an uneasy foreboding while he watched his massive custodian take notes. No lines, creases, wrinkles, or any other indication of feelings or fatigue radiated from DagReg. It wouldn't do to test the discipline of this man. Of course, he had already alienated the King's Protector. Jinmyn wished it could have been otherwise.

Jinmyn got a rush of self-respect. He warranted the attention of the elite, the top officer of the palace security. Take that, Rustbucket. How about your average operative now? They've taken notice.

He scootched to a sitting position, hating DagReg—and admiring him—as Fonely brought in a breakfast tray. It was the same fare as last night: a gruel made of local onion or garlic type plants, a thick slice of black bread, and water. He still had the bitter aftertaste from the previous bowl. When the mushy stench reached his nostrils, his stomach soured. He moved to the far corner of his cage for fear he'd be sick and collapsed into his blanket.

Fonely was all business and professional until DagReg left. "Good morning, Enemy of the King," he said. "The word is that you're to stand trial. It'll be broadcast live." He made a fist, shaking it up and down in short victory pumps. "You have done wonders for my career. A particular pompous shift commander, who used to make my life miserable, came to me whining and pleading to let him take my place watching you. DagReg squashed that. It was great."

Fonely smiled, obviously enjoying his new-found status. He pulled his log book from a satchel, took the chair, sighed, and made an entry. Pointing at the tray with his pencil he said, "You don't get anything else until you eat that. However long it takes."

Jinmyn had eaten the bread, drank the water, but the smelly, watery bowl of mush still rested untouched until well after mid-morning when his visitor arrived.

He was past middle age, average height with erect posture, well combed white hair on top of a friendly face now pulled into a frowning pinch. "What's that rotten putrescence?"

Fonely jerked his attention to the newcomer, Jinmyn saw the light of recognition in his eyes before Fonely bowed his head. "It's the tasga for the prisoner. It's been sitting out all morning. He won't eat it." Fonely gazed at the floor.

"Tasga doesn't reek like that."

"The king has the kitchen prepare this especially for the prisoner."

"Yes, he would. I'll be back."

Fonely waited until he was gone then scowled at Jinmyn, "You'd better not cause me any trouble when he gets back," he whispered.

The visitor returned. "Your prisoner is allowed to attend his necessary functions, is he not?"

Fonely rose to attention from writing in his log, "Yes, sir. Of course, I have to accompany him."

The stranger approached the cell door, "I'm Yorev, your appointed counsel," he said. "Let's go to the restroom."

Jinmyn searched Yorev's face. It didn't look deceiving but ever since he'd met Rustbucket things didn't appear as they seemed. "No thanks. I don't need to spend time with another stoolie of the king's."

Stoolie had been uttered in English causing Yorev to smile and raise his brow. "I don't know what that is," he said waving away the word, "but it sounds like you mean a confidant of the king. I assure you, I'm not, as your rigid overseer here can attest."

Jinmyn didn't move. "Why should I go anywhere with you?"

Yorev paused, his head dropping before regaining eye contact. "Because our king is feeding you a particularly detestable tasga. I believe he's using it to enhance all its undesirable qualities: gas, bloating, halitosis ... body odor." Yorev shrugged. "I apologize, but a shower would do you good. I've brought a toothbrush, too."

Jinmyn was on his feet. "Let's go."

"Tell me how you came to be here while you clean up as long as you'll have no privacy anyway. Sorry, I don't have fresh clothes for you. Maybe next time."

Jinmyn shrugged his shoulders: a universal gesture understood as dismissive. "A lack of privacy or clean clothes won't bother me. I'm an orphan raised in a system of substitute homes. It's the reason I'm here."

"I don't quite understand you," Yorev said, pointing the way down the hall. "You held the king hostage because you have no family?"

"No." Jinmyn covered a belch with his hand. "I mean it's the reason—or one of the reasons—why Rustbucket chose me to come here instead of someone else."

He noticed that Yorev had widened the space between them. "Sorry. How much farther?"

"We're here." Yorev pushed open a swinging door to reveal a barracks style latrine complete with showers, sinks, and partitioned toilets. Jinmyn headed for the nearest one.

Fonely followed. "Leave the door open where I can see you at all times," he said.

"Why doesn't he know that?" Yorev asked. "Is this his first allowed visit?"

"It is with me," Fonely answered.

"Unbelievable."

Yorev stopped by the sinks, out of Jinmyn's sight. Fonely stood in front of the open stall door but wasn't looking in. Jinmyn realized that both men were embarrassed. He was the one who should have been self-conscious. The realization that they were uncomfortable stirred him with a dab of supremacy. If the rest of the court were this easy to shame, he could play on their sympathies. He knew how to do that from his childhood days.

Yorev seemed determined to ignore Jinmyn's feculent necessities. "Who did you say chose you to come here?" he asked, his voice echoing off the walls of the empty room.

Jinmyn knew how exotic the name sounded in this solar system. He should use it every chance he got. "Rustbucket chose me. You call him the Regulator."

Fonely sneered and grunted, his gaze averted, his ear turned to Jinmyn.

Yorev waited until Jinmyn headed for the showers. "I remember hearing about you crashing the barricade when King Eborces closed the spaceport. You told the guards you wanted to see the king."

Jinmyn puckered his lips, "There was something like that. Yes."

"Then you finally get here, kidnap him and threaten him with a weapon. The Regulator has always helped Montibar, why would he send you to harm the king?"

"He didn't."

"You just said he did. You're not consistent with your story. If I don't believe you how can I defend you? Grabin sent you, didn't they?"

Jinmyn stood under the spray from the shower head and turned his face into the water. He found soap from a dispenser and lathered all over starting at the top.

Yorev's chin tilted up. "Well?" His hands were at the small of his back, a military parade rest position.

Fonely planted himself behind Yorev with his arms crossed over his chest.

Jinmyn recognized their body language. He had seen it in foster homes and principals' offices. He was already judged guilty.

Using his hands as squeegees, he got as much water off as he could and reached for his clothes, wrinkling his nose as he drew them on. "I'm gonna stink again. These are disgusting."

Yorev's face was withdrawing behind a wall of rejection. A startling realization jolted Jinmyn that he wanted this man to believe him.

"Look, I'll tell you everything, but first you have to realize that Rustbucket didn't send me to bother the king. And I didn't want to. All I wanted to do was convince him to disarm the Poison Pill System, and when he wouldn't do it, I tried to do it myself. That's all."

Yorev had taken note. Jinmyn saw his eyes fire and the change in his stance.

"What do you mean, 'Poison Pill System'?"

"I don't know what the official name is, but the King activated a killer bunch of asteroids. All it'll take is a slip-up, and they'll come crashing down. Little pieces already have. Anyway, Rustbucket was gone when the king did it, and now he can't get back in without causing the things to collapse."

Yorev held up a hand. "We have to go back to your cell. We'll talk there."

"I'm telling you now you'll think I'm crazy."

A FINE SENTRY

Fonely remained at rigid attention, sweat rings showing under his arms. His soft garrison cap may have kept perspiration off his brow, but his upper lip glistened with visible drops of moisture.

DagReg didn't scream, yell, or throw things. His firm voice outlined, point by point, where Fonely blundered. He held Fonely's logbook; his eyes fixed on the unfortunate sentinel. "I don't care how impressed you are with this counselor. I am the only one to allow the prisoner out of his cell. Not only did you let someone else release him, but he also walked to the latrine and back without restraints."

Listening to DagReg discipline Fonely, Jinmyn wondered why he didn't realize he could have made a break for it. He had fixated on the shower. He allowed a creature comfort to manipulate his actions. He'd have be aware of that weakness so they couldn't use it against him again. He needed to seize any opportunity to escape.

DagReg wasn't through with Fonely. "Perhaps you'd be better suited as a drummer in the Royal Marching Band. There's also room for another ex-palace guard at the rapidly freezing lake on the ice cap. Is that where you wish to finish your career? Do you miss your companions?"

"No sir."

Jinmyn laughed at the squeak in Fonely's reply, and he jumped into their exchange. "Get him, Daggie." He slapped his leg. "Phony looks like he needs to cool down."

"Then here's what you'll do," DagReg said, ignoring Jinmyn. "Set up cots in the far cell. You and I will live there until the prisoner leaves. If I am off duty when his advisor arrives, you will notify me. He talks to no one unless I'm present."

Sweat ran down the side of Fonely's red face. "Yes, sir."

"I am the only one to allow him access to the latrine."

Confusion evident, Fonely frowned. "Yes, sir, but—" He stopped at a cutting glance from DagReg.

"There will be a pail for the prisoner. You will keep it empty and clean."

Fonely groaned.

So did Jinmyn.

DagReg took a deep breath then exhaled in a drawn-out nasal expression that Jinmyn interpreted as disappointment and conveyed Fonely's final demerit before reassignment.

Jinmyn was at the bars. "Hey, Daggie, how about Phony and I trade places? I could do as good as he's doing."

He caught a quick shift of Fonely's eyes in his direction, but DagReg continued to ignore Jinmyn and spoke to Fonely.

"Before you return to watch the prisoner, hang some blankets around our cell and put bedding in it. I want a cot and some privacy, but you can sleep on the floor if you wish."

"Yes, sir."

"And get a haircut."

Fonely rose from his seat and motioned to the other chair. "Sir, you'll have to wait to speak with the prisoner."

"Yes, so the Captain of the Guard has informed me," said Yorev. "Would you please let him know I'm here?"

"Yes, sir." Fonely marched to the last cell in the row, now partitioned off with barracks blankets, spoke a few soft words and retraced his steps.

Fonely was halfway to sitting when he glanced at Yorev still standing. He aborted his maneuver in an awkward wobble to stand behind his chair causing Jinmyn to laugh at him.

Fonely's face darkened as he diverted his apparent frustration between Yorev, DagReg's expected appearance, and Jinmyn.

"Look as sharp as you can, Phony." Jinmyn pointed at the pail. "Don't forget that you're the Captain of the Bucket Brigade."

DagReg showed up in a creased uniform, alert, but with a blue-black inkling of new beard. The breach of less than Parade Ground perfection raised no comments. Not only had he returned to duty from his sleep schedule, Jinmyn doubted there was anyone on Montibar with the fortitude to tease DagReg.

DagReg nodded to Yorev. "Good morning, sir. Thank you for waiting to talk with your client."

Yorev smiled and tipped his head in return. "Not at all. We intend to follow all rules and regulations."

"Good. There is another rule to observe," said DagReg. He moved a chair from the table halfway to Jinmyn's bars. "You may sit here. You must remain well out of arm's length from the prisoner. I will inspect everything but words passing between you."

If the arrangement bothered Yorev, he didn't show it. "That seems reasonable," he said, taking his seat.

DagReg sat at the little table and waved at Fonely. "Get another chair."

Yorev pulled a notepad and stylus from a satchel, looked at Jinmyn and said, "Start at the beginning."

"You'll think I'm insane."

"I already do. Convince me otherwise."

CHAPTER FIFTEEN

EVIDENCE

SanMelo let her shoulders relax. She would meet King Eborces in the West Office. That's the way a monarch should act and use formal settings to receive visitors. Meeting in his private chambers made her uncomfortable where his entourage of servants, secretaries, and trustees of the many royal accounts shuffled in and out. The casual atmosphere left her feeling like she was in someone else's house. Formality required that she be identified as a State official, not stand by for an overstuffed monarch to squeeze her in between a muffin and a memo.

Today his staff was smaller than usual, but other dignitaries were present. She recognized Grabin Ambassador Lyram.

"Good morning, Sire." SanMelo bowed because she wore the uniform of her office. "I'm here as summoned." She mentally went over her prepared report on progress for the trial.

King Eborces smiled. SanMelo thought it strange since he wasn't holding something tangible and luscious in his hand. "Ah, yes, Head of Faithfulness." The king held the flat of his hand toward Lyram. "This is the ambassador from Grabin?"

SanMelo gave a small bow of her head. "I've seen The Esteemed Lyram on several occasions here at the palace, but have never had the honor of an introduction. How do you do, sir?"

Lyram returned the head gesture. "It is my privilege, Head of Faithfulness. SanMelo, is it not?"

King Eborces wiped a hand through the air. "Polite and formal, as I expected." He turned to Lyram, "Yet I remember that it was the Grabin attaché that brought the assassin onto the grounds," then he frowned at SanMelo, "and that it was your security that he made look foolish." He squinted from one to the other his fingertip tapping his pursed lips. "Collusion, perhaps?"

Did she hear that right? The audacity of the king's implications stunned SanMelo to the point of taking her senses away.

Ambassador Lyram, however, had a smile tugging his cheeks upward. "Ah yes, the reason for my invitation today. You wish to address the subject of our embassy's connection to your suspect."

Eborces squinted his eyes. "You admit to a connection?"

"As you said, Your Highness, one of our representatives escorted the accused to a meeting with your Office of Faithfulness. We are truthful as we always have been in our desire for peaceful harmony with Montibar."

"Why did you bring him here?"

"I wasn't involved, but I understand that he asked to meet with you. According to our Assistant Director of Security, he played a role in helping divert the space rocks from Grabin. To show our gratitude, we conducted him to your appropriate department." Lyram's honey voice added, "All in keeping with protocol."

SanMelo unclenched her fists. The calm Grabinian did not implicate her office as the cause of the trouble. Thank you. Would she ever be able to debate with enough skillful diplomacy to create a friendship after the way King Eborces handled the situation? Ambassador Lyram seemed genuine in his desire to coexist.

Her king was another matter. He picked at little details. Perhaps he already knew the information she was here to report.

Eborces matched Lyram's silky tones. "Your Assistant Director is on my world; we find a nest of Grabin spies, one threatened my life, but it's fine with you because of the proper protocol?"

Lyram shook his head. "Grabin would never condone violence, Your Highness."

"Then what's the link between Jinmyn and the Assistant Director? Have you got a rebellion going on?"

The silence grew as Lyram paused, a vee furrowing his brow. Shrugging he said, "I know of no covert assemblage. However, Assistant Director Velmere is here following rumors of a Christian sect. So far, they are just rumors."

Eborces indicated SanMelo to step forward. "Your report on the assassin."

"Yes, Sire." She would make it factual but try not to embarrass the Ambassador in return for his earlier kindness toward her office. "We find no record of any kind that confirms Jinmyn as a Montibaran citizen. His first noted appearance was at the Gaumen Shack over 0.214 cycles ago. He was naked and disoriented." She blushed but continued. "Subsequently he was apprehended and taken away by men suspected of being Grabinian spies at the time. We have since confirmed them as Grabin agents." She didn't look at Lyram.

"Jinmyn next arrived on Montibar in the same shuttle that brought the Assistant Director of Grabin Security."

She heard a small gasp from the diplomat. Either he just now learned that or else he was a good actor.

SanMelo consulted her notes. "Jinmyn didn't get off the ship before it was sterilized but survived and was cared for by the employee responsible for the decontamination."

"Wait." Eborces jerked his head up. "Did you arrest the worker?"

"No. You see he's a special—"

"Arrest him!" It was an official fiat issued from the Throne.

"Yes, Sire."

The King made a swishing motion with his hand as if he were reaching for his absent treat table. "Continue."

"Next we have Jinmyn seized by the soldiers at the barricade to the spaceport."

"Award them and make sure they attend the trial."

SanMelo nodded and recognized the King's finger tap to keep going. "He escaped from the holding area and later arrived here under the auspices of the Grabin representative. He's been on the palace grounds ever since." It wasn't necessary to recount how he escaped from her custody and reached her king. He would do that himself in lurid detail.

"So you see, Ambassador," Eborces said, turning to Lyram, "Grabin clearly set Jinmyn on the course to destroy the King of Montibar."

"I assure Your Highness that's not true." Lyram retained his calm demeanor. "I will have our resources track this Jinmyn as well. I'll be happy to report to you what we've discovered."

"Bring your Assistant Director of Security here. I'll hear his account personally," King Eborces said.

Lyram smiled and rubbed his hands together. "I think, Your Highness, to avoid any actions that could be considered rash, such as detaining a Grabin official, it would be better if the Head of Faithfulness and perhaps Jinmyn's council came to the Grabin embassy."

Eborces half arose turning red, his lips flattening. "You dare refuse me? The Ruler of Montibar and friend of the Regulator?"

Lyram turned his hands upward. "Only in the interest of decorum, Your Highness, to show the Regulator that we can indeed manage affairs between our two worlds."

It struck SanMelo that her king's irascibility could forever affect the welfare of both planets. How could she maintain peace when she was unschooled and incompetent in the subtleties of statesmanship? She shouldn't be here. She needed to talk with—"Sire, perhaps it would be beneficial if Yorev and I accepted Ambassador Lyram's invitation."

Eborces glanced at her as if seeing her for the first time and plopped down in his royal chair, his chin thrust forward. The skin tightened around his eyes, but SanMelo cut him off before he spoke.

"We could see, for instance, if there are more than the usual amount of troops billeted on the grounds, or any other preparations indicating anything other than peaceful intentions. Perhaps the Ambassador would give us a tour?" That sounded childish, but it was the best she could do.

It might work. Eborces relaxed. His squinty eyes and pursed lips showed that he was thinking about it. When he gave a small nod, SanMelo knew that she was on a spy mission.

"Fine then," Eborces said. "Tomorrow, Ambassador, San-Melo and Yorev will question your Assistant Director and tour the embassy."

Lyram made a shallow bow. "I'm honored, Your Highness."

Eborces' finger swept over both of them. "I want you back here day after that for your updates. Lyram, I expect you to vindicate Jinmyn's privileged status with your security."

"Certainly, Your Highness. Will that be all?"

FOREIGN SOIL

"I didn't know what else to do." For the second time, SanMelo explained why she and Yorev were in a transport going to the Grabin embassy. "I can't believe I said we would spy on the Grabinians right in front of the ambassador, but I was afraid the King would make matters worse." She held her face in her hands and groaned.

Yorev's soft chuckle floated through the open window as he admired the green parks, blue ponds, and towering shade trees their route traversed. He believed it.

"King Eborces is a master politician," he said. "It's what he trained in since the day he was born; it's his greatest strength. Especially if one underestimates him as a gluttonous fool. He is, of course, but that doesn't impair his ability to manipulate others. I imagine he knew how you would respond before you did."

SanMelo frowned. "It seemed spontaneous."

A paternal quirk gripped him. SanMelo was not a daughter, but closer than a coworker. Yorev wanted to protect her. However, she was Head of Faithfulness. "You are responsible for a significant portion of our government. Obey our Monarch, yes, but balance him. Stand firm, listen, then answer. Negotiate. You have strength. Use it."

The way she looked at him like he could give her the secret solution to all problems put an ache in his chest. "That's all I can tell you."

He sighed, pointed out the window and said, "Isn't it beautiful? They don't have much of this on Grabin. Have you ever been there?"

SanMelo's long pause caught his attention. He tilted his head, his eyebrows raised in question.

Her cheeks colored, she diverted her gaze to the view, her hand fluttered to her mouth almost hiding a tiny "No."

Gold-streaked green marble tile paved the floor of the colonnade and wide aisle of the arboretum. Exotic flowers offered tantalizing perfume, pastels, and vibrant colors. At the far end of the sunlit room, in front of glass doors overlooking the trimmed grounds, stood a conference table of dark brown wood. Its polished surface was laden with trays filled with fruits and prepared finger dishes.

DagReg was already there, standing at attention, resplendent in his formal Palace Guard uniform, waiting at the entrance for them. Yorev smiled to himself. SanMelo wasn't the only tyro to the nuances of subtlety. It was plain that DagReg wanted to scrutinize Grabin's armed presence on Montibar when he requested and received an invitation to join them.

Ambassador Lyram made the introductions.

Extending his arm to the uniformed person at his side, he said, "This is Velmere, our esteemed Assistant Director of Security. He has graciously consented to your interview." Lyram indicated a liveried person standing behind and to the left of Velmere, "This is Korfel, the Captain of our embassy guards. We thought the King's Personal Protector," he nodded to DagReg, "should meet his counterpoint." Lyram raised a hand to his chin. "Perhaps a better choice of words would be to say his reflection. We're certainly not on opposing sides here."

Yorev could have picked out Velmere. While the other two men in service garb wore flashy, almost gaudy, uniforms, their faces were neutral, bespeaking of training in the protocol used in palaces, Velmere wore military dress browns. His hair was short, not shaped to complement a service cap, but most telling of all were his frown and narrowed eyes, dark as the mysterious eclosus bloom.

Yorev caught his breath before it turned into an audible gasp. Was that why Lyram staged the meeting in here? Were eclosus growing in this very greenhouse?

Few ever saw the rare plant. They grew in the shade where direct sunlight wouldn't kill them. Their blossoms were deep space black with an aroma that drew reason from men and embraced them in an intoxicating madness while its allergens burrowed into noses and throats. Some didn't survive the aromatic embrace.

Though never documented, a common belief held that eclosus were root-walking plants that could show up near a house to portend death.

Yorev was far too rational to believe half the stories of the midnight-walking plants, but he still felt a tingle in his back thinking one might be behind him, propagating euphoric suffocation into his duped olfactory senses.

He breathed through his mouth and reassessed Velmere's eyes. No, they weren't evil. Those were the scared eyes of a soldier out of his element. Velmere didn't want to be here. He didn't trust them.

The aroma arrived before the carts. Yorev understood and appreciated Lyram's attempt to ease tension and promote goodwill by using a delectable lunch in the arboretum.

It wouldn't work unless something changed. Velmere had answered questions politely and to the point with one or two-word answers while eyeing the Montibarans: DagReg's frozen countenance and SanMelo's charm, now covered with a light sheen of perspiration. Why did she wear her cape of office in the botanic gardens where warmth and humidity must be adding layers to her discomfort?

Yorev shook his head. The things officials do for no reason but show, tradition or one-upmanship always amazed him. He'd try to seat her near one of the glass doors open to fresh air.

Maybe a fresh approach was what he needed too.

The luncheon table defined the schism of the meeting: Grabinians were settling on one side, Montibarans on the other. Yorev took SanMelo's elbow and steered her to the end chair across from Korfel. He took the seat facing Velmere and cast an approving glance at the offered fare. The meal, at least, was bound to be a success.

After the exclamations of appreciation for the delicious food, made mostly by SanMelo, had died down, Yorev lifted his chalice of dinvu, but then thought better of making a toast. An expensive wine known as much for the rubescent glow from the heart of the liquid as its elegant palate shouldn't be wasted by a mere, "Here's to a successful meeting" phrase.

He let a sip roll around his mouth, delighting his tongue and saturating his taste buds with the promise of sophisticated smoothness delivered.

The relaxing effects of the intoxicants were there, too.

The ability to stay away from such offerings while others indulged had helped Yorev navigate his long career. Still, he took another mouthful before returning his limpid crystal of living wine to the table enjoying the bouquet lingering in his nostrils. It was time to see if Lyram's dinvu was working.

He took a deep breath. "Velmere, I'm the only assistance Jinmyn has. Please help me understand.

"You say that Jinmyn identified with a group or mob that he called Christians. You didn't find evidence of them on Grabin or any here on Montibar. He states that he is not from either of our planets but was brought here by the Regulator. We have no record of him on Montibar, and Ambassador Lyram affirms that he can find no record of Jinmyn as a Grabinian. If such a man can hide his identity from both governments, don't you think a sect could conceal theirs too? Does that sound conceivable?"

Yorev paused to fork another bite into his mouth. Might as well keep the conversation convivial and enjoying food would support Lyram's intentions to do that.

Velmere kept his eyes on his plate. His body language gave no clue whether they would have a table conversation.

Yorev sighed and said, "There's a line of reasoning that Jinmyn is an agent with an identity manufactured by the Grabin government. That will be the circumstantial evidence that convicts him." He shrugged. "Unless I can make a case otherwise."

The others at the table were watching. Velmere continued with his meal.

"Velmere, if you want to repay Jinmyn for helping Grabin avoid disaster from the space rocks, now is the time. Are there Christians? What do they want? Are they a threat?"

Velmere used his serviette with light pats and glanced at DagReg.

Yorev noticed the Assistant Director's dinvu was untouched meaning his lips probably weren't any looser than earlier. DagReg's size and square-jawed visage didn't invite warm confidentiality either. Yorev decided that he might as well drain his chalice. It appeared to be the only thing of value he would procure this trip.

Velmere straightened. What was he doing, leaving? No. A tiny smile twitched at the corners of his lips to disappear as he inclined his head to Yorev.

"There are no Christians on either of our worlds, only where Jinmyn came from, although he said he wasn't a perfect one. They are followers of a belief system."

"Then you concur that Jinmyn is from somewhere other than our planetary systems?"

Velmere glanced up and down the table. Dining had stopped. "If Christians exist, they aren't dangerous. Jinmyn says they trust in a power greater than the Regulator. He even calls the Regulator by the name of Rustbucket." He shrugged and fell silent.

"Please continue," Yorev said.

Moist rings formed on the tablecloth under Velmere's water glass as he spun it in slow circles. "From our first encounter with him, Jinmyn seemed ignorant of some of our ways. But I watched him—the way he dealt with a little girl." A smile formed as he talked but his wrinkled forehead combined with it to make him appear forlorn. "She was brave but dealing with enough to break an adult. Her father was an administrator in the diplomatic corps when he died in an accident." He straightened, squaring his shoulders. "Within seven cycles the girl's mother developed grouping nodules and was confined to a hospital bed for the last stages of her life."

The air circulations faint breeze was the only movement as the guests waited for Velmere to gather his thoughts. Even Dag-Reg was attentive, eyebrows drawn together.

"It was to Jinmyn the girl went the night her mother died, and that was when he told her about Christian beliefs. It brought her peace of mind. Her name is Brimlet—"

Korfel jumped upright sending his chair flying backward. He ran around the table and caught SanMelo as she slid from her seat. He had an arm behind her, her head cradled in the crook of his elbow. Her damp face shone cold and white against the scarlet of his tunic. Korfel sought Yorev with a glance. "I saw her eyes roll up," he said.

"You responded correctly." Yorev understood the Grabinian was explaining the reason he touched a member of the Montiba-ran delegation. "Would you please carry her outside? It must be too warm in here for her."

Korfel gave Lyram a hasty peek, receiving a nod in return, before replying, "Certainly, sir."

The remaining four members of the meeting trailed Korfel, with SanMelo draped over his arms, to the shade of a spreading zelwur tree. The healing vapors from the green and gold leaves cured any number of ailments causing the tree to be a natural destination for sufferers.

SanMelo revived, stood and wobbled. She leaned on Korfel's arm, grabbed Velmere's service tie in a white-knuckled fist and locked him in wet-eyed contact. She let the tears fall. "My sister's dead?"

Jinmyn combed his fingers through his hair—greasy—scratched his scalp and rubbed the stubble on his chin. If he couldn't shave soon, it would be turning into a beard. He envied Fonely, sitting at the little table, having his uniform pressed, shoes shined, and hair trimmed. Jinmyn offended himself.

He stunk. He had kept the toothbrush Yorev gave him, and he brushed with water, but that was the extent of his ablutions.

How offensive his body odor had become was evident by the reactions of the workers that arrived to install the lights. Their wrinkled noses were the least of it. Fonely laughed aloud when one of them wrapped a rag around his face like an outlaw in an old western movie.

If such a smell had erupted from one of the boys in the foster care system, they all would have laughed and tried to create a worse one. This time, however, Jinmyn was shamed. He was a block of sour cheese leaving a rotten egg smelling, unctuous smudge to everything he touched.

The two technicians hurried to place tripod mounted construction lamps around Jinmyn's confinement. They started at the back wall and set the units one large step apart; all pointed at Jinmyn's cage. These they wired to junction boxes they left on the floor. They strung conductors from each box to a large circuit panel they left by the wall. One large cable from the big box ran along the wall and out the door.

They were checking their work when DagReg returned.

The lights were too bright. Jinmyn could see past them by squinting, but the only direction he could make out detail was toward the adjacent cell. The temperature became uncomfortable where the incandescence was converting energy to illumination and heat. Jinmyn went to the far corner, sat and hugged his knees.

"What is all this?" DagReg's voice carried a strength that stopped the technicians and brought Fonely to his feet.

"The King's orders, sir," Fonely said.

"Why?"

Fonely lowered his voice to a more conversational tone. Jinmyn kept still with his forehead on his knees.

"His Highness said that the assassin has a history of slipping away. He must remain under close watch."

Jinmyn tracked DagReg through slitted eyes. The King's Personal Protector turned his head first to the lamps, technicians, Fonely, and finally stopped on Jinmyn.

"Sleep deprivation," he said, nodding. "Very well."

DagReg loomed large as he pointed to one of the installers. "Nothing's gained by having these on during the day. You will turn them off every morning." He pointed at the other one. "You will turn them on every evening."

Both men acknowledged their orders then the man with the rag on his face asked, "What about right now, sir? It's still daylight."

Jinmyn didn't hear a response or see DagReg move, but he visualized that chilling square-jawed scowl. The lights turned off.

OLD FRIEND(S)

"We didn't do anything wrong. Honest. We didn't do anything."

The plaintive wail brought Jinmyn out of a fitful sleep and Fonely out of his blanketed quarters in the last cell.

Two muscular oziers escorted a crying prisoner, his toes alternately dragging and tapping out steps. DagReg held the entry of the middle cell open. The newcomer braced one foot against the bars, fighting his forced entry. It didn't slow down his jailers. His leg buckled and they shoved him through the door. DagReg closed and locked it. The wild-eyed stranger turned, shook the bars, babbled, and sobbed.

The scared mewling kicked in Jinmyn's recollection. "It's all right, Sruma. No one is going to hurt you. You're safe here, although it's a little inconvenient."

Jinmyn rose and straightened his clothes. "I suppose you don't remember me right now, but if you'll calm down and think back—"

Sruma screamed. "You hurt us. When our backs were turned. Get him away. Get him away." He stretched his arm as far as he could toward DagReg. "Please don't leave us with him." Sruma melted to the floor and wept.

"Pathetic," one of the oziers said inspecting the three-cell jail as he extended a form for DagReg's signature. His gaze swept the prisoners, the glaring bright confines, and partially dressed Fonely. "Pathetic," he repeated.

Jinmyn yelled at him, "What's pathetic is your total lack of compassion for someone who is obviously scared. And these two are the best of the royal guards. They're in here night and day. They're diligent and professional. You could learn something from them."

The ozier reclaimed his form and left without acknowledging the outburst.

Why hadn't DagReg used his leviathan bulk to shove the sarcasm back down the ozier's throat before the moment passed?

The old anger of arrogant family kids taunting the temporary homers rose with a memory. Kevin was wearing a new shirt to school, given to him by their foster mother. "Hey, look," a cowlicked loudmouth alerted his snobbish companions. "That's my old shirt. Mom put a bunch of my worn-out clothes in a garbage bag and took 'em to the needy church."

The most insolent of the bunch pulled his lips back like a donkey braying and declared, "You know what's worse than garbage? It's garbage wearing garbage."

John dropped his books and attacked. His peaceful roommate went along with him. Why did Kevin jump into the fight? It was two against five; he should have known how it would end. John had landed the first punch before fists started flying. He took a worse beating than Kevin did. The school suspended them both.

Different world, same results, he hadn't come far at all.

Jinmyn turned to DagReg, raised his shoulders and held his palms up, asking a universal body question.

The enormous jailer scrutinized his prisoner. A quick, cold tremble shot down Jinmyn's neck and arms. Had he overstepped? DagReg wasn't pointing a weapon, merely holding the receipt the ozier left with him, his head tilted, brows scrunched with—what? Curiosity?

Forget it. Let it pass. That's what teachers, agency workers, and foster parents told him.

Jinmyn sat next to the bars. "See, Sruma. I'm in here too. I'm a little dirty, but that's all."

"Jinmyn?" DagReg called his name.

Was it the first time the big guard had acknowledged him as anything other than a prisoner?

"Do you know this man? The transfer paper says he should be Frimox."

Jinmyn's first impulse was to have fun with DagReg but realized it would be at his cellmate's expense. He pulled himself up and indicated the huddled mass, weeping in the next cell.

"DagReg meet Sruma. When he calms down, you'll likely meet Tumrin before Frimox. There's a mean one, too, but I can't remember his name right now."

It was worth the honesty. Probably not many people could say they've seen DagReg confused.

CHAPTER SIXTEEN

THE TRIAL BEGINS

"This trial will be conducted in a different method," Yorev said. "There will not be a panel of justices. King Eborces alone decides everything from the rules of procedure to guilt or innocence—and the sentence." He shrugged at the expression on Jinmyn's face. "We can expect to lose."

Jinmyn took a deep breath followed by a long exhale. "Never thought otherwise."

Yorev swept his hand toward Tumrin. "I don't know the status of your friend. He wasn't assigned a defender, so he could be here as a prisoner or witness, but be aware of this: King Eborces is shrewd. Don't let his appearance fool you. He will use this man against you."

With his wrists strapped to a belt at his waist, his ankles gripped by leg irons connected by chains, Jinmyn commented, "Finally, enough belts to stop these pants from falling down. I thought they'd dress me in something else for the trial—not keep me in this filthy, stinky uniform."

Yorev touched his nose—a fleeting lapse of body language. "Those clothes are from the guard in Faithfulness. I think King Eborces is reminding SanMelo and the public just how far you managed to infiltrate security. Remember, I told you he is an able conniver."

A moan, more like a sob, turned their attention to watch Fonely truss up the other prisoner.

"They'll let you go soon, Tumrin," Jinmyn said. "There's no way that they can find fault with you."

The two prisoners shuffled on either side of Yorev. They followed a guide identified as a Captain of The Royal Elite Guards by the insignias on her two-tone blue uniform trimmed with gold-swirl sleeve embellishments. DagReg and Fonely brought up the rear.

"How much farther? This waltz is tiring me out." Jinmyn made a mental note to exercise more in his cell.

Waltz came out in English, which turned Yorev's head and elicited a whimper from Tumrin or one of his alter egos.

"We're taking the longest route possible," Yorev said. "Notice the cameras tracking us. All Montibar will see how bedraggled you are with every step to the North Gallery—our destination. Viewers will decide to identify with you or not before we enter the hall." Yorev snorted and managed a downturned smile. "They will choose not to."

Three steps later he added, "It was King Eborces' doing. You must admire his ability to manipulate people."

Jinmyn used his chin to point at a camera. "Too bad they can't detect a whiff of me. That'd help them decide."

Yorev rubbed his nose. "Yes, well, be assured that many reports will include your essence."

The newscaster's black suit and starched high collar white shirt topped by a golden bow tie were attire suitable for the palace though he sat in the studio. "Malaur here. Today we're bringing you a special broadcast from the Royal North Gallery. It's now a courtroom. There's seating installed along the sides of the Hall and a sub-throne from a receiving room for the Judge's chair. Take a look."

The view on the screen cut to the gallery showing a long rectangular room. A wooden partition barred the far end. It was tall enough to block the image of King Eborces from the chest downward even with the throne raised on a dais.

The seats on the right side were full except a trio next to the barrier. Small utility racks held crystal pitchers and glasses in front of the three padded chairs.

On the other side, four armed guards stood against the wall behind an isolated area surrounded by paneling. Inside were eight empty chairs.

Two small conference tables were in the middle of the room facing forward. SanMelo, wearing her cape of office, sat at the left one.

The view panned to the other end of the hall showing an overflow crowd standing near the entrance and occupying the foyer beyond.

Malaur's image returned. "I'll give you the details of this case while we watch the prisoners' march," he said. "They've included another prisoner as well as the man that attacked the King. There are confusing reports as to his name, but he must have been in on it."

The screen split to show a close-up of Jinmyn's shackled legs. The view pulled back until both Jinmyn and Tumrin filled one side.

Malaur consulted his notes. "King Eborces will act as the sole judge. It's legal although never applied before. The three heads of Parliament were given interested party status but no voice or vote as you would normally expect in trials of State." His attention flickered off-screen. "They're coming in now."

Two women and a man, all in official robes of the government branches entered and assumed the empty chairs. All three scowled. A frown fit the old man's face as a natural expression but soured the mature beauty of the women. The contrast of their elegance and bearing to Jinmyn' filthy clothes and shuffling gait was evident as a new view placed them side-by-side.

The officials took their seats while an undercurrent of noise directed the camera's attention elsewhere. A full-screen scene showed armed Royal Elite security force members escorting four handcuffed prisoners to the paneled area on the other side of the hall.

"Here," said Malaur in a voice-over, "come the spies captured from The Gaumen Shack. There's the bartender, he may be the owner, we haven't found out yet, and the server—she's heavily involved in this affair. All of them were there in the fight against our Montibarans. There are still some empty chairs; I don't know why. Maybe they excused some people just caught up in the melee at The Shack."

The camera scrolled across the audience recording the faces of the bystanders. Some, like the officials of Parliament, were frowning. Others sat up, eyes wide, mouths open. Their heads turning, pausing, and then moving on and back again. Some spectators were laughing and poking each other.

People, starting with those near the entrance, turned their attention to the arrival of Jinmyn's group. Silence slid inward through the gallery, a muted curtain muffling other noises. Padding steps and sliding shackles on marble floors boomed in the sudden quietness. More than a few people touched their noses as the group passed.

"Oh, my!" Malaur's voice croaked over the airwaves. "Look how filthy and unkempt he is. Information told to us says that his body odor is, frankly, very offensive."

The scene shifted as Jinmyn shuffled along until King Eborces was in the picture. His lower jaw hung among his chins, brows arched toward his royal headgear: the Crown of State for this occasion.

Malaur caught the king's expression. "See that? King Eborces is surprised at the sight of the prisoners. Why would that be?"

His question fell unanswered; the scene moved back to show that the accused had reached their destination.

Tumrin, Jinmyn, and Yorev took seats. DagReg stood behind Jinmyn, Fonely behind Tumrin.

The Captain of The Royal Elite Guards marched forward of the defense, faced the King and announced, "The prisoners are presented as ordered." She then paraded, stiff and taut, using a squared-off route until reaching the left rear leg of the king's throne. She assumed the same guard-at-post posture as DagReg and Fonely.

King Eborces, back in imperious regality, leaned forward, glaring at Yorev. "Who speaks for the accused?"

Tumrin sprang to his feet.

Fonely was on him with both hands, pulling Tumrin's shoulders back.

DagReg had his hands ready to place on Jinmyn.

The captain jumped in front of the throne, hand above her stunner. Eborces craned his neck around her to see.

Tumrin screamed, "I didn't do anything wrong! All I did was find him in the ship. We kept him until he attacked us."

Jinmyn said, "Frimox? Is that you?"

Fonely gave his prisoner a hard jerk backward, but the shackled man spun and head-butted Fonely. Wrenching against his restraints, the prisoner swung his elbows and tried to kick, as he was able. He growled a rumbling, "Leave us alone," as he bit at Fonely's hands.

Jinmyn whooped and bounced in his seat. "Ixet! How are you?"

DagReg stopped Jinmyn's frivolity by dropping a heavy palm on his shoulder. With his other hand, DagReg grabbed Ixet's tunic and shook him. If there was any starch left in the shirt, it was gone. Rigidity also evaporated from the combatant, leaving Tumrin limp, muttering apologies.

King Eborces' decree was louder than necessary in the horrified hush. "Return that man to his cell and keep him there until I decide otherwise."

At a gesture from the Royal Elite Captain, one of the guardsman left his post behind the Gaumen Shack prisoners and joined Fonely to escort Tumrin away.

Malaur's voice returned to the broadcast. "If the opening is any indication, it should be an exciting trial. I must say, I'm impressed with the King's Personal Protector." His chuckle came across the air. "The women here in the studio sure are. Stay tuned."

Yorev rose. "I speak for the accused, Your Highness."

King Eborces waved him down. "It's plain that the prisoner wants to disrupt our dignified proceedings. Before we listen to any of your long-winded speeches, I will give a summary of the reasons we are here and the rules of procedure." Eborces glanced beside his throne.

Yorev averted his gaze. Even here, now, the monarch would be nibbling treats if they were present. Yorev lifted one hand before dropping it in resignation and resuming his seat.

King Eborces turned, intimate and cozy, to the primary camera. "This would-be assassin was brought to Montibar on a Grabin diplomatic shuttle. He was aided by the other prisoner that was escorted out, and by the den of spies in The Gaumen Shack."

Yorev caught himself almost nodding in appreciation. Given a set of circumstances, King Eborces could arrive at facts that fit his purpose and make them sound believable.

Judge Eborces wasn't impartial. Yorev didn't expect him to be, but neither did Yorev expect Eborces to spend most of the morning portraying the Royalty as the last desperate defense against attacks from assassins, asteroids, and possibly Grabin. King Eborces explained that he had accomplished it all without the Regulator's help.

Yorev noticed hateful glances from the audience directed their way. Eborces was de-humanizing the accused. He leaned forward, shuffling papers on the desk, hoping to draw attention to his hands, then, without moving his lips, he whispered to Jinmyn, "Ask for a drink of water."

"Please, may I have a drink of water?" Jinmyn asked aloud, surprising Yorev with his smooth response as if in an act he and Yorev had practiced. Was the plaintive note in his request real?

Yorev turned to his client. "Only the King may allow you freedom of movement."

In the hush that followed, Yorev's statement hung heavy in the air.

Silence in the courtroom continued. Yorev was satisfied. Showing Jinmyn trussed up like a bag of trash deflated the image of the world terror Eborces described. Moreover, the king must now allow Jinmyn a drink, in essence admitting that there was no reason to keep him bound in immobility or else deny him a vital need revealing Eborces' inhumanity.

Yorev contained his smile as the King's face reddened. Yes, Eborces recognized the dilemma.

DagReg broke the impasse. Without waiting for specific orders, he loosened Jinmyn's left hand.

As Jinmyn reached for a glass, King Eborces squeaked through clenched teeth, "I have given my Personal Protector discretion to handle the prisoner."

Yorev enjoyed a satisfied tingle. He was in his element if he could debate Eborces. This could be a fun trial after all.

King Eborces glared at Yorev. "You may now speak for the accused," he said.

"Thank you, Your Highness," Yorev said rising to his feet. He strolled forward to the partition and turned to face Jinmyn, his back to Eborces. He addressed Jinmyn. "Now, before we discuss why you're dressed in a filthy uniform of our own Faithfulness Guard, or why, indeed, you're so filthy yourself, I'm sure everyone wants to know why you prowled around the palace."

The silence of a tomb filled the room. Someone in the far audience cleared his throat.

Jinmyn wiped his free hand across his mouth. "I had delivered a message from Rustbucket to the King earlier asking him to undo the dangerous position he placed Montibar and Grabin in, but he refused. So I was trying to disarm the asteroid hurling system myself."

"And who is Rustbucket?"

"You call him The Regulator. His name's Rustbucket."

Yorev paused while the spectators expelled their collective breath, some in giggles, some in derision, some in oohs and aahs. Whether they considered Jinmyn a lunatic or not, the name "Rustbucket" seemed to inspire wonder.

Yorev led Jinmyn through his explanation why Rustbucket couldn't return. An all-powerful Regulator that locked himself out? The assembly wasn't going for it. Yorev didn't believe it himself, but Jinmyn wouldn't sway from his story. They had to go with it, but he'd do what he could to make it sound plausible even if outrageous.

Yorev continued, "There are no records of your existence on Montibar until you first arrived at The Gaumen Shack. During this trial, we will hear you accused of being a Grabinian spy, but I've found out that there are no records of you on Grabin either until you arrived there after you were first on Montibar. Where are you really from?"

"Okay," Jinmyn said. "This is where people stop believing me and think I'm crazy, but here goes. I come from a different world than either Montibar or Grabin."

Yorev waited for the laughter to stop. He had listened to Jinmyn's explanation before, and it didn't make sense. Perhaps by having him tell it though, Jinmyn may receive some level of mercy. The fellow was obviously deranged.

"We know of no other worlds beyond Montibar or Grabin," Yorev said. "It must be very far away."

Jinmyn scratched his beard. "I suppose. I don't know where it is from here."

Bubbles of laughter and conversation popped up around the hall.

This wasn't right. To receive any semblance of favor for his client, Jinmyn's incompetence must be exposed. Yorev's mouth tasted like Jinmyn smelled. "You had to know how to navigate here; and where is your ship? How huge is it to hold all the life support necessary to cover such a distance? Were you the only one on board flying it?"

Mirth continued to effervesce among the onlookers. Eborces did not stop it.

Jinmyn shook his shaggy unshorn head. "There's no ship. Rustbucket brought me. I don't know how he did it. One minute I was in my world and the next I was naked on Montibar."

Unsubdued hilarity shook the gallery. The king held up a hand for quiet.

Yorev took in the image before him. Jinmyn, dirty, stinky, in ill-fitting clothes sitting bound in front of DagReg, who was perhaps the best model of male prowess and discipline on both worlds. Jinmyn was supposed to be the savior of those worlds and DagReg only the jailer. The logic of the situation was so skewed there was no need to continue. The trial was a farce for Eborces' pleasure. Its purpose had to be nothing more than to grab public approval for the king. Eborces never cared if anyone else suffered for his goals.

Very well. Yorev would finish this then slink away. He was just as much an idiot as Jinmyn to think he was ever suited for public service. He stopped his reverie and got back to questioning Jinmyn.

"Did The Regulator kidnap you—force you to come here?"

"No."

"Why did you agree to it?"

Jinmyn scratched under his chin and down his neck. "Seems strange, doesn't it? The fact is, in looking back, I didn't agree to come. I agreed to leave."

Yorev had never talked with Jinmyn about this part of his story. His interest perked up.

"What do you mean?"

"I thought I didn't matter. There was no one left where I was to care for me."

The gallery was listening too.

Jinmyn was answering questions but not offering additional information just as Yorev had instructed him. Now that Yorev wanted more, he'd have to coax it out of his client.

"So you risked traveling through space in some unknown way to save others. I'm sorry, Jinmyn, but it doesn't have the sound of truth."

Jinmyn balled his fist. "I didn't care about helping anyone else. But I gave my word, so it became an obligation."

"You created a lot of havoc fulfilling your obligation."

Yorev's statement drew some appreciative chuckles.

Jinmyn inspected the water glass, keeping his gaze on it as he answered. "It came to mean more to me when I met a little girl. A real person with her life ahead of her. She survived the loss of both her parents, but the royal lardo put Montibar and Grabin in the bullseye of annihilation. I want to help Rustbucket stop it."

Yorev didn't know the words lardo or bullseye. It sounded esoteric. The crowd was quiet—watching. Yorev saw what they saw.

SanMelo was on her feet, her face flushed, her glistening eyes fixed on Jinmyn.

Oh, no. Not here. Not now. Not another repeat of her arboretum performance. Yorev moved to place himself between SanMelo and Jinmyn, but she stayed put, gripping the edge of her counter.

She had Jinmyn in her gaze as if no one else were present. "If you care so much for a Montibaran child, why did you hold her king hostage?"

Yorev tried to over-speak her. "Head of Faithfulness, I believe it's my turn to address the accused and speak for him."

"Let her talk," King Eborces ruled.

Yorev held his hand palm outward to SanMelo hoping she'd stop as he turned to the king. "But Your Highness—"

"Let her talk." Eborces was leaning into the conversation.

Yorev saw the eager anticipation on his monarch's face and knew what it meant. Eborces thought SanMelo was on the attack.

Yorev clamped his teeth together. He may as well let SanMelo have at Jinmyn now. It was bound to happen. Might as well accept it. He would at least stand next to Jinmyn for whatever support he could offer.

King Eborces pounded his fist on the arm of his chair. "Answer the question!"

Jinmyn scooted around in his seat to face SanMelo. "What was the question again?"

SanMelo hadn't moved. "Why did you hold King Eborces hostage if you—"

"Ah, I remember," Jinmyn said.

"We were talking about a little girl," SanMelo prompted.

"All I was trying to do was reach the switch that would allow Rustbucket back so all people would be safe. I wasn't going to hurt anyone."

SanMelo's words struggled through the air, skinny and limp in the great hall. "Where is the girl?"

Yorev swallowed. SanMelo had to know that her career was dependent on how she handled this trial. When Jinmyn paused and looked at him, Yorev sighed and inclined his head toward SanMelo.

The head of Faithfulness stood with her arms stiff at her sides; hands gripped into fists. "What is the girl's name and where is she?" Such a dry, brittle voice could only mean SanMelo's throat was parched or stressed.

Jinmyn wiped his mouth. "Her name is Brimlet. She's on Grabin."

The gallery stirred. Eborces blurted, "Hah!"

SanMelo wasn't through. "Are you related in any way to this girl? Do you have ties to Grabin?"

"No," Jinmyn said. "I have no more ties to Grabin than I do Montibar. It was just there in the hospital that I met her."

SanMelo abruptly sat. "Was the girl hurt or sick?"

Jinmyn frowned at Yorev who shrugged. Jinmyn would find out soon enough where SanMelo was going with this. "Go ahead and answer."

Jinmyn used his free hand to lever himself back toward San-Melo. "No. Her mother was sick."

SanMelo appeared withdrawn and wooden. "What happened to Brimlet's mother?"

"She died."

"Was her name SanLemo?"

"I don't know."

It was time to stop this. Yorev cleared his throat and said, "Very well. Now if I may get back to stating—"

King Eborces banged the arm of his throne, de facto judge's bench, with a scepter. "What's going on here? Head of Faithfulness can you tie this man to Grabin spies?"

SanMelo wilted with her face in her hands. Loud, unprofessional sobs shook her shoulders. Her wailing Oh, Oh, Oh reverberated floor-to-ceiling, wall-to-wall, haunting Yorev. He wished SanMelo had gotten her cry over and done before now, or held it off until after the trial. Those things, though, will arrive when they must, outside of personal control.

Through her fingers and between weeping gulps SanMelo stuttered, "SanLemo is my sister. She married a man from Grabin."

WHO'S YOUR FRIEND

At the holding cells, DagReg freed Jinmyn from his security straps. While Jinmyn rubbed his wrists, DagReg inclined his head toward the figure slumped against the bars common to the first and center cells and asked Fonely, "How's he doing?"

"He's calmed down and been quiet. Nothing at all like he was in the North Hall." Fonely dashed a glimpse at the crumpled man and shook his head. "He's a strange one, though." Lifting his shoulders with his palms up, Fonely continued, "Since he was behaving, I had his supper brought in."

Jinmyn examined the two guards for a sense of attitude toward his fellow prisoner. There seemed to be no acrimony nor any desire for undue punishment. They were decent men doing their jobs. As for DagReg, in spite of his intimidating visage and adherence to discipline, he didn't abuse his position of power. Tumrin, Frimox, or the personality du jour would receive the same treatment as Jinmyn: no more, no less.

Jinmyn entered his cell and went to where Tumrin used their common bars as a backrest. The Montibaran ate from a plate of food balanced on his lap of crossed legs.

"Boy, you missed the fireworks, old buddy," Jinmyn said. "After you left, the king's Head of Faithfulness confessed to relatives on Grabin." Jinmyn laughed, clapping his hands. "His Royal Highness had a royal tantrum. He accused her of being in league with their enemies and removed her from the case. I wouldn't be surprised if she didn't show up as a guest here with—"

Jinmyn's fellow prisoner shrieked a primal war cry as he spun and buried a dinner knife shank-deep into Jinmyn's thigh.

Ixet had drool running from the corners of his mouth. "You did this to us! I should have killed you the first time I saw you!"

Jinmyn screamed and fell on the seat of his pants, his thumbs and forefingers forming a circle around the protruding knife handle without touching it. He caught a blur of movement outside the cell and saw DagReg level a stunner at Ixet.

"Don't shoot him! Don't shoot." Jinmyn scooted backward as Ixet clawed the space as far as he could reach into the cell. "You'll hurt all of them. Just wait." Jinmyn edged to a safe area where he pulled himself up.

Intense pain shot from his thigh to his stomach when he settled weight on his leg. Sweat covered his face and ran down his sides from under his arms. His body was responding faster than he could think. His vision paled, and he ducked his head to keep from passing out. That put the knife in full view. There was surprisingly little blood, which did nothing to make him feel better.

After getting his breathing, stomach, and eyesight under control, Jinmyn resumed a one-legged stance.

DagReg held his stunner unwavering on Ixet, but his eyes flickered between his prisoners. Jinmyn held onto a bar and with his free hand patted the air toward DagReg, "Settle down. Don't hurt him."

Turning his attention to the snarling face and the arm extending into his cell, Jinmyn began a one-bar and one-footed hop at a time toward the malicious personality. "Ixet please let me talk with Tumrin or Frimox. Please?"

Jinmyn kept his request soft, panting and repeating it as he hopped and shuffled forward. Ixet's arm dropped. Was it a real change or a ploy to get to him? Well, if he was wrong they might get to see DagReg's skill with a stunner.

Tumrin stood teary-eyed, looking at the shiny knife handle protruding from Jinmyn's thigh. "I'm sorry, Jinmyn. We all are. We couldn't hold him back any longer."

Jinmyn reached into the other cell to encircle Tumrin's shoulders as much as he could. "I know, and I know that I've messed up your lives. But I'll do everything I can to see that no harm comes to any of you." Jinmyn gulped and wiped sweat from his face. "Right now, I have to sit down." He lowered himself hand-under-hand down the bars, keeping his injured leg sticking straight out. "Oh, wow. It's getting a little pale and sicky in here," he said stretching out on his back.

DagReg holstered his stunner, motioning for Fonely, "Fetch Doctor Tetorm."

"Stick out your tongue." Dr. Tetorm had her bag open on the floor next to Jinmyn.

Anger, intense and sudden took Jinmyn. Why couldn't he ever get the assistance he needed on these enigmatic, backward yet advanced, worlds. "It's my leg that's hurt, not my throat. If you'll look, you'll see a knife in it, Quack." The word "quack" came out in English and was uncalled for since the doctor was trying to help him, but he was ready to lash out at someone.

If Doctor Tetorm was perturbed at his vitriol or strange language, she didn't show it. "Stick out your tongue," she said, holding a blue, oval wafer about twice the size of a thumbnail. "Suck on this."

The thin disc went straight to the roof of Jinmyn's mouth where he worried it with his tongue. It didn't loosen but began to dissolve in a pleasant minty flavor that took away the bile that had crept up his throat.

"Take a deep breath," Tetorm said. "It'll help you relax." She cut his pants leg from the cuff to his flank.

Jinmyn averted his gaze to the ceiling, "You know, Daggie, you really keep this place fit for inspection, don't you?"

"Another breath," the doctor said.

"Look, Doc. Give me a minute to get ready before you take that knife out, will you?"

"It's out, but I need to clean the wound. There's fabric and who knows what else in there. Stick out your tongue."

Jinmyn responded with an open mouth, eager for another relaxing dose. She gave him a red wafer that stuck to his hard palate and turned on his salivary glands. A delightful fruity sweetness diffused through his senses. He could smell the fragrance of cherries and roses. He loved everyone.

"While you're here, Doc," was that him talking? He sounded so far away, "would you look in on Tumrin there? I think he could use your help."

He couldn't feel anything but comfort and refused to look anywhere but the ceiling. Her answer came from a long way down a tunnel, "Who's Tumrin?"

It took all his effort to stay awake to reply, "Daggie can tell you."

Words fell into Jinmyn's comfortable repose. He tried without success to tune them out a little longer.

"You have the luck of an Ooshmer," Fonely said, referring to a mythical sprite that gives and receives good fortune.

Jinmyn stretched. He did feel good. That was surprising as his memories returned in a rush. He raised and looked at his thigh, naked and exposed by his cut-away trousers leg. A patch two thumb-nails in size glistened where the knife had been.

Fonely leaned against the bars, his left shoulder stuck between them. "Your tray of food is right there. I ordered it when you started waking up." He pointed to a table barely big enough to straddle the chair under it. The furnishings hadn't been in Jinmyn's cell before. "Thanks to Doctor Tetorm, you'll now eat what we eat."

Jinmyn glanced around and spread his hands over his bedding. "When did I get the furniture, and this cot?"

"Oh, you caused a whole bunch of changes and then slept through it." Fonely chuckled. "After you swallow some food, you get a shower and clean clothes."

Jinmyn took in his surroundings. "Where's Tumrin?"

Fonely looked at the empty cell. "Doctor Tetorm took him. DagReg had a long talk with her. I think DagReg was trying to help your friend."

THE FINAL SUMMONS

"It smells better in here," Yorev said as he entered the holding area housing his client. "Was it better for you or Fonely to get clean clothing and go three rotas without tasga?"

"Me!" Jinmyn and Fonely said it simultaneously.

All three smiled, Jinmyn understood the benefits were mutual.

Yorev dragged a chair to the spot prescribed by DagReg for visiting.

"You missed the evening meal," Jinmyn said. "I'll get as fat as Fonely if I keep eating like this. Not only has the food improved, but I also get to shower daily. The only thing left is access to the latrine. I still have to use the bucket in the corner if I can't include nature calls with shower time."

"Hmm," Yorev muttered. His smile had disappeared; he folded his hands in his lap and then wiped his palms on his legs. "Why aren't these lights on?" He swept a finger around at all the construction lamps.

Jinmyn followed his gesture. "Fonely tells me that Doctor Tetorm wanted them removed for my health, but DagReg said he couldn't because the king ordered them put here. They agreed to turn on the individual switches but shut off the power source. Obey the letter of the law, as it were. Is that right, Phony?"

Fonely bobbed his head in agreement. "That's it. Now we can all sleep at night."

"The doctor set you on a course of honorable treatment," Yorev said, "that extended beyond these walls."

"Oh, how so?"

"Several things really." Yorev stroked his chin. His eyes unfocused as if seeing elsewhere. "Montibarans are compassionate. They could see that you were dirty and mistreated. Then, SanMelo breaking down for her sister and niece touched many people. It's a family connection."

Jinmyn let Yorev talk. The more he said, the better Jinmyn's situation sounded.

"Public opinion, while not exactly in your favor, soured against King Eborces. Some have called him a tormentor for his treatment of you, and the way he expelled SanMelo from the trial."

"That's all good, isn't it? That's what we want."

Yorev's brow furrowed. "I planned to present you as pretending to bring the Regulator back because of your love for Montibar. That defense went away with your testimony that you didn't care about anyone else—that you were only acting in a sense of duty until you met the girl Brimlet." He shrugged. "I don't know if that was a good thing or not. It seems to have worked both ways."

"It sounds fine to me," Jinmyn said. "Is there another reason you are moping around?"

"These last three rotas weren't for you to recover." Yorev looked Jinmyn in the eye. "What drives King Eborces as much as his bakery is his perceived status. He started this trial as a wronged Monarch seeking justice—the victimized party. That changed, and he doesn't like it."

"What does that mean for us … me?"

"The king has called for the trial to resume. He will have a new strategy to regain his acclamation, and I don't know what it is. Furthermore, without SanMelo as the prosecutor, Eborces said he'd assume that role. I'll have to argue counterpoint as I see the debate at that time."

"You've done fine so far," Jinmyn said. "Why worry now?"

Yorev pinched the bridge of his nose; a frown pulled his brows together. "The king is shrewd, don't underestimate him. He could very well have me arguing in one direction and turn it around so that it made his point."

When Jinmyn didn't respond, Yorev stood and slapped his hands against his legs. "Eat early in the morning so your digestive tract will be settled by trial time. I'm sure we won't like the upcoming session."

Jinmyn sensed the change of attitude in the courtroom. Plenty of whispers still floated through the air as he shuffled in, but none of the sounds carried disgust. Perhaps his good luck would continue.

SanMelo's table was gone. His table had only one chair. Dag-Reg helped him sit down and unstrapped his left hand.

Jinmyn searched Yorev's face. The old diplomat's worry lines deepened, his eyes rummaged past the king's judgment seat. Jinmyn followed Yorev's gaze to the three heads of Parliament where he read their unspoken communication with his defender. All, it seemed, were wondering what the shift of prosecution would mean.

Well, Yorev had warned him to expect the unexpected. It probably didn't matter anyway since it was a kangaroo court in the first place.

The court ozier, Jinmyn thought of her as a bailiff, banged her staff three times calling the proceedings to order.

King Eborces rose and waited. Jinmyn was sure the king wanted to be the focus of every eye and camera. He wore a regal blue robe trimmed in luxurious ivory and umber midime fur that prismed a rainbow of colors as he moved. On his head was a scalloped crown of gold filigree. Identical deep blue gems glistened from each cleverly wrought spire. King Eborces was the monarch of Montibar and he exuded the royalty required of the position.

Jinmyn saw many in the gallery bobbing as if they were trying to bow while seated.

Eborces spoke into the hush, clear and without hesitation. "The trial of the assassin Jinmyn revealed that Grabin penetrated our peaceful society far broader and deeper than we suspected." He pointed to the space SanMelo had occupied. "Our own Head of Faithfulness admitted in this hall that she's close to Grabin. She's been removed as the court's voice."

Amid the gasps and murmuring Eborces continued by pointing at the holding area where LauNin, Mikara the bartender, and several others from the Gaumen Shack were ensconced behind partitions. "We have uncovered and dismantled a large den of spies."

Mutterings echoing in the hall had an ugly tone. Yorev leaned to Jinmyn's ear, "The king is cleaning away resistance to his prestige. I'm sure that's why I don't have a chair. Keep your wits about you."

King Eborces swung his ringed index finger to Yorev. "The assassin's voice and protector was relieved of his duties as Head of Faithfulness because of his very lack of faithfulness. Who would have believed at the time that he was grooming as his successor a Grabin sympathizer?"

The gallery grew louder causing the bailiff to bang her staff for silence.

Eborces kept his point at Yorev for a dramatic pause. "This court no longer needs his service. Remove him."

A Royal Elite Guardsman marched in military cadence and square corners to reach Yorev. The escort held his palm up toward the hall entrance indicating the way out. Yorev patted Jinmyn on the shoulder and left with his guide.

"Now then," Eborces said—from the way he stood, the king was obviously talking to the cameras—"to ensure the greatest safety for the security of Montibar, I have ordered the expulsion of the Grabin embassy staff and frozen their assets. One ship may land in five rotas to evacuate all Grabinians. If we decide to renew diplomatic relations with our devious neighbors, it will be under our terms."

Exclamations and wonderment sounded from all directions: "This is the first time that's happened ...," "Does this mean war?" The noise grew drawing another bang from the bailiff's staff.

King Eborces' face glistened with perspiration. "As for this trial, it has gone on too long. It has been allowed as a courtesy from benevolent Montibarans, but there is no longer need to continue."

Eborces glanced at the government leaders in their reserved side seats. "I am Lord Justice, the sole Judge, and Finder of Fact of these proceedings. Our heads of parliament serve in the role of Interested Persons by implication of consent to relinquish jurisdiction."

All three officials squirmed.

The king's pointing finger landed on Jinmyn. "You will now hear the justice you deserve and the largess of Montibar," he said.

This time, the king's hand trembled. "You will confess to spying for Grabin and attempting my assassination, and in return, you will spend the rest of your life in prison—or if you deny any allegations and fail to admit your seditious acts against Montibar—your sentence is death."

A thundering quiet sucked the air out of the great hall. Participants and spectators froze in place without a sound. No foot shuffled or chair squeaked.

Those weren't choices. Die in prison or die now? No, Eborces had to say something else—there must be more to come. As Jinmyn studied him, the king's face held a wide-eyed gaping incredibility as if he himself learned the options for the first time and now had to take responsibility for them.

LauNin's voice, commanding and rich in dark barroom timbre, broke into the cavernous quiet. "You have a snoot full of roggen if you expect anyone to believe that you gave him a choice."

Then she laughed.

It was the laugh that jolted Jinmyn across space and time. Back to a mirthful sound from a beautiful woman he had trusted. The woman that betrayed his love and wounded him so severely that he accepted Rustbucket's offer to run away.

Bile burned Jinmyn's throat and bit at the back of his tongue. It didn't matter where he was in the universe. His life was still the same. It would always be this way or become worse, but it wouldn't be life in prison.

He scootched his chair back and levered his free hand to rise. DagReg's hand gripped under Jinmyn's arm, helping.

Silence again claimed the gallery as Jinmyn rose. His heartbeat thumped in his neck and pounded in his ears.

King Eborces was pale and sweating, leaning on his scepter, but he had a tiny curl of a grin.

Jinmyn's heart banged harder, a physical presence in his chest, and he was cold. He surprised himself with how steady his voice was. "I remember all the times I was told that I was worthless, no good, and a pretender to decent society. Thank you, King Cupcake. It feels like home."

The utterance of the word "Cupcake" in English caused wonderment and speculating comments in the audience.

"However," Jinmyn continued, "you have given me a choice to admit to a falsehood or die. I'm not a liar, and I will not tell a lie just to die in prison. Since you want me dead, you'll have to execute me." He collapsed in his chair as his legs gave way. Not a man of swear words, nevertheless Jinmyn heard them most of his life, and if the time ever came to use one it was now. He pointed at Eborces and yelled, "You're an ingrown nostril hair." Where had that come from? That's far from what he meant to say. Rustbucket must have filtered his implanted vocabulary for profanity. A good thing, really, but he sure needed to vent—by toenail fungus.

CHAPTER SEVENTEEN

EVICTED

Captain Wimweg entered the first-class lounge aboard the Tap-Brid and sought Ambassador Lyram and Assistant Director of Grabin Security Velmere. He trod the plush carpet to their linen covered table in front of a man-sized oval window filled with a view of Montibar.

"I apologize for my late arrival, but the launch and atmospheric flight require my presence on the bridge. First Officer Stuzer is capable, and in fact commanded the lift, but we must follow regulations."

The men rose to greet him, Lyram in a shallow bow. "You're most gracious to honor us with your visit, Captain. We understand about regulations. Although with the recent events on Montibar, it seems rules and laws can be changed on a whim."

"Sit, please." Wimweg indicated their chairs and took another for himself. "I am the one who's honored, believe me." He turned to Velmere, "I've been wanting to thank you for the broadcast to rely on the 'Arr Bee assist'. Without it—well, you know the results as well as anyone. Catastrophe!"

Velmere dropped his chin and shook his head.

Wimweg thumped the table. "Don't be modest, my boy. You're a hero deserving of all the accolades we can give you."

"I'm agreed he deserves honors," Lyram said. "But the fact is, the Director had already issued a recall for Velmere. If Montibar had allowed a Grabin ship at the spaceport, he would be back home already."

Velmere shifted in his chair, sat straighter and tugged at the hem of his tunic. "Not for a parade," he said, giving a grinning Wimweg a negative headshake. "Unless there's a turnout watching me march to the stockade."

"I'm sorry. What?" Wimweg looked at his guests in turn. No one was smiling.

Velmere straightened. "Captain, you are a duty-bound officer of Grabin. As such, I place myself in your custody to be turned over to the Director upon our arrival."

Wimweg studied both men. They were serious. "Tell me what's going on."

Velmere paused, and then nodded. "The man responsible for the Arr Bee assist is the very man who was just sentenced to death on Montibar for attempting to assassinate their king. He escaped our custody while on Grabin. I tracked him down but rather than place him in confinement, I helped him reach Montibar."

Wimweg drew a deep breath. "Since when did we become a nation of assassins?"

"We haven't. And Jinmyn wasn't either. I place my oath on it. He was only trying to help the Regulator return." Velmere had a small grin. "Jinmyn calls him Rustbucket."

Wimweg rubbed his jaw. "This is not making any sense to me."

A new voice in his ear caused him to jump. Lyram and Velmere reacted as well.

"Perhaps I can explain."

All three men turned and twisted. Wimweg couldn't see who spoke.

Korfel's group and Lyram's retinue scattered throughout the lounge carried on their conversations seemingly unaware of strange voices.

"Pardon the intrusion, gentlemen. I know it's shocking to make my acquaintance abruptly and I don't usually communicate so intimately without invitation, but time, as you know it, is passing."

Wimweg felt beneath his chair and peered under the table. "Who is this?"

"You call me The Regulator."

"Rustbucket," Velmere whispered.

The color of Lyram's face matched the starched, white table-cloth. Velmere jumped to stand at attention, and Captain Wimweg looked for a prankster.

"Please sit, Assistant Director. I would like to hear the current news from Montibar. You mentioned a death sentence. Such a decree would be the first one ever proclaimed for this section of space. Is it for Jinmyn?"

"Yes, sir, uhh ... Lord Regulator?"

"Not Lord. I'm not sovereign. If I were, I wouldn't be asking questions. Now then, I monitored communications and broadcasts—there was a trial—what happened?"

Wimweg clenched his fists. "The Regulator wouldn't be so stupid. I'll find out who's doing this." He pushed himself away from the table and the voice spoke to him.

The Captain became aware of Lyram and Velmere staring at him. He also realized his mouth was open. Wimweg cleared his throat and regained his command posture. "Forgive me, gentlemen," he said readjusting his seat. "The Regulator has imparted to me certain information. His identity is confirmed. I apologize for my recalcitrance."

"I'll give you something to focus on," the Regulator said. "I've found it's easier for humanoids to converse with something."

Velmere and Lyram also turned to gaze at a translucent orb as large as two fists. It appeared in the center of the table, floating above the linen by a finger's breadth. Colors swirled and sparkling lights flashed inside the globe while the whole of it emitted a glowing soft white light.

"Now tell me. Did Jinmyn try to assassinate King Eborces?"

"Are you Rustbucket?" Velmere's voice was low, but his clenched fists and tight body language indicated explosive energy barely contained. He licked his lips. "Sir?"

The flashing in the sphere stuttered, paused, and then resumed. "Yes. Using the name Jinmyn does confirms you've been talking with him. Did he tell you I'm unable to return to either planet? He probably did, although space is mine. That's why I can talk with you here."

"A noble name," Velmere uttered and bobbed his head.

"What we believe, Your—uh," Lyram spread his hands.

A sigh whispered in Wimweg's ears. "You may call me Rustbucket."

"Yes, well, what we believe, Rustbucket, is that Jinmyn reached the King's chambers to deactivate the closet switch and was holding Eborces as a prisoner. It didn't work, but we don't think that the king was in danger at any time."

Lyram clasped his hands and stared. "Enthralling."

The dancing colors of the ethereal centerpiece captured Wimweg too. He could smell the enticing aroma of the exotic southern islands spicy dew trees emanating from the orb.

"Go on."

Lyram swallowed and cleared his throat. "Eborces was the sole judge at the trial, and he let things get out of hand. He tried to force Jinmyn to admit to spying and go to prison for life, or face a sentence of death. It shocked us all, but Jinmyn said he was through, and chose the death penalty."

"That's why the end of the trial wasn't broadcast," Rustbucket said. "Eborces censored it."

Velmere leaned toward the globe. "Will you help him?"

"I'll do what I can, but not at the expense of destroying two civilizations. Meanwhile, I intend to help you, Assistant Director Velmere."

"Me, sir?"

"Yes. I deduce that the Director intends to hold you responsible for Jinmyn's escape and the subsequent political mess with Montibar. Given his past responses allocating punishments, it won't be pleasant for you."

Velmere squared his shoulders. "That's what I think too. I'm prepared to face any consequences for my actions."

Color bursts popped into existence in the center of the orb. Intermingled hues rippled outward until the inside surface reflected them back to collapse in a whiteout before reincarnating as another blend in the spectrum.

The colors quit undulating. The sequence froze into a mesmerizing display.

Wimweg felt a nudge and dragged his consciousness away from the exhibition. "I'm sorry," he said glancing at his companions. "What did you say?"

Rustbucket was the speaker. Apparently the other men connected with the ethereal voice, too.

"I said that I prefer to have permission before interfering, but in this case, Captain Wimweg, your flight will halt half-way to Grabin to delay the Assistant Director's arrival."

Wimweg grabbed the tablecloth. "You're going to stop the TapBrid? I can't allow that."

"Your sense of duty is as firm as Assistant Director Velmere's," Rustbucket said. "I suspected as much." Wimweg experienced the breeze-sigh again. "It will seem to you and your crew that everything is progressing as it should. You won't discern when your ship halts. You will be blameless for the extended flight time."

"How long?"

"Until I am assured of Assistant Director Velmere's safety."

Lyram switched his gaze from Captain Wimweg to the globe. "You can do that? Make all the navigational instruments and personal perceptions believe an illusion?"

"Yes. However, I only do it when necessary. As I did with the Arr-Bee assisted life supporters."

Wimweg leaned over close to the orb. "Explain that, please." Once more the whisper of a gentle wind tickled the Captain's ears before Rustbucket spoke.

"Nothing I did detracts from your courage and determination, Captain Wimweg, but you know the life supporters' engines can't burn that long. I made them appear like they were still firing while giving you the extra push you needed."

"Impossible."

"True," Rustbucket said. Here's a quick test for you. If you touch the sphere, you will feel the smooth, crystalline surface, hard and round. You see the colors, and I can make my voice emanate from it instead of putting it directly into your ears.

"Like this," the globe said. "Yet no one else in the room sees or hears anything because there's nothing on the table. It's no effort for me. Simple. I admit gentlemen that my powers and abilities are so far beyond yours, that I must seem miraculous to you."

Wimweg considered this conversation and the past actions of the Regulator. He had no choice but to trust him.

Velmere spoke into the conversational lull. "Rustbucket, sir, I'm sure you have deep reasons that I may not be able to follow, but I'd like to ask a question."

"Go ahead."

"As long as it's only the planets' surface that you must avoid and can operate freely in space, why did you go to a faraway place to pick Jinmyn? Why didn't you select someone in transit between planets that Eborces trusts to tell him to disable the threat? Or perhaps modulate the communication frequencies before they reached Montibar to tell him what you want?"

The orb disappeared. In the stillness, Wimweg's heartbeat thumped in his temples. His ears rang over the buzz of lounge communications.

As the silence drew out, Velmere's eyes widened. "What have I done by questioning the Regulator?"

Rustbucket's voice wasn't loud but so near it startled Wimweg.

"I didn't think of it."

As the background noise of the lounge pervaded his hearing, the Captain's face hardened into a blackened blast shield. Perhaps he was too quick to place his trust in the specter.

ON MONTIBAR

DagReg's familiar twinge of guilt manifested in his stomach as he watched his only sister. Ephmel busied herself in her tidy kitchen, shuffling and re-stacking the cans and boxes on the shelves. Ephmel was the sweetest person he knew, and her life had not been easy. Her female figure was a smaller version of his, boxy and muscular. Her prospects for alluring a mate were bad enough, but no suitors would call on a young woman who blinked her eyes and jerked them in random movements while sniffing and grunting. At least she had outgrown most of that.

Still, DagReg couldn't shake the remorse that he had somehow ruined their mother with his birth. As if by being born he had imprinted the template for baby construction in her ovaries, and Ephmel had inherited the abnormal results. He would take care of his sister as long as he could.

DagReg placed his cup on the table, built like all the furniture in Ephmel's orderly house, sturdy and functional. "This is nice, Ephi. We don't dine together often enough."

"I'm surprised you took time off for it," she said, setting out plates. "I think your schedule would be worse than ever with your prisoner getting the death sentence."

"It's easier on me now that he doesn't have to be transported anywhere. He's strictly in lock-up. Fonely's posted on guard with nothing to do but make sure no one gets close to the cell."

Ephmel sat across from her brother; her eyes round and moist. "Dag, will you have to do anything—that is, will you be involved when—you know, it happens?"

His beautiful caring sister. Maybe this visit will work and put everything back in its proper order.

DagReg reached for his cup but only held it. "I don't know, Ephi. King Eborces hasn't declared the manner of execution. There's never been one before. However, I'm sure I'll be there and take part one way or another." He took a sip while he hoped she would understand his position. "Did you see the red handle of my sidearm?"

"No. What does that mean?"

"It signifies a lethal weapon, no longer a mere stunner. A select few of us have used them on the practice range. They're extremely powerful and kept locked in the armory. I'm the only person to carry one." He took another sip. "I will use it on him if it comes to that."

A tear spilled down Ephmel's cheek. "I wish you didn't have anything to do with this, Dag."

Here it was. The opening he came for.

"When you're cleaning the king's quarters, do you clean his closets too?"

"Yes, although his valet arranges all the clothes in there. Why?"

"Did you ever observe the switch that Jinmyn says is there?"

"Yes. The valet and I talked about it after you caught the intruder. It gave me a weird feeling to look at it."

DagReg took a quiet, deep breath. "Do you think you could flip it off and then right back on?"

He had poured an invisible glue over his sister freezing her in place. From the lines of terror on her brow to the grimace of her jaw, he may as well have asked her to bomb the castle. "Breathe, Ephmel. It's okay."

Ephmel trembled. Only her chin moved. "No, no, no."

"I shouldn't have asked, Ephi. It's just that I don't think Jinmyn is a bad man and if he's right, that might let the Regulator come back."

DagReg went around the table to hug Ephmel who was crying freely and shaking her head. "Forget I asked you, sister. We'll both do our duties to our oaths and king. Let's think about that dinner now."

Ephmel nodded and dried her eyes on her apron.

In almost all of his foster homes, someone cautioned him to watch his big mouth. Jinmyn finally learned his lesson but it was too late. He'd flapped his lips to spite the king, and soon his tongue would wag no more. He paced the perimeter of his confines alternately swearing with fluff words at himself and then Rustbucket.

He needed to stop this and do something constructive. For instance think of a reason to appeal the sentence. He needed help, or he would die, but Yorev was absent. Perhaps DagReg could tell him when his counselor was scheduled to visit.

"Hey Phony. Would you ask Daggie to talk with me for a moment?"

Fonely waved a hand toward the door. "DagReg is out for dinner. He should be back soon, though."

Nothing was going right. Jinmyn wanted to claw at something—do something. Act. His encaged tensions were upsetting his stomach and pressing his bladder. He sought his relief pail detesting the necessary exposure and lack of privacy he endured each time he was forced to use the heavy receptacle.

The pail. It was an idea. Maybe.

"Well, Phony, it looks like you're on the bucket brigade again."

Fonely groaned. "You couldn't have used it again. I just emptied it."

Jinmyn held the container behind his leg. "Don't look at me. Daggie is the one that said you had to keep it clean."

Fonely muttered as he unlocked the cell door and stretched his hand out.

Jinmyn pulled the bucket up by the handle in one hand and with the other grabbed the bottom. He boosted it in a motion that would have splashed the contents in Fonely's face had there been anything in it.

Fonely turned his head and brought his elbow across his eyes.

Jinmyn grasped the handle with both hands and from the height of his reach, swung the metal pot down on Fonely's head opening a deep gash above his right ear.

Fonely dropped but still moved in a slow, disjointed effort to right himself.

Jinmyn unholstered Fonely's stunner, breathed a quick, "Forgive me," and shot the guard.

He had a good idea where the king's chamber was and ran. His stab wound burned his thigh, but he couldn't slow down. He had to succeed this time. There would be no more chances. Dag-Reg would see to that.

He ran harder.

He tore down the long hallway and up the curving staircase, his lungs burning. At the top of the stairs, he passed a servant in the royal livery. The man threw up his hands and screamed. Jinmyn stunned him.

His leg aching and his lungs unable to breathe enough air, he reached the foyer to the royal bedroom chambers. Stop and remember. Which way did he go the first time? Queen Vinluc's bedroom was that way. He had it now and tore open the door to King Eborces' quarters.

As he bolted inside, he heard DagReg's voice behind, in the hall beyond the foyer. "Jinmyn, stop! Drop that stunner!"

A tingle went down his back as he tried to run faster. His peripheral vision saw Eborces collapse in a faint at the feet of a valet.

There was the clothing repository door and it was open.

Now.

Jinmyn spun as he dived into the closet and lunged for the switch.

For a nanosecond, a blinding white light seared his retinas. An explosion of heat engulfed him that could melt his flesh.

IT'S OVER

The weather was perfect, as usual, and the park across the street from the sidewalk café held couples strolling, children playing, and other folks enjoying pastimes in the natural surroundings.

Jinmyn had selected a table under the awning. He adjusted his sunglasses and scowled at a woman in the park. She was propped up against a shade tree reading a book. How could she be so blasé about recent events and appear so comfortable?

He pulled his hat lower and said it again. "I want to go home, Rustbucket. Today."

A dull red glow like a night vision light pulsed where another person might sit at the table. "Please, Jinmyn, it's only been two serotas. Can't you try it a little longer? Especially after Montibar deeded you the entire Polynee Peninsula with its vacation palace. Have you forgotten it has a staff of twenty-eight and you don't have to pay taxes? All expenses are met in perpetuity by the government."

"Don't care. This is a stupid place with mean people. Look what they did to me."

"Oh, Jinmyn. You only lost the hair on one side and it'll grow back. Dr. Tetorm said your eyesight would return to normal too. Even DagReg apologized for shooting you. You must realize that he didn't want to."

Jinmyn hunched down in his chair and pulled the collar of his long-sleeved shirt higher.

"Look," Rustbucket said. "I never abandoned you. I got to you a picosecond after your momentum threw the switch. In case you've forgotten, that's one-trillionth of a second. DagReg's shot was a two-second burst and I absorbed all but the first one-billionth of it. Refreshing, actually."

"Don't care."

"Don't you see? I'm telling you that DagReg started shooting before you turned off the trigger. He's quite a man. I don't think there's another on either world that is his equal."

"Don't care."

"What if I told you that Grabin has set aside a mountain lodge with a staff of thirty-nine for your use any time you want? It's much like the Canadian Rockies, beautiful snow-capped mountains with green, lush valleys and plenty of wildlife. Only three species will eat you."

"Don't care."

Jinmyn heard the soft whisper of a breeze that was a Rustbucket sigh.

"There's something else, Jinmyn. If I use the same pattern to take you back that I used to bring you here, you'll not remember anything that happened since you left the mental hospital on Earth. If I use today's pattern, you'll arrive home slightly burned and with no job."

While Jinmyn considered his options, Rustbucket spoke again. "Here comes someone you may care about."

Jinmyn looked up to see a young girl approaching in half steps. She clutched a doll to her chest as her searching eyes scanned the customers. Following close behind was a woman in the uniform of Head of Faithfulness.

His dry lips cracked into a grin. "Brimlet!" He took off his hat and sunglasses. "Brimlet, it's me, Jinmyn."

He rose as she reached for his hand. "Aunt SanMelo said you were hurt saving us."

"Nah, it's nothing. I'll be back in shape in no time."

SanMelo cleared her throat taking Jinmyn's attention. "If you're up to it, Brimlet and I hope you'll join us for dinner. We'd both like to know more about you."

A familiar suspicion nagged him. Attractive people had always seemed to hurt him one way or another, and SanMelo was pretty. "Dinner with you? You tried to get me sent to prison for life."

"Yes, and I think I would have succeeded if I hadn't got emotional." She blushed, a tiny smile pulled the corners of her lips. "I thought my career was ruined, but it turned out fine when your, uh, Rustbucket returned."

Brimlet squeezed his hand. "Please?"

Jinmyn gazed down into the face of the little girl who only had a rag doll and a beautiful aunt. "Rustbucket? Is there an arcade in that place Montibar gave me?"

A glow returned to the table. Fairy sparkles danced in the air between the three humans. Awestruck expressions indicated SanMelo and Brimlet saw and heard the omnipotent Regulator. "I'm sure King Eborces will be happy to provide the best and latest games."

"Brimlet will want them upgraded in a timely manner."

"Of course."

Was this sensation of tenderness what belonging felt like? Jinmyn liked the warm tingle and wanted to keep it. He wished to include everyone. Well, there were exceptions. He gazed into SanMelo's soft eyes.

"You haven't invited Rustbucket have you?"

SanMelo gasped and held her fingertips to her cheek. "We haven't asked him. Do you think we should?"

"No!" Jinmyn scooped Brimlet into his arms. "How do you feel about dinner on a peninsula?"

THE END

If you enjoyed Stranded Off World, would you
take a moment to leave an on-line review?

It's a huge help to readers when books
are seen in an unbiased review.

Of course, we hope yours will be favorable,
but if not, we'll learn from your comments.

Thank you.
Burton